George

George

Ramona
Lee Soo-Jun

Action Lee

ISBN 978-1-7392786-6-3

Cover illustration by Paul Harrison

"I understand that a man can have everything having nothing and nothing having everything."

— Mihai Eminescu

Chapter One
"Love Me Do"

George is my best friend, so I'd like to begin my story with his name.

"Cornelia, bless her... she shaped me, see? Changed me in ways I never quite put into words. She was mine once, if only for a blink, but she's with me still. In every heartbeat. Truth be told, I've been a selfish old sod... never really let her go," George said to me today. And I wonder if I hold onto his story the same way he's held onto Cornelia's ghost for the past sixty years. If I'm just as selfish, just as unwilling to let go. I don't know if he ever will. And I can't promise I will either.

I stare at George's old black-and-white photograph, trying to crawl inside his mind, desperate to know what he was thinking at that exact moment. Imagination, however, is all I have. So I grip that instead, like a rope in the dark.

I want to believe that somehow, somewhere, Cornelia knows. That George still holds his breath when someone who looks like her passes by. That every day he pats his front pocket before eating. I want to believe she knows he never forgave himself. But that he's learning. That he's finally making peace with the past. Maybe he'll hold his breath forever, and maybe that's just the way love works sometimes.

I know that one day, everything we've ever known and lived will be gone. But now that this truth is staring me down, I don't know what to do with it. Maybe we're only miserable because we misremember. Because we twist the past into something heavier than it was. And we hate on it so much that when we feel the present slipping away, we clutch at it, beg for it to stay.

When I put on minty lip gloss, it tastes like childhood. Like peppermint sweets that once melted in my pocket. It pulls me back into the stories I've been holding onto, the ones I thought I wasn't ready to release just yet. I still count the days until I might be strong enough to let go. Maybe one day, I'll forgive myself too.

George, though, was fearless enough to tell me his story. And that's something, isn't it? To speak the truth when your bones ache and your memories feel as though they are whispers from another life. So I'll share more of his story with you. And perhaps, if I'm brave enough, I'll keep telling you mine. Again, and then again. Until none of my words hurt me anymore.

＊

The old coffee machine lets out a tired squeak, dribbling weak, light-brown liquid into a grey plastic cup. Cars rush by and people shuffle into the corner shop next to me. I stand there with a shoebox full of hot, instant coffees, shifting my weight as I think through the next step. This ridiculous red tie's half-hanging out of my pocket, and I'm seriously debating whether it's even worth the hassle of putting it back on.

The machine sputters and hisses one last time and I place the full cup with the others. The frustration I've been holding in bubbles up. Lips sealed, I bend down and almost spit into every one of those sad little cups.

But then I catch sight of a granny leaning against the wall, hands resting on her cane, watching me with an eagle eye that could pierce through concrete. I freeze mid-spit, swallow, and paste on a smile. I give her a nod because everything's just lovely.

Flat sharing, working, living and breathing in Richmond—like in any other neighbourhood in London to be fair—has become an impossible task. Some of us are luckier than others, sure, but one thing we all seem to share in this city is that we're spinning the same never-ending wheel, all heading towards pretty much the same unknown destination.

Clutching the shoebox, I head back across the street to the gym, feeling my black trousers sag with every step, practically pleading for a belt. Either they stretched in the wash, or I've shed a few pounds. The trousers I can live with. That tie, though? That tie can rot.

Inside the gym, the TVs blare a VHS documentary about obscure churches. Fred, the gym's owner, sits at his small plastic table where he likes to greet guests. A few heavy lifters grunt in the background. Diego is here today, too. He's a former karate champion, current police dog trainer—probably in his late sixties—and the reason for the five coffees. Diego's tough to read and has a strange sense of humour.

"Fiona, your tie, please!" Fred calls out, waving a hand at me. "We got clienteles watching, darling girl!" I look around at the sweaty, focused lifters who couldn't care less.

"It's Julia, sir." I say.

"Fiona is the middle name of Julia Roberts. Very elegant woman, absolutely stunning—true Hollywood!" he adds with a proud little nod, as if he's just cracked a riddle. I bite back a sigh, holding my patience in check.

Fred and Diego go way back and their little friendship seems to impact every shift I work. Diego always downs those budget coffees without complaint, though I'm not sure if he actually likes them or just humours Fred.

Fred probably deserves an introduction of his own. He's a former bodybuilder, current alcoholic and the owner of this gym responsible for keeping my bills paid. Everyone here seems to be a "former" something, and I hope to add "former employee" to that list soon.

Fred's in his fifties, I think, with an accent I can't quite place. Rumour has it he inherited a tidy sum at some point, which would explain the extravagant water fountain and the gilded statue of Arnold at the entrance.

"Thank you, *madame*," he says in his theatrical voice as I set the shoebox on his plastic table. "Serve our guest, will you?" he adds as I try to slip back to my desk.

A televised prayer begins as I line up the coffee cups for Diego. "Continental breakfast, just like in Germany. What you reckon?" Fred asks him, and Diego nods, tossing back the first coffee in one go.

Fred fancies calling me "madame," stretching it out with a faux-French flair that never fails to give me the creeps. What I find even more disturbing is the fact that during his short-lived career as a bodybuilder, he managed to only work his upper body. But I'm not trying to body-shame bulldogs by associating them with him.

Finally behind my desk, I eye the stack of entrance cards waiting for my signature. I sneak a sip of a protein shake I made using powder from the bucket no one ever buys and hear Fred's laughter turn into a cough.

Looking up, I notice Silviu walking into the gym. He's once again wearing his tight shorts that seem to squeeze all of his body parts into one entity. He grins as he walks closer and I try to preoccupy myself with something, so I take another sip of protein shake.

In the background, a few guys grunt as they

lift weights. The prayers on all the TVs blur into a low hum and I feel the heavy pull of the dark circles under my eyes.

Man, what have I done with my life?

Photos from Fred's old bodybuilding competitions plaster the entrance wall. He's soaked in fake tan spray and resembles a rancid almond in all of them. Whenever he's scored a trophy, he's flanked by a lady or two gripping onto his biceps. Next to the photos hangs a framed article with a few quotes under his name:

"Life is a long lesson in humility."

"Professionals are professionals."

"Love your parents!"

The last quote is printed over half of Fred's foot. And on that note, I take my strawberry chewing gum out of my mouth and stick it onto his face. I turn my back to the wall and place my feet into the heated foot massager. I run this place when Fred's not here.

Fred's recent investment of a small fortune in CCTV cameras has resulted in the gym being completely covered. After Diego caught Tommy sleeping in the sauna last spring, Fred made it his mission to prevent a repeat. But Tommy still sneaks into the sauna every night and Fred's too clueless to check the CCTV footage properly. Whenever Fred asks me to show him some recordings, I conveniently skip the times Tommy comes and goes.

Fred's also got his suspicions about people sneaking into the gym without paying, and he's not entirely off base.

He's had it in for Auntie ever since he caught her slipping a few coins under the counter while a guy snuck in for a quick workout without a membership card.

Auntie's my only coworker, and she's the sweetest lady I've ever worked with. We work different shifts, so the only time we get to chat is when she's here to walk Fluf, Fred's neglected dog. She picks Fluf up every day at 2 pm for a stroll. Fred ditched eleven-year-old Fluf at the gym when he started dating a new woman who was allergic to everything but Fred's vodka breath. My feet are now Fluf's daily napping spot; we're good together, though he's not much of a conversationalist. Mostly, he's just snoozing and twitching in his sleep when he has a bad dream or lets one fly like a deflating balloon.

As the massage pillow digs into the ball of

my foot, a guy walks in and leaves his membership card in the little basket at reception.

"You again." he laughs as he walks towards the changing room.

"Guess I'm haunting the place now," I shrug, struggling to recall his name.

I can never seem to recall his name for the life of me. Don't ask me why. But he's a regular here, showing up pretty much every day, usually around 3 pm. Few use the gym throughout the day. People trickle in after 6 pm and clear out right before midnight.

Alright, I fibbed a bit. There's actually another co-worker: Dan. He's on the night shift duty. Fred insists on constant gym supervision. It's open for those one or two crazies who feel like hitting the treadmill at 3 am. Otherwise, Dan spends his shifts napping.

I wrap up my massage and slip my trainers back on. Fred's been trying to push me into wearing high heels, claiming it's part of the uniform. As if I care. Best I can do for him is wear the oversized black trousers, the tacky white shirts and occasionally throw on the red tie. Auntie doesn't bother with a uniform at all. The last time Fred gave her grief about it, she told him he could stuff it where the sun didn't shine.

Auntie and Fred, they're like oil and water. But Fred knows he needs Auntie, so he wouldn't dare fire her. Still, ever since Fred caught Auntie stashing some cash and giving out free passes, he's been keeping a close watch on her.

Everything I've picked up about being a receptionist, I've learnt from Auntie. I aim to be as astute as she is.

Auntie and I share the same taste in music. Fred's absence or inebriation grants us playlist control. Today the gym is listening to the "oldies but goldies".

I sidestep around Fluf and pop open the big white bucket to whip up a protein shake. I give my glass another quick rinse. I never seem to get these things properly clean. Nobody ever bothers ordering anything from this reception. They usually grab sports drinks, and I'm left jotting down their purchases on paper whenever one guy tosses some cash my way like I'm running a black market snack shop.

This summer is a scorcher, and this gym's got zero air conditioning. I'm baffled by gym-goers' stamina. Sometimes, the heat is so intense I can barely think straight. I hop onto my favourite vibration plate, punching a few buttons until it kicks into gear, shaking me so violently I lose all sense of self.

This shaky machine certainly isn't providing any answers, but it's a welcome distraction from reality. I glance out the top windows, seeing nothing but waves of stifling heat. Everyone's holed up indoors, anywhere but here. Sweat beads on my forehead.

Fred's car pulls up outside, next to his gaudy statues. I feel the urge to hit the back of my hand on the machine handle to feel that quick rush of cold flowing through my bones. I then hit each of my five fingers one by one on the handle, counting for the seconds of peace left. I scramble off the machine and shut it down.

Darting across the floor, I hurry downstairs past the framed photos, plucking the chewing gum from Fred's face and flinging it behind the bench by the foot massager.

I slip on my red tie and tidy up the reception desk, tossing all the crumpled papers behind the counter at my feet. Fluf shakes his head as a few stray bits land on his nose. I brush off the protein powder spilt across my notebook and straighten up. Fred can't stand it when I'm seated whenever someone walks in. I only stand up in his presence to avoid unnecessary conflicts. Well, on the days when he's not particularly getting on my nerves. On those days, he couldn't pry me off my chair with a crowbar.

I hear him shut his car door and saunter around to open it for Pussycat. Fred's taken to calling his new girlfriend "Pussycat," so I've followed suit. I couldn't care less about her real name. They started dating this summer, and with Fred never having been married or having any kids, he's got plenty of time and cash to spare on taking Pussycat on day trips and footing the bill for her Botox injections. They seem content together, and who am I to pass judgement?

Fluf wanders around the counter, his nose leading the way in his usual sleepy manner. Fred strolls into the gym, Pussycat trailing behind. He scans the room eagerly, attempting to tally up his clients. Meanwhile, the guy whose name forever escapes me does a few reps in front of the TV at the back. Over a hundred TVs, all blaring simultaneously, deck out the place—a megalomaniacal impulse choice by Fred.

Fluf comes to a halt at Pussycat's feet, and she kneels, her hand holding her mini skirt in place.

"Oh, you adorable little thing." Pussycat coos, reaching down to shake Fluf's paw. "How I wish I could snuggle you and take you home."

"Then do it." I interject, clearing my throat.

Pussycat shoots me a piercing glance, her mouth twisting into a sneer. "Why don't you mind your own business, Julia?" With that, she straightens up and heads into Fred's cramped office.

"How is business today, Fiona?" Fred asks as he approaches.

"I'm Julia."

His laughter is clear in the shake of his shoulders. He leans in, resting both hands on my counter. I muster a smile.

"It's not even 4 pm on a scorching workday, sir. I doubt anyone's eager to be here at this hour."

"Never say never, *madame*," Fred chuckles at his own quip before retreating.

Pussycat storms out of the office and stops at the top of the stairs.

"Turn this off, yeah? What's with all this old rubbish?"

"Weren't you dancing to this in your prime?" I hiss through gritted teeth, flashing a smile as I reach for the remote to switch to a different channel.

Pussycat flips me the bird as she tucks a strand of hair behind her ear. I resist the urge to reciprocate, mindful of the CCTV cameras. Instead, I pop another strawberry chewing gum into my mouth.

"Markus!" Fred growls as he bursts out of his tiny office.

Fred's office near the entrance consumes most of his time. It's lined with bodybuilding books and VHS tapes on display, and he loves boasting about having the biggest bodybuilding library in the world. But I'm not entirely convinced about his maths. Whenever I catch a glimpse of the office, all I notice are the vodka bottles on the corner bar. He's even got a leather sofa in there for his afternoon naps.

"Markus!" Fred bellows, scanning the room like a Roman emperor.

"Yes, sir." Markus materialises out of thin air, stumbling over the worn patch of carpet by the entrance.

Before Markus, Fred had another handyman named Don, who helped him clean around the gym. Last year, during a Christmas party, Fred had an epileptic episode. Don, thinking he was a medical expert, shoved his hand into Fred's mouth to stop him from biting his tongue. Fred bit Don's hand instead. Don got the sack, and that's how Markus ended up with the job. Make of that disaster what you will.

Fred hurls a mop at Markus' feet. "What I said before, eh? I return, this place should be sparkle like royal palace!"

"I'm sorry, sir, I'm on it now."

"Forget it. Leave it now. Focus on the machines!" Fred commands.

Fred treats Markus like his own personal lackey, and Markus follows his orders like a hungry mule.

"Sweltering out there, isn't it?" Markus sighs as he props his arm on my counter, the dirty mop dangling from his other hand.

"Yeah," I reply.

"I was at their place last night," he whispers, leaning in close, as he always does when he's about to dish some gossip. "Dirty underwear all over the floor."

"Classy."

"They're disgusting, I'm telling you," Markus continues, leaning in close. "I cleaned his entire flat last night while they were out. Gagged cleaning the toilet. But you know what I found?"

"What?"

"He's stashing cash under his VHS tapes."

"Markus!" Fred's voice booms from inside his office.

"Sir, yes, sir!" Markus jumps, rattled. "Catch you later, Julia."

As Markus sloshes his dirty water across the machines, I get back to cutting out more membership cards from the printed sheets.

Silviu strolls in, clad in the workout gear that makes him resemble the Pink Panther. I make a conscious effort not to look up as he approaches, his balls visibly staging a prison break through the spandex. He drops his card into the basket near my head as I remain seated.

"Julia," he greets me.

"Silviu," I respond, keeping my focus on my task.

He awkwardly fumbles about before speaking up. "Would you mind turning on the sauna for me?"

That blasted sauna! Whenever he's run out of small talk or ways to get me to stand up, he resorts to asking about the sauna. He knows starting it means I have to walk to the little metal cupboard.

I grab my keys and lead the way. Silviu trails along behind me.

"You know Tommy sleeps in there every night, right?" I mention as I unlock the door and flip the switches to get the sauna going. I wish I could adjust the temperature too.

"Tommy? Is that someone you're seeing?"

I scoff. "I don't think I'd date anyone who lives in a sauna."

Uncertain whether he should still be excited for his sauna session, he widens his eyes. I lock the cupboard door.

"Go ahead. You've got twenty minutes," I tell him, trying to step past him back to the reception.

But he leans against the door, blocking my path. "How about coffee this Thursday?"

Silviu has been pursuing me ever since I started working here. I made the mistake of listening to his MMA stories once, and now he thinks I'm interested. I'm not. Not in his sports career, nor in him as a person.

I duck under his arm and head back to my counter. "Did you catch my fight last Sunday?" he calls out as he follows me.

"No, I was working."

"Ah, always working, huh? Tell that old man

you need some time off," he remarks with a wink before darting off towards the sauna.

My time off since starting here is non-existent; and I'm surprised I've lasted so long.

By the time my shift ends, I swing by the corner shop to pick up a few carrots and potatoes for George. I toss them on top of my dirty uniform stashed in my backpack. A quick layer of sunscreen and I'm off, beginning my ride home.

The hot wind bites at my face, but I love it. I pedal faster, leaning into its warm embrace. As the road clears ahead, I rise from the seat, the bike almost lifting me as I glide through the streets. I count the intersections to track my progress, pressing my thumb against my palm. One down, two more to go before I turn left.

There's something about the rhythm of traffic which always feels like second nature to me. It's strange, though, considering I still can't pass my driving test. For some, not driving by twenty is just a fact of life; for others, it's a quiet disappointment.

But George never saw it that way. He was always proud of me. After I spectacularly flunked my first driving test, he handed me this bike. After the second and third fails, no more bikes appeared, but he did promise I could take his car for a spin if I ever managed to pass.

I pass the third intersection, and as I prepare to turn left, I bend my middle finger next to my index, counting my way home.

My flat is in the fifth building on the street, right next to George's cottage. I hop off the bike, leaving it outside, and hurry over to Bluebell Cottage.

My childhood charity helped me find a modest, affordable room in this peaceful side of Richmond after I left the shelter two years ago. They didn't require repayment—just that I look after the retiree assigned to me. That's how I met George, and how he became the best friend I never knew I needed.

Photos of George's late wife, Hilde, their two children and only grandson line the hall. Hilde passed away a while ago, and the kids visit seldom. Smelling earthy tea always fills the air like it's part of the house's heartbeat.

"I got your carrots." I call out over the music blaring from the old vinyl record player. Jimi Hendrix, I'm sure, still frequents this place to some degree. Next to the entrance door, I take my shoes off and throw them.

Nick Drake's 'Pink Moon' plays in the background, mixing with the familiar smells of old furniture. George's living room has shelves packed with everything from the classics to the obscure: Velvet Underground, Silver Apples, even the occasional Rihanna album—George swears it helped him recover from losing his appendix.

I spot George near the TV, absorbed in a dusty book.

"Have you had lunch?" I ask.

"Define lunch." he answers without looking up.

I drop my bag on the wooden table. "George, we've talked about this. You need to eat," I say, then head to the kitchen with the groceries. He follows me, the music getting louder with each step.

"What's with that look on your face?"

"What look?"

"That one. The 'mother-in-law's being a dick again' face." George calls Fred my mother-in-law, always teasing me about the way he bosses me around. I stop and face him. But no words leave my lips.

As the song plays on, George taps his foot to the beat, nodding at me like he's waiting for me to join in. I hesitate, then give in, swaying to the rhythm as the music fills the room.

I've known George for two years now and he's never changed his whisky stash. It's always tucked just behind his red armchair. He sneaks a sip whenever he thinks I'm not looking.

Approaching his kitchen table, he shuffles over and examines the paper-wrapped bag of potatoes, squinting suspiciously. From his shirt pocket, where he keeps his trusty pair, he pulls a single chopstick and uses it to pry open the bag with one precise slice, like a tiny samurai sword.

"What's with the paper bag? Is this supposed to be saving the planet?"

"Did I just hear a complaint?" I say, passing the hallway to get to the kitchen. "And global warming is real, by the way. I can show you a TikTok if you need proof."

"I don't need no *thick rock* to tell me it's getting hotter. Been cooking up in this world since I was born. And guess what? Spoiler alert: we're all checking out, eventually."

As I walk, I pass the wall lined with framed photos. I never met Hilde, George's wife. They got married in the seventies and had two kids who went on to have their own kids. Every morning when I come in, I see their pictures covering every stage of life, from toddler to teenager to adult. George told me Hilde had passed away years ago from throat cancer. His kids don't visit. He says when they did, it was only to see Hilde. Now that she's gone, it's like he vanished along with her.

"Did you take your meds?" I ask as he tucks his chopstick back into his pocket.

"Maybe. Could be. Could also be a jellybean."

"Not a debate. We talked about this."

"And I said I'd consider it. That's practically a handshake in my book," he grumbles, wandering over to his barely used, second-hand computer and wakes the screen up. "This Facebook account you set up for me, I started using it."

I see a string of comments when I examine the concert page more closely.

"And you're using it to start fights?"

"I'm educating. Can't help it if some kid thinks The Doors were *'mid.'*"

"George, are you arguing with strangers about sixties rock?"

"Damn right I am. History's under attack. Now, how the hell do I block someone?"

I owe George more than I can ever say. He's

been my rock, the one person who always has my back. With his eighty-first birthday coming up, though, I have no clue what to get him. George has it all.

Chapter Two
"Please Please Me"

I'm on the late shift tonight. Auntie took Fluf for a late stroll and then rushed back to catch some live competitive swimming on TV. As I fasten my belt around my oversized trousers in the changing room, I glance at the music videos playing on the TV overhead.

Back at the desk, Auntie left everything neat and orderly, as she always does. A few people wander in and out, but it's still too early to call it a busy afternoon. I try to catch a glimpse through Fred's blinds, and with a bit of squinting, I can just make out his office. Every few seconds, his fan stirs the blinds, giving me brief snapshots of Fred at his computer, laughing sporadically.

Sometimes, I entertain the idea of starting a YouTube channel. It could be my ticket to wealth or maybe just a stroke of dumb luck—who knows? I jot down a few ideas, but they quickly seem ridiculous, so I scratch them out. Earlier, I found a straw in the cupboard under the cashier counter and now I'm using it to sip my protein shake.

The laughter from Fred's office stops abruptly. I look up just in time to see Emily leaving, exchanging a friendly goodbye with Fred as she shuts the door. She catches me watching her.

"Hey, Julia," she greets me as she walks closer, somehow perching on my counter at the same time.

I scoot my chair back so I can look up at her.

"How's life?" she asks.

Before I can answer, she leans in, glancing over her shoulder towards Fred's office. "Listen," she confides in a hush, "I'm thinking of cancelling my membership here. I'd rather pay for one somewhere else."

We're all entitled to a free gym membership as employees, but with work hours from dawn until nearly midnight, few of us ever use it. Curiously, Emily's membership hasn't expired, even though she left the team the day I started. "I just had a chat with Fred and told him I won't be dropping by anymore. I just don't feel safe here," she admits.

I take a sip from my protein shake, pushing my YouTube notes aside. "What do you mean?" I ask, leaning in as she checks over her shoulder again.

"Fred's a creep," she replies, her voice cold and dripping with contempt. "Earlier, he asked me to stay a minute after my workout. He started telling me about his trip to Thailand. Then he put his hand on my leg and when he started tugging at my leggings, I knew it was time to leave. He's disgusting." She jumps off the counter. "Just be careful, Julia. That's all I'm saying."

I chew on my straw, my eyes drifting back to Fred's blinds fluttering under the steady breeze from his fan.

Outside, the heat presses down relentlessly and the gym remains quiet. Soon enough, Fred emerges and I stand up from my desk. Dressed in white sneakers, white shorts and a sleeveless button-up revealing his tanned, wrinkled skin and shaved chest, he strides over, holding one of his beloved Mr Olympia VHS tapes.

"*Madame*, kindly, do be a darling and put this inside the player, yes? It's time to create… how you say… legend," he says with a theatrical grin, handing me the tape.

I take the tape, push my chair aside and bend down to feed it into the dusty VCR, which never works without a few hearty slaps. Finally, it accepts the tape and I grab the remote, aiming to switch from music videos to the workout tape. The room falls silent except for a few metallic clinks in the background. Fred clears his throat.

"*Madame*, just a small but gentle reminder: put on your tie, always. Always tie. It is... professional standard!" he says pointedly.

I nod, wrestling with the remote, which badly needs new batteries.

"And don't forget, eh? Stand tall. Smile big. Welcome the clients like they come from Buckingham Palace."

A guy wanders in, his backpack slung over one shoulder. He tosses his membership card into one of the little baskets on my desk as he passes by.

"Hey, Julia," he mutters, heading for the changing room.

I catch Fred momentarily rising on his toes as if to check if I'm wearing heels. He appears disappointed, but for some reason, he doesn't bring it up. With a defeated air, he retrieves the guy's membership card from the left basket and transfers it to the right.

"Remember, cards without faces, they go in basket number two, not number one," he instructs, tapping his fingers impatiently on my desk. "Now tell me, the tape—is it in or not?"

I nod, still grappling with the TV remote.

"No, no, Fiona," Fred interjects, exasperation creeping into his voice. "You always need to press little arrow first."

"Sir, it's still connecting," I say, jabbing the remote.

"No, no, take it out, Fiona," Fred says, waving his hand like he's conducting an invisible orchestra.

I comply, and Fluf lets out a loud fart as he strolls over my feet.

"Now, put it back in and press little arrow," Fred commands.

I follow his directions.

"Nice," he acknowledges, waiting patiently for a few seconds as I stand there, expressionless. "Does it work now?"

"No, sir, it needs to connect first," I reply matter-of-factly.

"OK, connect the machine." Fred orders.

Another guy walks in, casually waving his entrance card. Fred eagerly redirects his attention.

"Young boy! Shoes OFF!" Fred bellows, pointing at the poster on the door. "*No shoe from outdoor. Change into training shoe.*" He shakes his head in disbelief. "What's going on? America, is it? You walk in your home with mud shoes? No, thank you!"

The guy wordlessly removes his shoes and enters the changing room holding his trainers between his fingers. Fred turns back to me.

"Is it connected now?"

I give the machine one final slap and all the right lights illuminate. Shirtless young Arnold Schwarzenegger appears on all the screens, eliciting a satisfied grin from Fred.

A guy across the hall shoots me a strange look.

"*Madame,* I need you to run errand for me," Fred declares, clapping his palms together. "Follow me."

I leave the remote on my desk as the earlier dude walks past me in his white socks.

Fred leads me into his office and I wait sceptically at the entrance.

"Come on in, come on in," he urges, as he rummages through a few envelopes on his desk.

I step closer, taking in the sight of the trophies displayed on the old wooden shelves. Being surrounded by only posters and tapes, the office is practically concealed from the rest of the gym. It's essentially a tiny box in the middle of the gym, shielded from everyone's eyes. That thought unsettles me.

"*Madame*, if you can, please be so kindly to make a small trip… to the post office, yes?" Fred requests.

"Sure," I reply, shadowing his every move.

He retrieves a stack of cash from his safe and tosses it into an envelope. Then he tears a page from one of his notebooks and places it over the envelope.

"Here, send this. Use this much for post. On the way back, stop at the corner shop. Buy me big tomatoes, juicy ones. And cheese, proper cheese. Oh, and say hello to Martha for me. Tell her I still waiting on her stew."

I glance around. "What about the reception?"

"Don't worry about it, *madame*. I will take care." he reassures me.

As we converse, Diego enters the gym, offering a friendly wave before heading for the changing room.

"I salute you, Diego!" Fred grins and presses the envelope into my hand like he's passing me a secret mission. "And grab a few coffee too, OK?"

Stepping out into the burning heat, the first thing I do is remove my tie. As I make my way to the post office, I contemplate whether to run away with the money or not.

The streets are restless, cars darting past with barely a soul walking around. Ducking out of the gym mid-shift feels strangely exhilarating, as if a jailbreak with no real escape on the other side.

At the post office, the line's short enough to breeze through. I pull a wad of bills from the envelope, handing over the rest. I grab a form and quickly scribble down the name and address Fred gave me.

Outside, a wave of dry heat smacks me in the face, evaporating the last traces of sweat but leaving a heaviness behind. I cross the street to the little corner shop.

"Well, look who it is." Martha calls out with a grin.

"Surprise, surprise," I laugh, owning my predictability.

"One kilo enough?" she asks, lifting a bag of tomatoes.

"Yep. And some cheese too, please."

As she bags up my order, I shuffle awkwardly.

"How's it going?"

"Surviving this oven, same as everyone." She seals the bag and punches a few keys on the register.

She hands over my bag and I count out the money, dropping a couple of coins for a tip.

"Oh, and Fred says hi."

She rolls her eyes and slams the register shut. "Tell Fred he can bite me."

"Message received," I say as I head for the door.

"Try not to melt out there." she shouts after me, winking.

I grab an empty apple box from the entrance and head over to the coffee machine outside the shop. The machine churns out a flimsy cup, followed by a stream of lukewarm coffee. I wait, filling the carton one by one and mumble in frustration as I fasten my tie once more.

Balancing the box on one arm, I clutch the bag of tomatoes and cheese in the other. A few cars honk as I dash across the street, tomatoes threatening to tumble from the bag. Near the golden statues, I catch a glimpse of Noah slipping into the gym.

Ah, Noah.

Something flickers in my chest—annoyingly warm, like a spark I didn't ask for. I adjust the groceries, trying not to look too eager as I step through the gym doors. I've had a crush on him since I first started here, but I keep telling myself it's just a fleeting thing, nothing serious. But it's tough not to notice the way he walks, like he has his own personal soundtrack. And then there's the smile. It's not fair. Sometimes, I catch myself staring at his membership card, wondering what kind of life comes with that grin.

As I burst inside, joy propels me into a happy pirouette, only to realise coffee has spilt on my chest.

"Oh, come on," I mutter, brushing at the stain.

"*Madame!* I need you now, immediately, with great urgency!" Fred's voice booms across the gym.

Everyone turns to look. I'm grateful Noah's still in the changing room. Seeing a line forming at the reception, I abandon my coffee and groceries on Fred's plastic table and dash upstairs, dabbing at the stain on my shirt. The gym is waking up, filling with chatter and clinking weights. Diego walks out, his tank top showing off his big arms.

"All good, Julia?" he says, giving my desk a

friendly tap.

I nod, smiling back.

"Diego, come here, my friend!" Fred calls, gesturing him over to his table.

As I take copies of new members' IDs and cut their photos for handwritten membership cards, I steal glances over the desk, hoping to see Noah when he emerges. Something about cutting out faces for the cards always feels oddly unsettling.

Silviu saunters in, squeezing himself among the newcomers. He's wearing yet another outlandish spandex bodysuit and I resist the urge to avert my eyes.

"Hey, Cinderella, how's the kingdom?" he smirks.

"Yeah," I say, distracted as I finish up another card.

Silviu pipes up again. "Did you catch my fight last night?"

"No, I missed it, sorry."

"No worries," he replies, grinning. "Maybe we could watch it together sometime. I could show you some of my moves, too."

I ignore him, handing out cards to the newcomers. Then, just in time, I spot Noah as he steps out of the changing room. I cover my stained shirt, suppressing a grin. He leaves his card in my basket, the wrong basket, and I feel like I could melt into the floor.

From somewhere nearby, Silviu's still talking. "So... Wednesday?"

"Hi, Noah," I mumble as he walks by.

"Hey!" he replies with a friendly nod, joining his friends at the back of the gym.

"Earth to Julia!" Silviu's voice cuts through, snapping his fingers in front of my face. "So... how about Wednesday?"

"You know I'm working. Go sweat it out or something."

"Wait—let me show you something." Before I can protest, he grabs my hand and peers at my palm. "Ever had your palm read?"

"Don't be a creep, Silviu," I say, trying to pull away.

"Trust me, just look," he insists, tracing lines on my hand. "This finger shows courage." He taps my thumb. "And this one here," he moves to my index finger, "suggests affection."

I frown, but he keeps a firm hold on my wrist, which pales under his grip.

"Now, your middle finger," he says, examining it closely, "is quite delicate. In Greek mythology, this would imply cleverness."

Over his shoulder, I notice Noah reappearing, making his way towards the stairs, sweat glistening on his forehead. He looks as though he's just doused himself in water. My heart races and I try to stifle a gasp as he passes. He smiles just enough to make my stomach flip. I barely notice Silviu tugging on my finger anymore. Noah smiled at me!

"Hello?" Silviu snaps his fingers again, shaking me from my thoughts. "So you're free Wednesday?"

I exhale, more firmly than I mean to. "I'm not! I don't want to go out with you."

"Ouch. Fine," he says, backing off before turning back with a sheepish grin. "Can you at least turn on the sauna?"

The lights flicker on in Fred's office as membership cards trickle into my baskets. I catch an odd smell at my desk. I glance around, half-expecting Fluf, but he's nowhere in sight. I shrug, resigning myself to the gym's unique bouquet of aromas.

Fred's voice booms from his office, louder than usual. "You don't know nothing, Marcela, nothing!" he yells, clearly on the phone. "I gave you everything! To you, to Mama, to your daughter! All of you, takers! Bloodsuckers!" A loud crash of glass. Gym members glance at his door, then at me. I meet their looks briefly before they carry on. Diego strolls by with a grin.

"That money is for Mama, Marcela! Not for you, slut woman! You are no sister of mine! Finished! Done! FINITO!" Fred bellows.

I blink rapidly, forcing myself to focus on counting the money from today's energy drink sales. Then, his office door swings open and I freeze, bracing myself for what's next.

"Fiona, do something for me," he mutters, swaying over the counter. His stench of alcohol hangs in the air. "Turn the TVs louder... so guests can enjoy, you know? Like cinema." he slurs, gesturing vaguely towards the TVs.

One of our regulars, Chris, shows up behind Fred, wearing his usual yellow t-shirt like it's part of his uniform.

I comply with Fred's order and raise the volume a few notches, earning a couple of puzzled looks from gym-goers. Fred claps a hand on the counter, looking at the bustling gym. "Busy day, huh? Is good, is good for business. But Fiona," he says, wagging a finger, "nobody comes in free, okay? No free pass, no 'just looking around'—that old lady, she must pay or she must leave! They think I'm fool? I am not fool. Good luck with that!" Fred's voice climbs like a siren. Meanwhile, Yellow-T-shirt-Chris mimics his gestures, flapping behind his back. I press my lips together, fighting a laugh.

Fred props himself against the counter and Yellow-T-shirt-Chris clears his throat. "Good evening," he says.

"Oh, good evening! Welcome!" Fred immediately straightens up.

Yellow-T-shirt-Chris takes his backpack off and places it on my desk. Our hands brush as he hands it over and I spot a banknote tucked beneath it. He gives me a quick wink as I tuck the bill out of sight. "Mind holding onto this for me?" he asks.

"Of course," I reply, slipping his bag behind the counter.

"How are you this fine evening, young man?" Fred asks.

"Doing alright, sir. You?"

"Excellent! Busy evening, as you see." Fred gestures at the gym floor.

I notice Noah heading out without picking up his membership card. For a second, I think about chasing after him, but Fred's exhausting presence has me pinned to my desk.

Around 11 p.m., Fred finally locks up his office. He gives a half-hearted wave goodnight, and I nod back. It's weird seeing him here this late. As he heads out into the night, I settle in to finish counting the day's cash, just as Dan shows up for his shift, looking tired but kind of ready to go.

"All yours," I say, passing him the notebook and locking the cash in the cupboard. Outside, Yellow-T-shirt-Chris waves through the glass door. I wave back, my hand brushing the taped banknote under the register.

The TVs are still rolling muted workout tapes. I flick off a few lights. Fred hates it when the lights stay on, though the TVs are apparently fine.

Just then, Fluf bolts out the door to greet his auntie, who's waiting outside, giving him a good scratch behind the ears. Auntie spots me and smiles as she makes her way to the desk.

"You look exhausted," she says, plopping into the chair next to me. Fluf curls up by her feet, tail wagging.

"Saw that old fool leaving a few minutes ago," she says, nodding towards the door.

"He was here all day."

"Like a bad rash."

I laugh, gathering up my backpack. Auntie springs up, her face lit with a mischievous gleam. I wonder what she's doing here so late, and... is that spiced rum I smell on her breath?

Before I can ask, she pulls a set of keys from her pocket and unlocks Fred's office.

"What are you doing?" I follow her.

"I'm making myself a drink," she mutters, pushing the door open. "You stay put; no need for both of us to get in trouble."

"Where did you get those keys?"

"He wanted me to clean his office last week and forgot to take them back."

"And did you?"

"What?"

"Clean his office."

"Do I look like I'd do that?" She raises an eyebrow.

I follow her inside, where bottles of alcohol line the shelves, gleaming in the TV light. Auntie picks one up, unscrews the cap and gives it a sniff.

"I know this is a bad influence," she says, holding out a cup, "but care to join me?"

Auntie's husband, András, passed away a

couple of years ago from lung cancer. She still tells me stories about his Olympic days as a swimmer. Fred hates her for it, thinking he's the only real "athlete" in town. But we all know he's more barstool than barbell.

She pours a splash into my cup, then takes a swig straight from the bottle. "Cheers to us."

"Cheers." I tap my cup against her bottle.

We settle down on the floor next to Fred's sofa, surrounded by shattered glass. The TVs flash as the workout tape cycles through body parts, each one bulging with biceps and Arnold's usual charisma.

After a while, Auntie breaks the silence, leaning over conspiratorially.

"How are you, my dear?"

"I'm... OK." I nod as she offers a faint smile. "And you?"

"Oh, I'm fine, just fine." She chuckles. We both know it's a lie, but tonight, we're okay with silence. Dan's already snoring, stretched across the plastic table like a very unconvincing guard dog.

"Auntie, can I ask you something?" I say, glancing over at her.

She shifts to face me, her expression softening. "Of course, sweetheart."

"It's a little random, but there's this guy here I kinda… like."

"Well, he's a lucky young man."

"I don't know about that." I laugh, a bit nervous. "I barely know him, but I want to. Should I just… ask him out?"

"Ask him out?" She raises her brows. "My dear, it's simple. Men love the thrill of a good chase."

"So… what then?"

"Talk to him. Give him a chance to notice what a clever young woman you are. If he's got half a brain, he'll be the one asking you out."

I nod, still a bit unsure where to start.

Fred has a camera crew at the gym today, shooting a commercial to showcase his flourishing business. He's flanked by two young women who look like they're not totally sure why they're here, sitting on either side of him at the plastic table. He introduces them as his "most devoted clients." Pretty sure I've never seen them before in my life.

Markus scurries around, setting the table while the crew prepares to film.

"*Madame*," Fred calls, spotting me as I'm trying desperately to look like I don't work here.

"Would you be so kindly to bring coffee for the gentleman peoples?"

The camera crew immediately shakes their heads and I take the hint. Just then, Silviu strolls in, catching my eye as he crosses the threshold.

"Morning, Princess! How about a steamy sauna for the two of us?" he asks, stopping by my desk with a grin.

"Silviu—" I draw in a lungful of air,, fighting off the thought I probably shouldn't say out loud. "I'm sure you'll manage just fine on your own."

"Thought about you last night."

"Shocking, really," I say as I unlock the control panel.

"You'd be a killer in MMA. I'm serious." he insists. "Your fist could be your signature move. Your secret weapon."

"Enjoy your workout, Silviu." I lock the panel, heading back to my desk as he sighs and ambles towards the changing rooms.

Meanwhile, Fred begins his monologue as the camera zooms in on him and his breakfast.

"I am man who needs big energy," he declares, waving at his food like it's royalty. "I burn so much, you don't understand. It's crazy. So I must eat, yeah? No 'portion control'—what is this?

Eat what you feel. This is my advice."

The two women beside him awkwardly nibble at a slice of banana, exchanging a look like they're not sure if this is a real shoot or some weird prank.

"Listen," Fred goes on, "Life—it is every day. You must live it. You eat good, you move your body, you feel amazing. So come here, to my gym. Live your best life, with this balanced breakfast I am showing now." He finishes with a thumbs-up, beaming like he just solved world hunger.

A couple of guys lifting in the background give me a look and I shrug.

Tommy stumbles out from the saunas, face flushed. Crap. Poor guy looks lost. I dash around my desk and guide him towards the back door to avoid Fred's cameras. All of them. Seeing this, Markus springs into action. He intercepts Tommy, steering him discreetly away from the front entrance.

Fred waits for the camera to zoom in and catch him in a close-up like he's auditioning for a documentary.

"I don't like to talk about me. I like talk about others. But OK—if I must..." He places his hand on his chest. "I was born very small. Tiny, like this."

He pinches his fingers together. "Doctors, they say, 'maybe he not make it.' My mother come one time per day to give little milk. Only once. No touching, just milk." He pauses, clearly digging for more backstory. "People don't believe I become something. But now look! I am big boss."

He stops, milking the silence, but then realises he's out of words. He clears his throat.

"When I was boy, I was skinny. So skinny, you see through me." He chuckles. "The kids, they laugh. They say, 'Look, is stick man!' But then... I find the lifting. I lift pots, trees, meat from the freezer. All the things. I make my body strong." He nods proudly. "No one laughs now."

He shifts his focus to his fruit bowl.

"What we got? Banana, apple, grape..." He trails off, and one of the women jumps in with a smile.

"Pears," she says, a bit too eagerly.

"Yes! Pears, very good," Fred says, giving her an approving nod. "And because I talk about myself now—which is rare—I tell you, I eat two breakfasts. Always two. First the power food, then the fruit. Fruit gives you Vitamin C. And also Vitamin E... for the ladies. Good for skin." He chuckles at his own wisdom. "Also, cereal gives me all the Vitamin Calcium I need. So I'm covered."

As he drones on, I exchange a look with the camera crew, who seem just as entertained as Markus is.

Soon, the camera crew pack away their gear. Diego, who's squeezed in a workout while Fred gave his interview, saunters over to hear all about it.

"So, tell me—who you say is more handsome, eh? *Stallone"*—he rolls the name like he's ordering fine wine—"or Arnold?" he asks, nudging Diego towards his office.

"You, of course," Diego replies, laughing loudly at his own joke.

"Fiona!" Fred shouts just as he's about to close the door. "You mind making us salad, yes? Add the tuna."

I want to refuse, but I kind of need this job. I grab the tomatoes and cheese, feeling a few judgemental glances from regulars as I pop open the tuna. Just then, Auntie arrives, and Fluf is already scampering excitedly around her feet.

She doesn't even look towards Fred's office as she walks past. "How are you today?" she asks, clipping Fluf's leash. She smells like whisky and stale cigarettes, and I notice she's had a bathroom accident. I open my mouth to say something but hesitate.

"I'll be out of your hair from now on," she says, looking straight ahead. "That old coot gave me the boot. Guess he finally figured out I kept a key to his office."

"No! He can't just—what'll we do without you?"

"You'll manage. This little guy's the only one who needs me." She nods at Fluf, who tugs impatiently on his leash.

I stare after her, feeling a strange finality in the way she leaves. The tuna can slips from my fingers.

"Are you going to be OK?" I call.

She turns with a small, warm smile. "Always, my dear."

I carry Fred his salad. Diego is sprawled on the sofa in Fred's office, sipping a soda. From the corner of my eye, I see Noah entering. Why is everyone here this morning?

"Fiona, have you ever considered doing the workout yourself, hmm?" Fred asks, still riding high on his interview energy.

"I don't have the time, sir."

"Come on now! You are here all day, all the

time! People take train just to come here. You, you are already inside the magic, and you do not use it?" His voice grows louder, and Diego exchanges a tired look with me.

"I'm just not interested," I lower my voice.

"Ay-yay-yay, you are so skinny! You need some meat. Proper muscle, like the girls from earlier. They are looking strong, fit! Not like wind would blow you away," he says, pushing a bowl towards me.

Out of the corner of my eye, I see Noah walking over to my desk, and my heart does a little flip.

"Sir, can I have a day off next week?"

"Day off? For what kind of reason?" Fred laughs.

"To… relax."

"Relax?! Ha! I never hear such fantasy in my life. In Germany, people work two job! No need for rest. They know the value of hard working! Is why their sausages are the best." Diego shoots him a look but stays quiet.

"Sir, there's a client," I deflect.

"Yes, yes, go do your clienting." He waves me off. I realise I'm still wearing my tie and quickly try to tug it off, but the knot's too tight.

Near the front desk, I spot Markus holding Noah's pass just out of reach, teasing him to kiss his cheek. Noah laughs and gives him a quick peck.

My heart sinks. I want to disappear, to melt right into the floor, salad and all.

"Hey, can I get a protein shake?" Yellow-T-shirt-Chris pushes a crumpled bill into my hand, snapping me out of it.

Markus gives me a wink as he walks by with Noah. I consider running out after Auntie or just screaming into the sky.

"When'd you get here?" I ask Chris.

"Just now."

"Seems like only you and Diego actually buy these drinks. This powder might well be expired." I start preparing his protein shake.

"Meh, we're both not dead yet. Diego just seems to get fatter, that's all."

"*Madame!*" Fred's voice booms.

"I better get going." Chris picks up his drink.

"*Madame!*" Fred repeats, emerging with a stack of poster ads, all spelling out "PRIVATE TRAINING DISCOUNTS." I'm sure Diego typed them, given Fred's total inability to read and write.

"Let's go stick these up! We promote, we inspire, we sell greatness!" Fred says, rushing over with tape in hand. He grabs my arm, pulling me down the hall towards the men's changing room. I glance back in the hopes to see Noah one more time, but he's gone.

As Fred turns to face me in the doorway, the only light is the neon glow behind him. My thumb curls into my palm involuntarily and I count. One.

"I can't go in there."

"Why not?" He glances over his shoulder. "There is no one—empty like desert! I just did inspection."

I step past him and take the posters from his hands. Inside, I pin one to the wall, but his stare weighs on me, prickling my skin. The room feels smaller, tighter, pressing in. My index finger curls in, and I count. Two.

"Summer is prime time for body transformation." he says, hands on his hips like a coach.

My middle finger curls in. Three. I don't want to be here anymore.

"*Madame,*" he then says, "if you would kindly grab us some coffees after this?"

I can't take it any longer. I let the stack of posters fall onto the bench and push past Fred, escaping back into the hall.

Stepping outside the gym, I gulp down air. My bike is leaning against the wall and I fix my gaze on it, counting. Three intersections, then a left and I'll be home. I visualise each step of the way, drawing in steady breaths until my chest loosens.

I want to go home.

"All hail Julia!" A voice calls out as I straighten up, wiping my cheeks. I turn and see George striding towards me.

"All hail Facebook!" he shouts.

I let out a relieved laugh, realising it really is him. He stops in front of me, pulls out his phone and starts scrolling.

"Please don't tell me you started more fights on Facebook."

He holds up his phone and shows me a blurry photo of his computer screen.

"George, I can't see anything. You need to focus when you take photos."

"I *am* focused," he insists, swiping through more images until, finally, a clear one appears. I squint at it, a profile photo of a woman in her early sixties with red hair threaded with grey.

"Who's that?"

"Cornelia's daughter," he says softly, nudging me to step aside from the gym's entrance.

"Who's Cornelia?"

"My first wife."

"Your first wife? Isn't that Hilde?" I don't know why I'm whispering too. "George, are you drunk?"

"No, but I wish I was. I've been married twice."

I pinch the bridge of my nose, collecting myself. George leans closer, his voice hushed. "She has her mother's smile. It's unmistakable. And... her mother's maiden name."

I pause, steadying myself. "So this is what you do on Facebook when you're not arguing about music? You stalk your first wife?"

"It's not stalking," he replies defensively. "I couldn't find Cornelia anywhere. But I found *her*." He points to the woman on the screen.

"How do you know she's Cornelia's daughter?"

"She's wearing the necklace I gave Cornelia in '64." George points at the screen. "Custom-made. Blue enamel and silver. No one else would have it."

I close my eyes, conscious Fred is waiting for his coffees.

"OK, what is all of this about?"

"Listen to me," George lowers his voice again. "Facebook says this young woman by the name of Christine Whyler was born in August 1965."

"I'm not sure I'm following."

"Cornelia left me right before Christmas in 1964."

"Maybe it's time to let go of the past."

"She looks like me. Christine Whyler looks like me."

I take another look at the Facebook photo in George's hand, just to find a reason to talk him out of whatever this is.

"It's all my fault." George adds as he packs away his phone. "I've been a fool." his voice almost fades.

"Ah George, I'm sure there's an explanation. Many people resemble each other without being relatives. Maybe you and Cornelia looked alike?"

"No... no. I'm uglier than a rusty Model T Ford next to her."

"Well, why would Cornelia run away with your unborn child?"

"Because it's all my fault."

"Then there's only one way to find out! Drop Christine a message. I'm sure she wouldn't think it's weird at all."

"No, no. We're going to New York."

"What are you talking about?"

"You and me," he says, his face serious. "I need you to help me find Christine Whyler."

"How do you even know where she is?"

He holds up his phone. "Facebook told me. She's a journalist. I know who she's writing for. There's no such thing as privacy in that dictionary of living people they call social media."

"Are you in your right mind, George?"

"Was I ever?" he retorts with a mischievous grin. "Besides, I can't just message her. I don't want to scare her off. This might be my only chance."

He has a point, sort of. Still, I shake my head. "I can't just fly across the world with you. I have a job."

"When was the last time you took a break?"

I think back. "Before I started working here."

"Exactly. You're wasting your life in that fluorescent hellhole."

Before I can protest, George marches into the gym. I hurry to keep up.

"Good afternoon," he announces loudly as he stops in front of Fred's office.

Fred stands up, looking puzzled. "Welcome,

welcome! What can I do for you, good sir?"

George clears his throat. "I want you to find yourself a new employee because this young lady here is leaving today."

"George, stop. I need this job," I plead under my breath, tugging at his arm.

He shakes his head. "No, you don't."

Fred's gaze shifts between us. "If I may do ask, who am I speaking to?"

George raises his chin. "The name's George."

"Alright, well, Mr George, I think Fiona has a tongue of her own to speak for her own herself. Right, Fiona?"

I stare at his ugly face, reminding myself how much I hate him, this place, and what two years here have done to me. I despise that gold statue, the useless TVs sucking up more power than half of London. I hate what this place did to Auntie— and since when is Markus gay? I hate myself for the choices that led me here and for never being adopted.

"My name is Julia," I say, locking eyes with Fred. I slip off my red work tie and drop it to the floor. "And I don't want to work here anymore."

Fred's mouth tightens. "Very well, if that is what you want. After all I have done for you...

offering you job, training, the chance to meet people from all over life."

"Oh, you keep your chances to yourself, you mother-in-law, you," George interrupts, grabbing a tomato from the open bag on the table. He hurls it at Fred, who dodges. George fills his arms with tomatoes. "Your stupid salads too!" This one hits. George takes aim again, throws and this time Fred shields himself behind his office door as tomato pulp splatters the glass, dripping onto the carpet.

Heads peek up from around the gym.

"Bastards!" Fred spits, stepping around the mess.

"Run." George shouts, piling into me to push us both out of the gym.

Outside, George makes a beeline for my bike, hopping on like he's sixteen again. He pedals off and I chase him as he rounds the corner, leaving Fred's angry panting behind.

"I haven't felt this young since 1981." George whoops in the summer heat.

"What happened in 1981?" I gasp, struggling to keep up.

"Long story. Everything's a long story." Cars honk as we take up too much of the road. "And it all begins with Cornelia."

Chapter Three
"I Want to Hold Your Hand"

Summer 1964

I sit at the back of George's story, and it's a bit like sliding into one of the cracked seats in his father's old cinema. The air around me thickens, with the ghostly scent of dust and stale popcorn. It feels like I've fallen straight into the memory itself. George's voice has that pull, like the quiet charge in the air before a storm.

He tells me he's just twenty then, but the way he talks, it's like he's still right there. Restless and curious. He says his movements are always carefree, like he's just about to crack a joke or brush off some minor disaster. Nothing rattles him. Not a customer with a complaint, nor a stubborn film reel refusing to play nice. I picture him leaning back, watching it all with that boyish grin.

Beside him, his father is calm, his hands precise as he waits for the cue mark to flare on the screen. George remembers it like a spell—timing, rhythm, the low animal purr of the machines, the small, devout motions that kept everything alive. His father never falters, eyes locked, as if he's conducting something only he can hear, something breathing beneath the static. George knows every part of the ritual, the way you know your own heartbeat.

But that night, George's thoughts start to drift. He talks about the smoke in the room, heavy and curling through the projector's beam. Someone in the front row—an older woman—sprays perfume around her neck, attempting to mask the smell of cigarettes. And the way he describes it, I can almost smell it too. It's all there, settling in around us like dust.

Then his voice falters, just for a second. I can feel him looking out into the dark, into the old auditorium. He's searching for something, or someone, even if he doesn't know it yet. And then he sees her.

She's alone, sitting in the flickering light from the screen. There's this glow about her, he says, something soft which makes it feel like she's part of the film herself. He can't look away. She laughs out loud when it's funny, and when the story turns sad, she wipes her tears without a hint of self-consciousness. There's something so real about her, so open and unguarded. He's completely hooked.

He forgets everything. The projector, the reel, even his father beside him. All he can see is *Cornelia*. She stands out so clearly it feels as if the rest of the world falls back, as though it exists only to frame this one scene.

The reel runs out with a click, snapping him back. His father's already setting up the next one, but the feeling doesn't go. George says it's like the whole room changed all at once. Like something bigger happened, even if it looked like just another movie night.

"And? Did you talk to her?" I rush to ask.

"I did," George replies, shifting in his seat and fumbling with his seatbelt.

"And what did you say? I can't believe you've never told me about her. What did she say?"

"I can't remember. I was high as hell."

"George." I press in a low voice as I look around.

One of the passengers across the aisle gives us a dirty look. I stare at the screen in my seat and see the flight map to New York. Four hours left. I can't believe I'm flying to New York. I can't believe I quit my job to fly to New York. I can't believe I quit my job to fly to New York to find George's girlfriend that he had never mentioned before.

George watches as one of the young women heads back from the toilet. "Why do girls walk around with holes in their jeans?"

"I bet you wore that back in the '70s too. Come on, stop it."

"Looks messy. Not in a good way."

"Shh!" I caution. "People can hear you. They're not deaf like you."

"I'm not deaf; it's tinnitus."

I cross my arms, sensing George hadn't finished his story. "So, what happened next?"

George reclines his seat, making the person behind him grunt in irritation. "I stared into the heart of everything..."

Summer 1964

George stumbles a little as he reaches the bench where Cornelia is sitting, her face a serene island in a sea of swirling colours. The world feels strange to him. Colours are brighter than they should be. Shadows stretch and shift like they've got minds of their own. Every edge feels soft, slightly off, like he's moving through thick blankets.

He tries to focus on her, but her silhouette seems to shimmer, just slightly. Her eyes are steady, curious, but he keeps getting distracted by the way the light lingers around her when she smiles. He blinks, fighting to clear his vision, but everything just gets more intense. The ground beneath him feels like it's pulsing, alive with each shift.

When he lowers himself onto the seat, he misses the edge by a bit and adjusts with a small jolt. The wood feels weirdly textured under his hands as he straightens up. He turns to Cornelia, his mouth dry as he clears his throat. Her hair catches the sunlight from within the movie, each strand a fibre-optic filament dancing in the breeze.

"Hello," he says, and even to himself, his voice sounds a little far away. He forces a smile, his face not quite doing what he wants. Cornelia smiles back—easy, warm—and that alone helps him settle. Her smile catches the light, and for a second he's completely caught up in it.

"And then? What did you say? *'You come here often?'*" I fix the blanket on my lap as turbulence makes the inside of the plane clatter.

"I'm not that big of an idiot."

"OK, well... did you ask her out? Did you start dating?"

"We did." George smiles.

"Can you move your chair back up, old man?" the guy behind us asks as he punches the top of George's seat.

George shifts just enough to see between our seats. "Can you ask me nicely?"

The guy groans, visibly annoyed. "This is my airspace—"

"Then no." George turns back around.

"Why have you never told me a single word about Cornelia?" I wonder, still processing the fact that we're flying to New York. I've never been to America.

"Sometimes when someone isn't in your life anymore, you learn to live without them. And you don't often talk using words you unlearn to use, or do you?"

"I told you to move the fucking thing back up." The guy behind us shakes George's seat. "Are you deaf, old man?"

I turn to look through the gap behind us. "It's called tinnitus."

"Fuck off!" he hisses.

George turns again. "No, you piss off, Steven Seagal. Stop slapping the seat. Some of you Millennials have never been hit with a reality check and it shows."

"I'm Gen Z." He rolls his eyes.

"Oh, whatever." George turns back and relaxes in his seat.

A flight attendant rushes to the guy behind us. They chat over each other. The flight attendant then leans in closer to George. "Everything alright?"

"Thank you, sir. Everything's okay."

"Wonderful. By the way, I'm a 'she/they,' not a 'sir'." The flight attendant chuckles.

"A *sheeday*? What's a *sheeday*?" George asks with genuine curiosity, while the guy behind kicks his seat again.

"I suggest we lean back *this* seat as well. This way, it'll feel like everyone has a bit more space." The flight attendant shows the guy behind us he can recline his own seat.

"I don't want to do that. I want him to move his chair away from *me*."

"What's a *sheeday*?" George looks at me.

"You just assumed they're a 'he'."

"But he has a moustache."

"See, you did it again."

The flight attendant rushes to assist another passenger.

"*They* have a bloody Freddie Mercury moustache." George whispers to me.

"So do my legs if I don't shave."

"But you don't wear your legs on your upper lip. Or do you?"

"You can't assume, though."

"What can I assume, then?"

"Simply put, George, you can't say that."

The guy behind kicks George's seat just to make a point. George shows him the middle finger through the gap behind us.

"Why are we doing this, George?" I sigh.

"Because I've done a lot of stupid nonsense in my life. And I owe Cornelia an apology."

The plane propels us ahead through the clouds.

Summer 1964

Just a week after meeting at the cinema, George and Cornelia are having dinner at a small diner, sitting across from each other in a booth. George tells me the story like it just happened, and it's easy to picture, like I'm right there, sitting next to them.

Cornelia's in a soft yellow dress, as if made for her. It moves easily with her, tied at the waist and falling in loose folds. She's twenty, with a brightness in her eyes impossible to ignore. Observant, curious, a little playful. George is completely taken.

Over dinner, she talks about her father's plans for her. Teaching. A steady life. But Cornelia wants something else. She loves poetry, writes in secret, even turns some of her poems into lyrics. She laughs when she says she can't sing, and doesn't play any instrument either, but it hasn't stopped her from dreaming.

"Sometimes I just want to run away," she says, almost to herself, and pulls a pair of wooden chopsticks from her dress pocket.

George gives her a look. "What are those for?"

"My friend went to a Chinese place once, kept the chopsticks, but didn't want them. So I took them." She grins, then uses them to pluck a piece of lettuce out of George's sandwich. "I'm practising for when I finally get to Asia. You think it's weird to try to learn from other cultures?"

George shrugs. "I don't know. Never really thought about it."

His parents came to America from Romania just before the war with his older sisters. His father never talks about the life before. He just keeps busy at the cinema and blasts classical music on his old speakers. George has learnt to keep his focus on the present, to not look back too much.

Cornelia leans closer, eyes sparkling. "Would you come hide away with me, then? I know a place."

Before he can say anything, she grabs his hand and they're off—running into the night like a pair of kids who've just got away with something. The air smells like flowers and city grime, the streets half-asleep around them. A train hums in the distance, a dog barks somewhere behind a fence. Streetlights flicker as they pass beneath them, skimming fractured light across their faces.

They stop at a small overlook, the city stretching out below, glowing dimly under the stars. Somewhere nearby, soft jazz drifts through the air. They absorb the music, letting it settle around them. Everything slows.

George wraps his arms around her, pulls her in. Her face is soft in the moonlight, and he can't stop looking at her. They start to move with the music, gently, without planning to, the lights of the city blinking below them like a secret just for two.

I slam the hotel window shut as a drunk outside yells at a streetlamp.

"Welcome to New York," I whisper to no one in particular, turning to take in the room. I peel off my socks and toss them near the bed. None of this feels like it adds up. But maybe it doesn't need to. I shrug and pull off my shirt and trousers, heading into the bathroom for a shower.

I like long showers, especially when I'm not the one paying the water bill. I like hotels too—for the same reason. *Take shorter showers, save our planet,* I read on a placard glued just above eye level on the tiles, one corner curling where the tape's lost its grip. I read it while rinsing shampoo from my hair, eyes stinging. I'm probably not the most admirable person, I think. Somewhere, better people are showering in thirty-second bursts, collecting rainwater for their plants, saving the world one tepid rinse at a time.

Back in the room, I wrap a towel around myself, hair dripping, heat already sticking to the back of my neck.

Then—three knocks. I scramble into my same sweaty t-shirt and trousers and check the peephole.

It's George.

"Fancy a drink?" he asks, dressed for something almost ceremonial—patterned shirt, dark trousers, shoes that gleam.

"Right now?"

"Yeah."

"Am I even allowed to drink in this country?"

"Oh, don't worry about that."

I glance at my phone. It's nearly midnight. Which means it's practically breakfast time back home. Jet lag is doing its thing, and George clearly doesn't sleep much. I follow him out into the hallway.

Downstairs, the bar is ablaze with conversation. The hotel itself is modest, functional without frills. The bar feels like an odd mix of regulars and people just passing through.

George leads me to a table already in progress: five older friends, mid-conversation and mid-drink.

"These are Alan, Anne, Anthony, Rosanna, and Humphrey," George says. "And this is my good friend Julia."

Alan, white beard and round glasses, has an arm slung casually around Anne. He's in a floral shirt, half unbuttoned, with a second pair of sunglasses hanging from the front pocket. Anne sips from her wine. She gives me a once-over, not unkindly. She's just more curious than anything.

Anthony tops off his whisky. Rosanna peers over her glasses to get a better look at me. Her silver bangles clink loudly when she raises her hand in hello. Humphrey nods with a small smile, his cowboy hat dipping slightly.

I feel like I'm on a Whodunit film set.

"What are you wearing, honey?" Rosanna asks. I should feel offended, but somehow, I'm not. I glance down at my sweaty t-shirt and shrug.

"Come on, join us."

"Care for another round? Perhaps with a splash of water?" Anthony asks George as he sits next to him and opens the whisky bottle.

"No water in my whisky. I'll hydrate enough after I die and they incinerate me and throw me overboard to the sharks," George replies.

Alan leans in closer to Anne while I find my seat opposite them. "Explain to me once again why you want to go to France?"

"To eat Ortolan," Anne replies, as if she's had to explain herself repeatedly.

"But it's been banned, darling. You're a few

years too late, I'm afraid."

"It's not. They ate it in that documentary."

"The one you watched after smoking my pot? I don't think so. Eating Ortolan is illegal." Alan turns to me. "Tell her it's illegal."

"Are you French, Julia?" Anne asks and I realise everyone's a bit drunk. I shake my head.

Alan tries to conclude, "Eating Ortolan is illegal."

"It's not," Anne interjects in a low voice. "You just gotta eat it with a napkin covering your head."

"Why? Because of the shame?" I feel involved now.

"No, because the aroma is better that way. You eat it with feet included, but you leave out the beak," she says. "And you eat it alive."

"Alive?!"

Alan lets out a low groan.

Anne shrugs. "I mean, you eat oysters alive."

"Yeah, but those don't have feathers." Alan leans back against the leather booth.

Anthony taps George on the shoulder. "That lady over there looks like she's got an eye for you," he hints, motioning towards a woman at the bar with her Chow Chow. No sooner does she catch us looking than she winks at George.

George grimaces, trying to avoid her gaze by turning back to our group. "She looks like she's ready to invite me over to her Tupperware party. Not to be judgemental."

"Are you married, George?" Rosanna asks.

"I'm widowed," George says.

Anthony's shoulders hitch upward. "Well, perfect timing then, I'd say. Dog ladies are easy to deal with. Usually, the moment you find out they have a dog, even if you don't like dogs, you say, *'Dogs? I love dogs. Dogs are my favourite.'*"

Rosanna turns to face me. "So, Julia, tell us something about yourself," she smiles. "But first of all, would you like some wine?" she asks as she already pours me a glass. "Do you have a boyfriend?"

"No," I say, finding their company strange but oddly enjoyable.

"How old are you?" Rosanna asks.

"I'm twenty."

"Ah, to be twenty again..." Anne sighs. "I was twenty-five when I first met Alan. He looked like a young Tom Selleck. I wanted to bang him all the time."

"Oh, really?" Alan raises an eyebrow. "What

changed?"

Twenty. It feels like nothing. Like I've barely made a dent in the world, unless I'd been Greta Thunberg or something. And yet too old to not feel like I should have figured out at least one thing by now.

Summer 1964

Cornelia was twenty when she met George.

Later, after dancing under the flickering streetlamp, they find themselves near Nobody's Children, the church where Cornelia's father preaches. It's late, but Cornelia assures George the Sunday service always runs long, and there's a room downstairs where they can hang out.

They slip in through a back door, Cornelia holding George's hand as they duck behind rows of wooden chairs. The stage lights give off a pale, hazy glow, casting long stains across the faces of the congregation. It feels like stepping into another world. People are standing with their arms raised, swaying and chanting softly, completely absorbed in the preacher's voice. George holds still. Cornelia's father is on stage, his voice booming, his gestures astute and forceful. George can't make out the words, but the intensity of it, the energy in the room, sends a chill down his spine. There's something both fascinating and unsettling about it all, as though the crowd is suspended in a collective dream.

George grew up around religion too. Icons above beds, long tables at Christmas and Easter, but it never meant much to him personally.

Cornelia smiles and squeezes his hand. They rush through a wooden door into a narrow corridor leading to a basement. Cornelia opens the door to a small studio room, a cosy space with warm colours and low furniture. Vinyl records line the shelves and a record player sits in the corner. George steps into the room, taking it all in. With every detail he uncovers about Cornelia, his desire to know her only deepens, leaving him yearning for more. She lifts a record and sets it on the turntable. "I Want to Hold Your Hand" by The Beatles begins to play, and the music fills the room. Eyes closed, Cornelia glides to the beat, her movements soft and unbound.

She gets closer to George, inviting him to join her dance. There's a playful glint in her eyes as she tugs at his shirt, fingers teasingly attempting to unbutton it. George laughs, grabbing her hands gently in his palms.

"Isn't this a holy place of worship or something?" he asks, a smile playing on his lips.

"There can't be a God, not when there's war and kids dying and people breaking each other's hearts," she says, pausing to look into his eyes. "This place used to be a sock factory before it went under. My father bought it cheap. You can listen to rock music in a cheap sock factory; there's no religious law against it."

As the night deepens, they lose themselves in the melody, the room alive with laughter and the soft shuffle of feet.

The song fades into the background, a faint pulse threading through the quiet.
"I Want to Hold Your Hand" starts playing at the hotel bar.

George shoots up, knocking the table with his knees. It wobbles as he storms off without a word.

I slide my chair back, muttering a quick, awkward excuse, and follow him. The hallway feels weirdly long in the dim light. It's stretching with every step. The carpet muffles my footsteps, but the silence somehow makes them louder.

I find George sitting against the wall, his back pressed to it. His shoulders shake with quiet sobs, each one heavier than the last.

"I slapped him," he says.

I sit down next to him.

"I slapped him. In front of the board during a meeting." He stares at his hands like they still hold the memory.

"Who did you slap, George?" I wonder how drunk he is.

"Jesse. My eldest. He walked into my office one day—thirteen years old... unlucky thirteen. First thing I see? His shoes. Bust open, caked in mud, laces hanging on for dear life. He'd been playing football in those things for years. And I got mad. No—worse, I got embarrassed. What would the board think if they saw him like that? So I stood up, walked right over, and slapped him."

He pauses. His voice tightens.

"A week later, I bought him new shoes."

In the two years I've known George, he's only ever talked about his family with a glowing sort of pride. He's told me about Hilde, how much he loved her. How proud he is of his kids. But sitting here now, slouched against a cold hotel wall, that pride feels different. Not gone, just heavier. Like loving them so much has stripped him bare. His pride doesn't just lift him; it seems to shrink him, too.

"He never wore them," George adds. "The new shoes. Kept wearing the old, filthy pair. His mum bought him another set later on, and he wore those." He nods to himself. "I think that was it. That day was the start of him keeping his distance. I don't know if it was the slap, or the shoes, or if he just started liking me less."

He scratches at his temple.

"I think about that day a lot lately."

The hallway is quiet. It's waiting with me.

"I raised Jesse to believe he could always do better," George says. "That's the only way you get anywhere, right? You don't tell a smart kid he's smart. You tell him to try harder. He had potential, loads of it. If I went soft on him, he wouldn't have done anything with it. My father never pushed me. Just nodded along, said as long as there was food on the table, it was enough. But it's not. It's effort. That's what matters."

He glances up.

"Jesse didn't always take it well. But he's done great for himself, and I'm proud of him. So maybe I wasn't all wrong in the end." George stares back at his palms. "He hates The Beatles, he says." George chuckles softly, shaking his head. "I reckon he hates a lot of things I like, truth be told. That's how it goes with boys, isn't it? When they get to a certain age, all they want is to be the opposite of their old man. I can't say I blame him. I was Jesse once. We've all been there." He pauses. "When he was a nipper, he'd dance 'round the living room to "I Want to Hold Your Hand" every time Hilde put it on the stereo." George smiles. "My little boy grew up too fast."

I think for a while, but I don't know what to say in reply. I think pride can look an awful lot like regret if you sit with it long enough. But I don't say that out loud. George is still staring at the floor.

"The sound of that slap," he says, "sometimes reminds me of clapping—loud, sweaty, impossible to escape."

Summer 1964

The grand hall of the Nobody's Children church reminds George of a Catholic chapel. The high ceilings, the quiet devotion; but something feels different. He slips into a seat at the back, running his fingers along the smooth wooden bench. Around him, fifty people sit silently, their eyes fixed on the stage. But to George, it might as well be hundreds. He feels their presence in the air: the soft rustle of movement, the stillness, the quiet tension hanging between them. There's a strange rhythm to it all, like a heartbeat.

He closes his eyes. For a flicker of time, he doesn't feel separate from them. The bench under him seems alive, like it remembers the tree it once was. He imagines himself in that tree, a tall white oak, perched high in the branches as a boy. He can almost see the fields stretching out forever, the wind tugging at his shirt like the sky wants to lift him up. He feels small, like a single piece of something vast. He's never believed in God, not really. But here, in the white oak, it almost makes sense.

Sudden applause snaps him back. George blinks and grips the bench. There is no God, he reminds himself, only the answers within.

His mind stirs, scattered by the effects of the LSD. The church's name still makes him laugh a little: *Nobody's Children*, just like the movie from 1951.

Cornelia's father, Jeffrey "Bobby" Dean, steps into view on stage. He's in his early forties, and George can already see where Cornelia gets her striking features from. Bobby wears a light blue shirt, a few buttons undone. It hugs his frame neatly. His long hands move as he talks, sometimes curling into fists, sometimes sweeping through the air. His face is expressive, his eyes wide and open. He has the presence of someone used to holding a room.

His warm and steady voice rolls over the crowd like soft music. "Be careful," he says, "of what people whisper into your ears. The Devil doesn't visit you in your sleep. He shows up as someone close. Someone new."

The room is silent, listening.

Bobby walks slowly across the stage. "Just last week," he says, "a friend came to me in tears. 'Bobby,' he said, 'I think I hate you.' I asked him, 'Why, brother? What's made you feel this way?' He said a neighbour told him to stop trusting us. That our church wasn't real. That he should leave. He said, 'I don't even know why I feel this, but it's in me now. And I think I have to go.'"

Bobby pauses. "So I hugged him," he says. "I prayed with him. And together, we pushed that doubt away. Just like it came, in whispers, it left. If you ever feel that way, if the doubt creeps in, come to me. My arms are open."

Applause rises. Bobby stands still, then raises his arms slowly, soaking in the room's energy.

Everyone is on their feet.

At the back, George stays seated. He watches. He feels out of place. Cornelia sneaks up behind him and wraps her arms around his shoulders. He leans back into her. He's late. He was supposed to cover for his father at the cinema.

They slip out of the church and run through the streets, laughing as they duck inside the projection room. George threads the film just in time. As the projector whirs to life, Cornelia kisses him.

They stumble and fall to the ground. As he slips his hand under her blouse, he sees in her something so divine. She is the God he found in the branches of the white oak, the one who pulled him into the skies. Her lips are so soft, warmer than a glass of milk before bed. The applause of the cinemagoers carries as the names of the main cast members appear on the screen. George pins Cornelia's shoulders to the floor, just to look at her. In her face, he sees traces of Bobby. Of faith, of something worth believing in. She's the only religion he's ever needed.

Chapter Four
"She Loves You"

"Absolutely not." I exclaim the next day as I watch Alan, Anne, Anthony, Rosanna and Humphrey standing in front of a vintage VW Kombi. The 1960 Kombi has a two-tone paint job in mint green and white, round headlights that seem almost too innocent and a front bumper covered in stickers from places it's been. The vehicle screams 'flower power' with its oversized side mirrors and the unmistakable VW emblem in front and centre.

"Why not?" George throws his hands up, more playful than frustrated.

"Because we're not a bunch of hippies with nothing better to do," I retort.

"Oh, come on, it'll be fun," George insists.

Alan opens the Kombi's door, revealing an interior, clearly old but lovingly maintained. The seats are upholstered in retro plaid and there's a faint scent of cedar mixed with the lingering aroma of decades-old coffee spills. Cool boxes are already packed and neatly stacked, ready for the journey.

"It'll be fun, Julia," Rosanna says, leaning against the Kombi's rounded front. "Let's help George fulfil his last wish." She sounds as though George is on his deathbed.

"It's not like he's dying," I mutter. "Are you dying, George?"

"I'm not. Not yet," George replies with a wink.

I drag in a breath. *"Just breathe,"* people always say, *"and everything will make sense."* Nonsense. Breathing doesn't do shit.

"So, three days, yeah?" George continues, barely containing his excitement as he takes out a map. "Day one: We get to Woodland Valley Campground and stay the night. Day two: Woodland Valley to Hudson. Day three: We drive to Woodstock, just in time for Christine's conference."

Alan went through all of Christine Whyler's latest posts and found out she'll be at a conference in Woodstock in three days.

"Storytelling in the Age of Social Media," I read the article title myself as I scroll through my phone. *"How journalism can evolve while staying true to its roots. Integrity, local relevance, fake news, the role of*

independent media and reporting on social movements."

"I still don't get why we can't just call her." I say.

"Imagine how you'd react if some old bloke called you, claiming he might be your real father." Rosanna chimes in.

"Oh, so ambushing her at a work conference is a breeze to process instead?" I fire back, but the acidity of my own words cuts me in return.

I wonder if Christine ever feels the absence of someone she's never known, the faint trace of a presence she's unaware exists. If she truly is George and Cornelia's daughter, I wonder whether Cornelia ever spoke of him. I glance at George as he cheerfully folds his oversized paper map.

"Those shoes don't exactly scream 'road trip,'" Anne points at Alan's feet.

"Better to be overdressed than underdressed," Alan quips.

"But we're going on a trip. How are you going to be comfortable in those?"

"Last time, you told me to dress smart, and everyone else was in T-shirts and jeans."

"That was on April Fool's Day, Alan," Anne shakes her head.

"And I'm still not over it. You've got a cruel

sense of humour."

"Whatever. By the end of this trip, even your blisters will have blisters in those shoes."

"I'll manage. Someone has to maintain some standards around here," Alan says with a mock sniff of indignation.

"Standards or not, we're in this together," Rosanna cuts in, patting the Kombi's hood. "So, let's hit the road before George starts acting again like he's on his last legs."

The van groans like it's dying. Alan grips the steering wheel with all the intensity of someone convinced they're in a high-speed chase, even though we're barely scraping 40 mph. It feels like we're racing in the summer heat until a bigger lorry overtakes us and we feel small again.

George and Anne sit in the front, chatting like co-conspirators. Meanwhile, the rest of us—Rosanna, Humphrey, Anthony and I—are crammed into the back row like mismatched puzzle pieces. I've claimed the extra fold-out seat shoved near the boot. It's not so much a seat as a flimsy excuse for one.

Rosanna slaps the side of the van's ancient radio. "Alan, seriously. Music. This feels like it's going to give me the Stockholm syndrome."

"You're welcome to walk," Alan says without missing a beat, his eyes still on the road. "Besides, do you even know what the Stockholm syndrome is?"

Undeterred, Rosanna twists the radio dial, searching for anything free of static. The first hit is an upbeat polka tune which makes Anthony visibly wince. She skips to the next station, landing on an overly cheerful televangelist declaring salvation through mail-order holy water.

Rosanna groans. "Does this thing even work? I swear this van is older than George."

"Careful, Rosanna," George quips from the front. "I'm old enough to write you out of my will."

The jab earns a chuckle, but Rosanna's not done. She swivels in her seat to face me, her bracelets jingling like wind chimes. "Julia, you're French, right?" she asks, tilting her head like she's already decided I am.

"I'm not."

Anthony groans while waving his arm. "Oh, Rosanna, please don't start this now."

"But you're European?"

"Yeah…?"

"So, what do you hate most about the US?"

She looks at me expectantly, like a crazy cat lady with the enthusiasm of a dog.

I blink. "What I hate? Nothing, really—"

"Bullshit," Humphrey cuts in, his lanky frame sprawled across the middle seat. "Nobody likes everything. Spill it."

"There's a lot to like about the US. I mean, the people. I like you guys, for example." I say, glancing from the road to Rosanna, hoping the interrogation will stop soon.

"It's not about what you like—it's about what you don't. Nobody likes everything. You kids are so scared of offending people, you can't even speak your minds anymore."

I pause before speaking. "I guess... when people leave their fridges open in movies? Like, they just stand there, staring into it, eating straight from the shelves. Who does that?"

Rosanna tilts her head as though I've just unlocked a universal truth. "Huh. Interesting."

"And shoes indoors," I add quickly. "Like, walking around the house and then hopping straight into bed with them on. Why?"

"Oh, we definitely do that," Rosanna says, turning to Humphrey for confirmation.

"Of course we do," he agrees, as though

walking around barefoot would be an act of treason.

"Speaking of movies, I have this great idea for a movie," Humphrey says. "What if the United States never existed, right? Like, poof." He gesticulates wildly. "Imagine only one country colonised the Americas. Say… the Greeks. Imagine Greek diners everywhere. Toga-wearing politicians. Democracy 2.0."

Alan snorts. "Why Greeks?"

"I don't know," Humphrey says with a shrug. "They're badass. Ancient as hell. Just picture the vibe."

"Ugh, you'd ruin even a Greek diner," Rosanna mutters. "Anyway, Julia, what are your hobbies? Tell us more about you." she asks as the van takes a slightly sharper bend, almost pressing my cheek against the window.

"I—don't think I have a hobby."

"Oh, come on," she presses. "Knitting? Scrapbooking? Deep-sea diving?"

I shake my head.

"I know what you need!" she raises her voice. "Meditation."

"Oh, leave the poor girl alone." Anthony rolls his eyes. "She doesn't need you to teach her how to open her fifth eye through her butthole or whatever." He leans in to look at me. "She's like this with everyone. Just ignore her."

"Sounds like a pretty cool idea." I smile.

"Don't be such a people pleaser." Humphrey shakes his head at me. "Nobody wants to meditate with her."

"Oh, Humphrey, don't be such an ass!" Rosanna slaps his shoulder.

I can't tell if these people hate me or like me. I look out the half-open window. Cars race past us from the opposite direction. Hot wind blows into my face. I wonder if this is how families feel when they go on holiday.

By the time we arrive, the van door jams, Humphrey trips over a cooler and George somehow manages to pop open a bag of marshmallows before we've even unloaded the tents. He pulls out his phone, taps the screen a few times, then lifts it towards the sky.

"No signal for Facebook out here."

The campsite is busy, buzzing with the sounds of crickets, distant guitar strumming and the occasional whoop from the teens camping nearby. Setting up the tents quickly becomes a group exercise in frustration. Alan refuses to read the instructions, Rosanna keeps offering helpful suggestions nobody asked for and George spends five full minutes lecturing Anne on "proper guyline tension" before she storms off.

I wrestle with my tent for what feels like an eternity before finally securing it. It's small. So small I half expect to find a kennel logo stitched onto it somewhere, but it'll do.

As the night deepens, our little campsite transforms into a drunken circus. Anne is sprawled on the ground, having what seems to be a very philosophical debate with herself about the superiority of red wine over white. Alan tries to play the guitar but keeps forgetting how to tune it, so it mostly sounds like he's wrestling a dying cat. Rosanna is dramatically reenacting what she insists was "the single best scene from Titanic," but nobody seems to remember the part where Rose monologues about chakras.

The group of teenagers camping nearby are lounging around their fire, vaping in near silence like they've perfected the art of stillness. They occasionally let slip faint plumes of vapour that rise into the air. The smoke carries a subtle, fruity scent that drifts intermittently in our direction.

"They're definitely judging us," I mutter to

Anthony, who's busy balancing a plastic cup on Humphrey's head.

"Let them," he says, straight-faced. "We're living. They're… inhaling raspberry clouds."

Hours later, the laughter dies down. Most of the group has retreated to their tents and the teens' fire has burned low. I try to sleep, but the air feels heavy, my thoughts louder than ever.

I slip out of my tent and find George sitting on a rock just beyond the campsite, his silhouette outlined against the stars.

"Couldn't sleep?" he asks without turning.

I shake my head as I sit beside him, wrapping my arms around my knees. For a while, we just sit there, letting the night fill the silence.

"Do you think I'm boring?" I ask, making George lift his head.

"Boring? You're the most hilarious person I've ever met."

I laugh.

He picks up a small stone and tosses it into the darkness. "What's this about?"

"I just… I feel stuck. Like, everyone's out there chasing something, and I'm just… here, not even sure what I'm good at. Man, I sound like a total pick-me."

"What's a *pick-me*?"

"It's fine. I've said worse. I probably got kicked out of feminism five opinions ago. Who even knows what the rules are now?"

George leans back on his elbows. "Sometimes the world makes you feel small. Like you've got to stay quiet when all you want to do is scream. I get that."

I look over at him, waiting.

"But you don't always have to scream," he says. "Sometimes it's about knowing when to be quiet. When to just… take things in."

He then gestures towards the tree line. "You don't have to be extraordinary. Just notice what is. Be here. That's enough. One day, you'll look back and miss it."

He nods to himself, like he's having a quiet word with the trees. "Truth is… the things I used to say to my kids, the way I went about it all—I look back now and think… maybe I mucked it up more than I got it right. Maybe I didn't quite understand what being a dad really meant. Or maybe I just didn't have the measure of the world at all, not properly."

I pick up a pebble and toss it, watching it

disappear into the night. A couple of birds fly from one tree to another, making branches swing. "Have you been to this place before?"

"With Cornelia." he says. His voice is quiet now, almost fragile.

Summer 1964

George borrowed a friend's 1957 VW Kombi. The engine purrs softly and is worn just enough to divulge stories of past road trips. It's not flashy, but it has character.

The road ahead winds through a patchwork of sun and shade. Maples lean in overhead, hushed and observant. George keeps sneaking glances at Cornelia, unable to help himself. Her bare feet are on the dash, toes tapping along with the scratchy rock 'n' roll spilling from the radio. Her skin glows in the light, and the breeze carries a warm mix of pine, dirt and wildflowers.

The campsite is tucked between tall conifers. It feels hushed, abandoned. They pitch the tent in a clearing, taking their time with the poles and canvas, laughing when things don't quite fit. Eventually, it stands. Not perfect, but good enough. Later, they lie inside, curled up, the faint sound of a tinny song drifting from their little radio. Outside, the lantern paints faint patterns across the tent's walls.

Cornelia stretches out on her back. George props himself on one elbow, gently twisting a strand of her hair. She giggles, and the sound slips into the night like it belongs there. Her hair slides through his hand and he thinks of it as water. She isn't just Cornelia. She's a mermaid, her laughter luring him further out to sea.

"You know what really gets on my nerves?" Cornelia says, breaking the quiet.

"What now?"

"People who take a bite of food, spit it out halfway, then just jam it back in. What the hell is that?"

George grins, leaning in a little. "Don't sweat it. I'm never going to spit you out. Once I get a taste, I'm all in."

She scrunches her nose. "You're gross, you know that?"

He kisses her, his hand drifting lightly along her neck.

"So tell me," he says, his voice dropping low against her skin. "What do you love the most, then?"

"Besides Paul McCartney? Probably you."

"Well, I'm a George. That's practically a Beatle already." he teases, his fingers brushing along her arm.

The night wraps around them in soft colours. Crickets buzz and leaves rustle. A creek gurgles somewhere nearby. Under the wide, starry sky, George and Cornelia feel both small and alone in a world seeming endless.

"I wrote you a poem," George announces then, sitting up. He reaches into his chest pocket and after some fumbling, pulls out a crumpled, poorly folded piece of paper. He unfolds it with exaggerated pomp, holding it up like a royal decree.

Cornelia raises an eyebrow. "Oh, boy."

Clearing his throat dramatically, he begins,

"The birds have tholdeth me
That, beneath the shelter of a noisy church,
Dwelleth a princess with her music even louder.
With rivers of hair cascading,
And suns that doth sparkle therein.
The songs within the secret room only sungeth for
her,
And I walked into her world,
And now she's dancing in my arms."

He wraps up with a look of quiet triumph,

tucking the paper away as he meets her gaze. Cornelia stares at him, her lips twitching. She collapses into laughter, doubling over and covering her face with her hands.

"I love it, I love it! I love it!" she cries, hiding her face against his chest as laughter shakes her shoulders.

George pulls her close, kissing the top of her head. "I love you, I love you, I love you," he whispers, holding her tightly.

Later, they sit by the fire with their new friends—travelers like them, drawn together by chance and shared wonder. There's Eloise, the artist from Lille with paint-stained fingers, and Thomas, a soft-spoken history graduate who sees stories in every pebble. Beside them lounges Violet, who sings old songs with a voice like smoke.

George and Cornelia sit side by side, hands clasped. Each time their palms connect, their bond feels stronger. Cornelia speaks his language, and he speaks hers. Yet, it is in the silent stretches, when he holds her hand, when his embrace surrounds her, that she truly speaks to him in languages he has never known.

George's father had always found English tricky. He spoke it with a heavy accent, careful with his words, sometimes getting stuck between what he wanted to say and what he could say. Still, he'd always insisted there was no language more beautiful than Romanian—the tongue of his parents, and their parents before them. When he spoke of it, his voice filled with a kind of quiet pride, anchored to a world he left behind that still talked to him in dreams.

To George, these stories felt like chapters from a fairy tale. His father described fields ripe for farming, the laughter of children playing games on dusty roads and cities brimming with youthful promise, and dreams crushed by the heavy hand of history. He recalled theatre plays shared with his mother, books devoured in lamplight and music that once spoke of freedom. And always, in his stories, there was the fresh, open air of the countryside. A current of possibility in a land which seemed destined for greatness.

But his father knew, painfully, that those promises were lies. He left that place not because he wanted to, but because he had to. For a better future. For the family. It cost him something, leaving. George could see that. He carried the ache of it on his shoulders and in the way he held on to his language like it was the last piece of himself he could still protect.

He wanted to pass it on. Not just the words, but the meaning behind them. A way of keeping the past alive while building something new.

George, though, never quite saw the point. The stories felt distant. The language now awkward in his mouth.

"If it's me, or two of me, or a hundred clones of me, it won't make a difference, Dad," he'd once said, half-laughing, half-exhausted by another long tale of "what once was."

In the end, George didn't carry the language forward. He didn't speak Romanian fluently. He didn't feel the same connection to old movies, or the same pull towards music his father spoke about.

But now, holding Cornelia's hand in the stillness of the evening, something shifts.

He thinks of his father again. Not as a man stuck in the past, but as someone who just wants to share something of himself. A kind of love that's bigger than words.

In Cornelia's eyes, George sees a version of the future his father might've wished for. A love steady enough to hold the burden of everything that came before, and light enough to carry them into whatever comes next. Her smile makes music matter again, like every song is quietly watching them, translating their story into its own tune.

And for the first time, George wants to speak a language other than his own. He wants to learn hers.

"Where there's love, there's music," Cornelia says, her voice soft by the campfire. The flames flicker between their small group. Thomas strums a guitar, while Violet plays along on her harmonica, the two of them swaying gently, their shoulders brushing.

The music is slow and easy, tempting them into a space where life simply is, without reason or consequence.

George runs his fingers through Cornelia's hair. It's soft and warm, and he moves like he's figuring out a melody, one strand at a time.

"I wrote you a poem too," Cornelia says, fishing around in her pocket. "It's kinda dumb, but it's my comeback to yours."

Instead of opening it, she pushes it into George's hand and folds his fingers around it.

"Here," she smiles. "Go on," she teases. "Read it to me."

George unfolds the paper to find it blank, save for a single coffee stain splashed across the white.

"It's... empty?" he asks, confused.

"It's our unwritten future," she says, her smile tilting playfully. "We get to fill it with whatever we want. No one's going to stop us. Not the world, not the past. It's wide open."

George doesn't say anything right away. The guitar keeps going, low and steady in the background.

"Well?" she asks, leaning closer.

"I think," he says, pausing with a dead-serious face, "this might be the laziest present I've ever gotten."

Cornelia laughs, and he pulls her into a kiss. George doesn't just want to understand her—he wants to know her, really know her. He wants to walk through her memories, hear what moulded her, learn the language of how she loves.

Out of nowhere, the group jumps to their feet, peeling off clothes and racing down to the lake. George and Cornelia don't even hesitate. They follow, splashing into the freezing water. The night is pitch black around them, yet their laughter lights up the world around them, sending birds scattering from their nests.

It is the height of summer and the peak of a

romance blossoming so quickly, so deeply, it feels eternal. Floating in the cold water, surrounded by nothing but starlight and each other, they understand; there is no light without the dark.

I find a strange sort of comfort in George's story. Comfort in knowing he once had Cornelia, that he once loved someone like that. The kind of love people are always banging on about. I can picture her now: her smile, the way she carries herself, the way her hair moves across her back when she turns to look at George over her shoulder. No wonder he was mad about her. I think I would've been too.

"Cornelia wasn't a redhead, was she?" I ask George.

"Nah. Why?"

I shrug, not quite sure why I thought she was. I'd just pictured her that way, I guess. But now, thinking back on everything he said, I can see her clearer: dark brown hair, brown eyes.

I let out a big yawn. It's late. Time for bed. The night air has gone cool again and my tent is calling. I push myself up with a groan, like someone twice my age. Honestly, I creak like I've been through the 60s myself. My body's a mess.

But I don't get far. George doubles over,

clutching his stomach. His face tightens, eyes shut, breath coming out in laboured little gasps. I freeze, heart hammering, not sure what to do. Then I shake myself—standing there gawping isn't helping.

"What's wrong?" I say, but my voice comes out thin, almost drowned by the rush of blood now pounding in my ears.

He waves a hand like he's fine, but he's clearly not. I glance around. Everyone else is drunk or fast asleep. Anthony's somewhere nearby, still throwing up from all the whisky. Brilliant.

No help to come. No staff, no adults. Just a group of teens over by the campfire, doing absolutely nothing useful. I mean, I'm not sure how it works over here, but I wouldn't trust a teenager to drive my car, let alone handle this. I realise I have to do it.

I steady myself and focus. I stretch out my hand, count my fingers. Thumb in. "One." The rest curl into a fist. "I've got this."

"You need to drive me to a hospital," George says, his voice all tight and strained.

"I haven't got a licence," I panic, yanking out my phone, hands shaking as I try to load Google. The nearest hospital is about an hour away. "You know that. I can't actually drive."

"'Course you can," he mutters, struggling to stand, grimacing all the way.

"I've only ever driven automatics," I blurt, still full of panic as I help him to the Kombi.

"It's not rocket science. You kids act like everything's a crisis," he grumbles, chucking me the keys and collapsing into the passenger seat.

I stare at them in my hand. Then glance back at the group. No choice.

Sliding into the driver's seat, I adjust it as best as I can.

"Right," I mutter, sliding the key in.

"Watch the gear stick diagram," George says, head resting against the window. "Clutch down every time. You'll be fine."

"Stop saying it's fine," I snap, turning the key.

"You've got to press the clutch to start it."

"Yeah, alright." I press it and turn the key.

"Clutch down, first gear," George says, doing the handbrake for me. "Bring the clutch up slowly, feel for the biting point, then more gas. Then let go of the clutch."

Somehow, the Kombi starts moving.

"Clutch down, second gear," he says softly.

I follow his lead, even though my brain's

spinning. "Now slowly let the clutch go while giving gas."

The car jolts, but we're off. Out the car park, onto the road.

"I said *slowly*," he mutters.

We wind through the hills.

"Clutch again. Fourth gear. Let it go slow, gas. Just feel for the bite."

"Are you alright?" I ask, watching the road, sneaking glances at him.

"I'm fine," he says, waving me off again.

Eventually, we make it. The Kombi flies into the hospital car park and I stop badly across two bays. Hazard lights on. I run to his side and help him out.

Inside, the doors close behind George. I'm left sitting there with too many thoughts.

I've never really lost anyone to death before. Not properly. I don't know what it's meant to feel like. But I do know what it's like to miss something and not know why. Is that what loss feels like? Like something's gone missing that you never got to really hold in the first place?

I've tried replacing my parents in all sorts of ways. But the thing is, I didn't even know what I was replacing. It's challenging to fill a gap when you're not totally sure what was there to begin with. After a while, I stopped looking for people to stand in for them. I couldn't picture them properly, anyway. Instead, I started looking for comfort in places, in new memories, in smells. They say you never forget the smells from when you were little, and for me, that's the closest I've got to family. To a past I don't quite remember, but still somehow miss.

The smell of mint sweets and butter biscuits is the nearest I get to a grandmother. That and the scent of a chimney, a crackling fire, and old furniture that's started to go green. And old books—not just how they look—but how they smell. That dry, dusty smell of time. Years I never lived, but kind of wish I had. It's weird to feel homesick for a time you don't even remember being in.

Sometimes, our orphanage smelt like that. Like books and old wood and the sort of furniture people don't make anymore. It was like stepping into someone else's past. Like being looked after by a made-up grandmother from another life. I used to imagine walking into a cool, quiet house on a hot summer day. The windows were so old they felt more like cling film than glass, with those white, lacy curtains someone probably sewed by hand. The walls were all uneven, layers of paint flaking off like lebkuchen. Big black-and-white photos on every wall. Outside, tall walnut trees moving gently in the breeze. No one else in the house, but the wooden floorboards still smelt alive. Like they remembered.

My parents smelt like the 80s. Even though they were supposed to be younger than that, to me they had that grown-up smell I imagine adults had back then. Hairspray, shaving foam, coffee, cigarettes, that thick hand cream, and the weird plastic scent of Polaroids just after they've been shaken and the colours are still forming. Sometimes the photo would just be of an empty room, but even then, it smelt like someone had just left. Like something had just happened.

One single face, though, stays clear in my memory: three-year-old Norina, with her light brown hair and green eyes. My sister, Norina. She's the closest thing I have to understanding what loss feels like. Actually, she's the only one I've ever really lost. That tiny memory of her, at three years old, is all I've got left. They took her away, and all I had after that was the soft, comforting smell of her baby hair.

I lie down across the blue plastic chairs in the waiting room, the ones rusty and prone to bending if you move too much. I curl up, knees tucked in, head resting on my arm. I start remembering those nights as a kid when I couldn't sleep. The cold kept creeping into my bones, and I'd lie awake wondering where else I could be. I'd imagine fields—huge ones. The grass would be hot and tall, brushing up against me as I ran. Dandelions bursting around me, drifting like dreams. I'd picture myself running free, through endless rows of maize, like I was inside a living, breathing Monet painting.

The orphanage had a garden out back. It wasn't exactly a garden, just rows and rows of tall maize, reaching up to the sun. I'd run through them whenever I could, trying to part the leaves without getting tiny cuts on my palms. I was small. Way too young to do anything about my life. But I knew beyond those green walls was some version of me I hadn't reached yet. Someone older. Happier. Someone free.

My thoughts start to slow. I can feel myself slipping into sleep. So I let go. I close my eyes and drift away.

In the dream, I reach the edge of the garden

and push through the last of the maize stalks. I squint into the light. And there she is—Cornelia. She's sitting under a plum tree, reading. Her back is resting against the trunk, long legs stretched out, the ruffles of her summer dress moving gently in the breeze. She looks peaceful. Like nothing could ever touch her. She's everything I hoped I might be someday.

I step closer. She doesn't look up. It feels like I've walked into a private world. One where I don't belong. But she doesn't send me away. She just stays there, being her, letting me exist beside her.

The wind picks up and I hear the leaves rustle behind me. The book in her lap flips open, pages flying until they stop near the front. I lean over her shoulder and glance down. The publication date stares back at me: the year I was born. These old, yellowed pages I always thought belonged to another time… they're not older than me. Not anymore. We're the same age now. Somehow, time caught up with me. Or maybe I caught up with it. It used to move slow, like it was waiting for me. But now I'm not sure where it's going.

Cornelia looks up and smiles.

I jolt awake and sit upright. The waiting

room's still quiet. A few people here and there. It's early, still dark outside, but not for long.

George is here. The sound of the door must've stirred me.

A nurse wheels him in, the chair gliding beneath him. While still in motion, George waves the nurse off and gets to his feet. There's more colour in his face now than before. He nods, thanks her, and she folds up the wheelchair with a tired smile.

"What happened? Are you okay?" I ask, already halfway to him.

"Constipation," he says, like it's no big deal. He just keeps walking. "They said I was constipated."

I follow him. "That it?" I ask, without meaning to sound sarcastic, but it kind of comes out that way.

"Yeah. They cleaned the shit out of me. I'm good as new."

"Does that mean you're driving back?"

"Bloody right I am. Never want to see you behind a wheel again."

We pull back into the campsite. Alan is throwing up in the corner of the parking lot. The group of students watch him like they're witnessing a crime scene. We park the Kombi right next to the mess, and Alan looks up as we get out.

"What're you two up to, early birds?" he asks, wiping his mouth and making an effort to pull himself together.

"Running some errands," George answers smoothly, and I just stand there, lips half-open, ready to say something real, but I don't.

Because the truth is, I'm scared for George. This trip is draining him. He's old, and he's not keeping up the way he wants to. His meds, his energy, the way his body is dealing with all this— something's not right. This place is taking something out of him.

Before I can say more, Rosanna flies past and grabs my arm.

"I know exactly what you need," she says. "Dhyana."

She drags me over to the old firepit, where she kicks a few blankets into place.

"Come on. Sit. Meditate with me."

"I—Uhm." I start, unsure, but she pushes me down before I can finish. I land cross-legged, and she sits in front of me.

"Trust me. It'll bring you peace. Maybe even a new hobby."

I don't have the heart to tell her that no amount of meditation is going to fix the way I feel. That my constant, low-key anxiety, like everything I do is probably wrong, won't just disappear because I find my centre. But whatever. I let her have this one.

She closes her eyes and slips into lotus position. I try to copy her.

"A door is always open if it isn't closed," she breathes. I open one eye, just to check if she's serious. "Let that sink in for a moment. Let that energy flow through your body."

I keep that one eye open just enough to spot George in the distance. He's sitting in a little camping chair, eating ramen with his favourite pair of chopsticks. And somehow, that tiny, quiet image throws me right back to the second part of his story from last night.

Summer 1964

A Capitol record spins on the turntable, jangly guitars and tight harmonies filling the air. Cornelia and George step into the outdoor party, voices and laughter pressing in around them. They hold hands so tightly George feels his knuckles go white. They're both welcomed with a can of beer each.

Cornelia breaks free from George's grip and spins to the music. Her movements are unbothered and free, her hair gliding over her shoulders as she dances away. One of the guys in the group stuffs a nearly finished cigarette into George's lips. George grabs the cigarette between his fingers and takes a drag, grinning at his good fortune. He's watching the most beautiful girl dance, and she's dancing with him.

He gulps from the cold beer, moves the can into the same hand as the cigarette and joins Cornelia. He grabs her hand and helps her spin around. She twirls a few times until beer spills over her dress, the liquid glistening in the party lights. She laughs out loud and hugs George, his shirt becoming wet with beer as well.

They dance away, surrounded by others moving to the beat. The crowd is a tide of mismatched outfits and raw delight, the music threading through their limbs. George downs his can of beer and crushes it in his hand before tossing it to the ground. He moves in and steals a kiss from Cornelia. She takes the cigarette from his hand and places it between her lips. She breaks away and dances off.

In a blink, she leaves the cigarette in her

mouth and tugs at the back of her dress. She pulls one strap of her bra out from underneath her dress and, in a flash, the entire bra is flung out and lands on the floor. George stares in disbelief as Cornelia dances back to him, grabbing him behind the neck. She bumps his nose with hers and smiles. He gazes into her large, gentle eyes and wonders if he's the luckiest man on earth.

George slides his hands down to her hips, swaying with her. She takes his left hand and moves it up to her breast. The music blares in their ears as George leans in for a kiss. She tastes of beer and nicotine, a heady mix that makes his heart race.

"What are we gonna do when summer ends?" Cornelia says, raising her voice to be heard over the music. "Am I gonna end up some boring teacher while you take off for a real job and we just… stop seeing each other?"

George tucks her hair behind her ears to admire her fully. "We'll figure it out. We're not just gonna drift."

"Let's get out of here," she says. "Right now. Let's not go back. Let's find somewhere new. Anywhere."

He grins. "Alright, I have an idea. We'll get a little place, maybe some land. Have a dozen children and make them work for us. We'll kick our feet up and drink all afternoon while they milk our cows."

"Not like that, silly," she laughs, touching his lips.

"Alright, whichever way then. I'm in," he says with a smile. He knows, in his heart, he'd do anything for her.

The music covers them like a blanket of hope.

The same catchy tunes play faintly in my mind, fading like a distant echo. I watch George sitting in his camping chair, methodically packing away his empty plastic bowl of ramen. He wipes the chopsticks clean with a tissue and tucks them neatly into his front pocket.

Anne emerges from her tent and immediately spots mud on her trousers. My gaze shifts from her to Humphrey, who springs up to help her clean it off.

"I can't hear you," Rosanna tries to get my attention. "Ommm," she intones, looking so relaxed she almost appears asleep.

"Ommm," I reply to keep her happy.

I follow George with my eyes as he gets up and starts cleaning up the empty alcohol bottles scattered in the grass.

I watch the way things get picked up off the floor. It reminds me of Norina and me when we were little, gathering our toys.

Norina was only three, and we'd pick up each plushie together and set it by our beds. Sometimes we got gifts at Christmas. One year, Norina got a tiny elephant with two different-coloured eyes. She named it "Tutu" because she thought it was the sound elephants made. I'd just read in a book how elephants can live a super long time, sometimes even longer than the people who take care of them.

"What do you wanna be when you die?" I asked her once.

"Pepper salami," she said, giggling. "That one's yummy."

Nobody at the orphanage ever told us what death was. Every kid had their own idea, and sometimes we'd argue about it.

Norina was so small when they took her from me. I watched her cry and kick, desperate to get back to me. But I just stood there, frozen, while the caretakers walked her away. I'll never forgive myself for what I thought right then: Why wasn't I adopted? Was I too messy? Not pretty enough?

Those thoughts came before I even wondered where she was going.

I knew I'd miss Norina so much. She was the only thing feeling like home to me. As they carried her out, she screamed my name. My chest felt heavy, like my heart had turned into a rock. It was so heavy I couldn't breathe. Then I felt nothing. I imagined Norina turning into a slice of salami.

"Ommm." Rosanna pulls me back to the present.

I close my eyes and feel warm tears gathering fast.

Our orphanage was a big, old brick building, once a hospital in the war. It had a church chapel we used for plays and events. We used to imagine that if we had parents, they'd come pick us up there after school. From books and the few TV shows we were allowed to watch, we learnt that normal kids—kids from the outside—got dropped off at school every morning with packed lunches: a sandwich, a piece of fruit and a snack. After school, someone would pick them up—a parent, a grandparent, or a babysitter who cared more about her boyfriend than their homework.

The idea of a packed lunch felt weird to me. It was like a faraway tradition from another world.

Their parents worked all day, earned money, and went shopping—buying bread, margarine, ham, apples and chocolate snacks. That's where the lunches came from. So easy, so out of reach. Every time I thought about it, it reminded me that their world wasn't ours. And even though I wanted to be part of it so badly, it always felt out of reach.

I used to wonder what it'd be like to have grandparents. To know someone who raised your mum or dad when they were little. To meet someone old who looked like you and like your parent. I wondered if sharing stuff like that made people feel closer.

The orphanage had two smaller buildings stuck to the sides of the chapel, kind of like train cars. From the dorms, we could take a back stairway to the canteen, and to the basement, where we played hide-and-seek.

If I was the oldest in the group that day, I'd take charge. I'd line the younger kids up and have them say their names. Then I'd pick one girl to set a "price" for everyone, including herself. They'd say stuff like "One million dollars," "A billion trillion hundred," or "All the gummy bears in the world." Then I'd tell them they were being "sold"—and that was the cue to run.

Right behind the orphanage was a large maize field. We spent long summer days out there. The tall rows were like a maze. We'd get lost and find each other by following the sound of our own laughter.

When I was the one "selling" the girls in our game, I never chased them. But they'd still run every time, like someone really was after them. I never let Norina play the game. Even though it was just pretend, something in me couldn't put a price on her. I just couldn't. I loved her too much.

I think I usually do a good job of pushing all these memories down. But sometimes, they come back, one picture after another. I try to shove them away until they stop chasing me. Until I feel like nobody, with no worth and no real past. That's when I finally feel calm.

I open my eyes and see Rosanna. I wipe the tears off my cheeks.

"Oh, darling, I *knew* this would help." she says, crawling over to hug me. "Whenever I do this routine, it feels so freeing. Like it strips away all the built-up junk and leaves you with nothing but pure peace." She leans back, watching me. "Right? Don't you feel it?"

"Light as a brick," I say, forcing a smile.

Anne runs over and spins around. "Can you see the mud marks? I fell on my butt."

"Nah, you're good," Rosanna tells her.

Chapter Five
"I Saw Her Standing There"

We're headed to Hudson, New York, all crammed into the old Kombi. The pop-out front windows are open, letting the wind rush through, bringing along the hum of the road. Cars zip past us.

"Back in the day, you'd hear cars whooshing by," Humphrey says, a touch of nostalgia in his voice. "Now everyone's locked in with the A/C, shutting the world out. Right, George?"

George chuckles. "Back then, the world smelt like freedom. Now it's just detergent in our clothes."

Summer 1964

George and Cornelia sit on the roof of their Kombi at the Hudson Drive-In. The air is warm, the night full of the smell of grass and pavement. The sky is just starting to go dark, caught between sunset and stars. Rows of parked cars stretch out, each with a tinny speaker perched on a pole.

The sounds of summer drift around them. Laughter, low voices, the quiet purr of engines and the odd slam of a car door. The beam of the projector slices through the dark, casting *The Sword in the Stone* onto the big screen. Shifting light plays across Cornelia's face as she pops Milk Duds into her mouth. Beside her, George crunches on nachos.

The smell of hot dogs and popcorn hangs in the air, drifting through the scent of fresh grass. Underneath it all is the acrid bite of car exhaust. The little speaker by the Kombi's window crackles with static, but it's just clear enough to follow the story. Sometimes the movie gets drowned out by a shout or a honk, but the energy of the place draws them back in.

George looks over at Cornelia. The glow from the screen softens her face. She's completely absorbed in the movie, her expression tender and unguarded. It stirs something in him, a kind of ache he doesn't have words for.

When the movie ends, Cornelia turns to him out of nowhere, breaking the spell.

"You should never say no to a dance, no matter who asks, no matter how ugly they look," she says. "That's what my Nana used to say. She had a way of seeing people that was... I don't know, special."

George laughs. "Is that why you're dancing with me? Am I that bad?"

"No, dummy!" she swats his arm. "She just meant… everybody deserves to be seen."

"Well, you're the one dancing like a star," George teases. "The real Uranus."

"What in the world are you talking about?"

"Uranus used to be called *George's Star*," he shrugs. "So, you're my star."

Cornelia's face softens, her eyes staying on his. Behind them, the movie screen glows as Cleopatra makes her grand entrance.

"If you had to teach after summer," George says, "what would you teach?"

Cornelia sighs and looks down at their hands, still linked.

"I wouldn't want to teach. But if so, they wouldn't call me a *teacher*, they'd call me *a spiritual guide*."

"What's the difference?"

"It means," she says, quiet now, "that summer's almost over."

She traces the back of his hand with her thumb, silent for a while. When she finally speaks, it sounds more like the end of a conversation she's just had with herself—an answer she's only now ready to say aloud. "We put the best God could create into the worst man could imagine," she whispers, her voice trailing off into the night as Cleopatra's opening credits begin to roll.

We're all crammed into a corner booth with red, worn-out leather seats. The bench stretches awkwardly to meet an armchair, with two tables shoved together like a bad blind date. The waitress leans over the back of the bench, giving us a once-over.

Before she even says anything, my stomach growls, loud enough for everyone to hear. That's when it hits me. I haven't eaten all day, and I've not had a proper meal since we got here. I tighten my belt to stop my jeans from slipping off what's left of my bum.

The windowsills are lined with candles, all lit, and crystals catching the light. The whole place smells like hamburgers and essential oils, a weird mix, but sort of calming in a strange way.

"So, what can I get y'all?" The waitress's voice cuts through. She's giving us the up-down again. "We've got the best, fresh burgers in town. Freshly melted cheese, too. I'm not making this up."

"Alright, get us some burgers then," Alan says, slamming the menu shut like he's settling a court case. The rest of us nod in silent agreement. She doesn't bother writing anything down, just strolls off towards the kitchen.

"You know what might be the biggest hustle ever?" Humphrey pipes up, in his usual philosophical tone. "You go to a big chain—like, not a place like this, obviously—and you order five burgers. Then you tell 'em one's missing. What are they gonna do? They can't prove anything, and the kid working there doesn't care enough to fight you on it. Bam. Free burger. I mean, I'm just saying— metaphorically—screw big corporates."

"What are you even talking about?" Rosanna shakes her head, exasperated.

The lunch crowd starts trickling in, groups and families filling up the place. Alan flips open the drinks menu and holds it at arm's length, squinting at the small print.

"I'm craving something strong," he declares.

"I'm getting the *Petit Champignon*," Rosanna says, leaning over Alan's shoulder at the menu. "That's French, right, Julia?" she adds, propping her elbow on the booth. "What's it even mean?"

"No clue," I say. "It's a cocktail."

"But it's French, right? *'Petit'* is definitely French. And that other word sounds French too. Even more French."

"It sounds French if you say it slow," Humphrey adds, waving his hand.

The waitress returns, balancing all our plates on a white plastic tray. She parks it by the table and starts unloading.

"That was quick." Alan exclaims. "You sure all this is fresh? Got a butcher out back? Milk the cows yourself?"

The waitress laughs, rolling her eyes.

"Don't mind him," Rosanna cuts in. "What's your name, honey?"

"I'm Amy," she says, standing a little straighter and wiping her hands on her apron. "Any coffee? Free refills."

"I'll have the *Petit Champignon,*" Rosanna says eagerly.

Amy nods, again skipping the notes. "So, where y'all from? Not around here, right?"

"Well," Rosanna starts, "we're pretty boring, but these two—" she gestures at George and me— "these two are here on a mission."

Amy's eyes light up. "A mission? Like a

secret mission? Undercover spy stuff? I love a good spy story."

"Less spy, more love story," Rosanna grins, glancing at George. "This gentleman came all the way from England to find his long-lost daughter. We're helping him."

Amy's jaw drops. "Oh my God."

"Isn't that exciting?" Rosanna claps her hands like she's on a talk show.

George stays silent, picking apart his burger. Rosanna presses on, because of course she does.

"If we're lucky, we might even find George's old girlfriend from back in the day."

Amy beams. "Wait, you're looking for your ex too? Like, digging into Pandora's box?"

"It's going to be great!" Rosanna squeals.

Amy turns to George. "You have a daughter you never raised? That's… naughty."

"Hey." I cut in, my voice more muted than I meant it to be, like I choked on air. George chews on a pickle.

"Sorry," Amy says quickly. "That was a bit much. I get carried away. But honestly, I love relationship drama. Had a bunch of it myself. Like, right now? I'm dating this totally toxic guy. Massive mama's boy. Drives me absolutely nuts.

And I mean *literally* drives my car nuts too. Every time he gets behind the wheel, it's either a ditch or nearly wrapping it round a tree. Last week, I told him, *'If you don't start making your own money, I'm done.'* You know what he said? He said—and I'm not even joking—*'There's nothing I'm good at, except loving you.'* Like, come on. That's not romantic, that's just lazy. And he gets away with it 'cause I'm a complete sucker. Sometimes I honestly think about strangling him. Not really," she adds with a shrug, "but, you know. Like, he'll leave the toilet roll empty and never replace it. The man would never wipe his ass if I didn't keep the damn bathroom stocked. And if he smells like some homeless druggie, it's apparently my fault for not changing the roll fast enough. The worst bit? His mum doesn't even want him back. I tell him, *'Go stay with your mama,'* and she's like, *'Nope, he's your problem now.'* And I get it. I do. He doesn't clean, doesn't earn, just—ugh."

"Why are you still with this guy?" Humphrey asks, setting his burger down because this conversation needs full attention.

Amy shrugs. "He's got nice chest hair."

Then, a teenage boy in a recycled cotton tee and scuffed sneakers sidles up to our table, juggling a stack of flyers with tiny trees on them. He hands Alan a shiny metal straw. "Free straw?"

"Sure, thanks," Alan says, barely looking up as he drops the metal straw straight into his whisky glass. The boy hesitates for a second, hand hovering over a stack of flyers. Meanwhile, Anne's quietly arranging breadcrumbs into a little lump on Alan's plate, like she's working on sculpting something.

The boy opens his mouth like he's about to say something, then shifts his weight and sighs. He clutches the flyers tighter and shuffles off to the next table.

Then, out of nowhere, a four-year-old comes charging across the room like a sugar-fuelled torpedo. Before any of us can react, he smacks right into Alan's knee.

"What the hell!" Alan yells, grabbing the kid like he's just caught a sick raccoon.

The mum waves from her table and mouths, "He likes you! He's bonding."

Alan puts the kid back down and nudges him off. The boy giggles and carries on tearing round the restaurant like nothing happened.

"So, what's the plan?" Amy asks, clearly used to the chaos.

"Woodstock in two days," Rosanna replies. "We're meeting George's daughter there. She's a journalist."

"Wow, y'all are so cool," Amy says, leaning on the booth. "You look like you're heading to the Woodstock music festival, not a conference."

"Wasn't that in Bethel?" Alan asks, scratching his head.

"Yup," Anne confirms, now building a breadcrumb snowman on Alan's plate.

Before anyone can answer, there's a sudden whoosh. We turn, just to see the curtains on fire. Wide-eyed, the four-year-old is holding a crystal. He then sheepishly sets it back on the windowsill near an upturned candle.

"Oh my God," Amy whispers as her manager bursts out of the kitchen with a fire extinguisher.

Alan picks up the crumb snowman creation from his plate and pops it into his mouth.

As we stand to leave, Amy looks at George, flames flickering behind her.

"Hey! Good luck! I hope you find love again. I hope we both do."

"Please don't be scared to ask dumb questions,"

Steve-the-gallery-owner says, as he ushers us in. Quite the Freudian slip.

Anne grabs one of the free glasses of white wine and tries to press another into my hand. I resist. She shrugs, deciding she can manage two. She's got two hands, after all.

"Fill the space, don't be afraid," Steve says with a sweeping gesture, his voice booming like a motivational speaker at a paint-and-sip class.

"Thanks," Humphrey replies, polite but non-committal.

George insisted we check out a gallery—muttered something about it being part of his "side quest bucket list," whatever that means. So we wandered into the first free one we spotted, just a few blocks down from the restaurant.

Steve nods, satisfied, and steps back, clasping his hands behind him like a proud curator of chaos. From his new vantage point, he watches us like a zookeeper studying monkeys.

One wall is covered in pairs of paintings, each a spot-the-difference puzzle.

"Imagine having to do everything twice. Aw jeez," Alan mutters, attempting half an eye-roll, though it's more of a twitchy glance upward.

"Done!" announces a guy near the back of

the hall, his arms folded smugly. He strides to the next painting, dragging his girlfriend behind him. She leans in to examine the details, but before she can even begin, he says it again: "Done."

Alan leans towards Anne. "What's with Steve wearing his granddad's old knit tank? Hell, even my dad wouldn't step out looking like that."

"He needs to compensate for the freezing air con, honey," Rosanna interjects, her tone as dry as Anne's chardonnay.

"You know that's not what I mean," Alan says, plucking one of Anne's wine glasses.

I wander off on my own. With all the paintings, the dividing walls and the sculptures placed in strange spots, it feels like the space itself is part of the art, designed to make you lose your way, in every sense.

As I pass the first huge placard of art dangling from the wall, I count: one. I glance back to make sure George hasn't vanished. He's still there, not far behind.

I remember how simple it used to be to get to our house from the main road: take a left, go straight, another left, and the house would be there on the right. Two tall walnut trees stood in front. The gate was long and made of metal, and the garden door was never locked. One of the bricks in the front wall could be pulled out by hand. It sometimes slipped loose on its own after the rain.

I used to want to tell the police everything. That the house smelt like wood cleaner and cigarettes. That it was enough to prove Norina and I had a family.

The walnut trees were still there, if anyone had just looked closely. But after all the articles and court orders, it felt like nobody remembered we once had a home.

If only someone—anyone—had remembered Norina and me the way we remembered those trees.

Strands of hair hang from the walls, glued in place as part of the exhibit. They shift slightly whenever the entrance door opens, stirred by little gusts of air. The piece is called *"The Last Haircut"*.

I look closer at the different kinds of hair: long, straight, dark, curly, blonde, permed, natural—dyed. There's even some that's been completely fried by bleach, left with a tragic chicken-orange tint.

George and I find ourselves standing side by side in front of the display, equally baffled. I can feel a story brewing inside him, waiting to spill out.

But before he can invite me into his world, I follow him there. I step into his story, uninvited and greedy, and for a moment, I feel like a thief.

Summer 1964
Cornelia stops in front of a painting of a pair of eyes seeming to gaze into eternity, their stare piercing through her. She freezes, staring back, locked in a silent conversation. George steps beside her, draping his hand over her shoulder. He tilts his head to see the painting from her perspective.

"What are you staring at?" he asks, his tone light, the question directed equally at her and the painting.

"I think it's looking at you," she says.

"Then we're both looking at you," George says. "It's looking at me, I'm looking at it, and somehow we've teamed up to admire your lovely eyes."

Cornelia laughs, a sound that's warm and unguarded.

I stand next to them in George's imagination. I'm a quiet intruder. I'm mesmerised by Cornelia, too. The way she smiles when she listens to George, her confidence so innate it's almost enviable. She carries herself with the weight of many more than twenty years. Like she's already danced through a lifetime of experiences. She knows she's beautiful, but her beauty doesn't dominate the world around her. Instead, it enhances it, like sunlight making everything it touches more vivid.

"Let's move to London," she says. "I read there's this whole American crowd settling in. We could find work at a record shop, maybe even open a little café of our own. Something different. Something that matters."

George narrows his eyes at her, a soft smile tugging at his lips. "What is it with you and running away? What are you running from? Tell me. Maybe I can scare the monster away." He leans closer, his voice quiet and sincere.

Cornelia doesn't answer right away. Her eyes stay fixed on the painting, the silence feeling intentional. Then, like she needs to shake something off, she steps away. No rush, just steady and sure. She stops in front of another piece: a tangle of wild roses, bold and full of colour. Standing beside it, she turns to face George. The painting stretches tall behind her, the blossoms curling around her like a crown. She closes her eyes, and for a second, George sees it differently. It's like she belongs there, like she's part of the canvas, resting right where she's meant to be.

"You know what, George? When I die, I want to be sent off on a bed of roses."

It's not exactly the answer George expected, but he can't help but notice how the roses seem to fit her. They don't just frame her; they seem to pull her in, wrapping around her like they were made to highlight everything she is.

What is Cornelia running from, though? I wonder the same thing, my curiosity gnawing at me. Twenty-year-old George doesn't have the answer, but the older George standing beside me today must. I need to know before my own memories catch up with me.

"I do wish I could time travel," George says, his voice soft, almost wistful. "I wish I'd known when it was the last time I did something. Last times, they sneak up on you, don't they? And then they're just gone, final, like a door closing without your ever seeing it open. I'm glad this wasn't the last time I visited a gallery. Haven't been to one in nearly fifty years. Haven't been camping in fifty years either. My kids probably think I'm mad for it. But I couldn't bring myself to do anything that reminded me of her." He pauses, a flicker of something in his eyes. "I tried to be careful with my memories. Wanted to remember her the way I chose to, on my terms. Didn't want her bursting into my life whenever she felt like it. I wanted her close, but not so close that she consumed what was left of me." His gaze drops. "I'm glad we're here, Julia. Glad we're doing this. Everyone talks so much about first times. The first time you do something, the first time you meet someone. But what about the last times? The last time you say goodbye to someone you love? You never see it coming. Cruel, really, don't you think?"

George's voice blends with my own thoughts, drawing me back in time. I've been so good at locking all of this away, burying it deep. But now, it's all tumbling out, unstoppable.

I brush Norina's fine, silky hair to bring her comfort, and to calm myself down. We'd been told if we made any noise, we'd die. Norina and I told each other that if dying meant we could go home, then fine—we'd die.

Locked in a basement, terror flooded our hearts. It felt like being trapped in a giant, abandoned well, just deep enough to make you realise there's no way out. We could tread water, but only long enough to know we were sinking.

The walls were covered in cheap, peeling wallpaper. A small oil lamp in the corner gave off just enough light to show the terrified faces of the other seven girls with us that night.

We were lost. Hidden away where no one seemed to be looking. All the little girls started to blur together. Our faces, our fear... It all melted into one, like we'd become the same person.

We stayed in the basement for days, weeks, maybe months. Or maybe it was only one night. I tried to count the time by how many nights we pretended to sleep. But sleep was impossible down there, especially for Norina, without her favourite blanket.

I held Norina's hand tightly while we were pressed against the wall. My grip was so strong, I worried I might hurt her tiny fingers. I didn't say anything. Fear kept me quiet, but my mind wouldn't stop. It drifted far, far away from where I was.

The kidnappers seemed extra focused on Norina and another little girl, who was around three. They kept muttering about a "special place" for them. There were maybe four, five, maybe six men in the room. Broad-shouldered, with huge hands, they paced back and forth, their blur sweeping over us as they moved.

Pressed against the wall, we were stared at like objects. Every strand of hair, the contours of our fingers, our age—they were measuring us like we were items on a shelf.

But I thought of my walnut trees. I thought of them so deeply, it felt like I was there, climbing one, hiding in the thick, sweet-smelling leaves. In my head, I walked the road home over and over. Left, then left again, until I could almost see our house on the right. Then I'd go back to the start and do it again—left, left, and look for the house. Again and again, just to be sure, I wouldn't forget the way. But sometimes the house wasn't there. The turns got mixed up. Left and right started to look the same. And I lost my way in my own memory.

Little things faded. Was it three walnut trees or just one? Maybe two? I clung to my parents' names, whispering them in my mind, but even their faces started to slip away. I tried so earnestly to hold onto every street, every turn, so I could get back home.

When the police finally burst into the basement and found us, they said we were the luckiest nine girls in the world. We'd been meant to be sold in a group of ten, but the traffickers hadn't found a tenth girl.

And while I'd been trying so desperately to remember—while all I wanted was to go home— my parents' faces had already faded, like dreams right after waking up from a nightmare. All I had left was the garden, the brick wall, the walnut trees, and the smell of cigarettes which never quite went away.

"Done!" the guy at the end of the hall exclaims proudly, patting his girlfriend on the head while she's still scanning the paintings for differences.

"I read this book the other day," Humphrey says. "There was this experiment, right? At a supermarket, they always kept soda near the checkout. One day, they swapped it out for bottled water. And guess what happened?"

"People asked where the soda went?" Rosanna replies.

"Nope. People just started buying more water."

"Sure, 'cause that's how the world works, huh?"

"You know what I've had to unlearn since leaving the States?" George says, addressing the group with a faint smile. "The way we write dates. Look at this." He gestures at one of the inscriptions on the wall. "Day, month, year. Small, medium, large. Makes sense. But Americans insist on putting the month first, treating the rest of the world like they can't count to twelve."

"Give me a break, old man," Alan rolls his eyes.

"Nah, he's got a point," Humphrey says, squinting at the wall like he's thinking it over. "But he forgot the bit where all of this was started by the English."

Chapter Six
"Can't Buy Me Love"

I skip dinner with the team. I feel sick to my stomach. The hotel room walls feel like they're closing in a little more with each passing second. The kettle clicks, done boiling. I clutch my cup in a trembling hand and head towards it. Hot water splashes in, steam rising between my fingers.

I need to know where Cornelia is. I need to know what happened to her and George. Without answers, it feels like the floor's giving way underneath me. My own memories won't leave me alone. They're right here, clawing at the edges of my mind.

I look around the room, searching for something to ground me. The bathroom door. The entrance. One window, right in the middle of it all.

At the orphanage, we got a bit of free play before lunch every day. They didn't sort us by age, but by how we were "developing," or how tangled we were with each other. If a kid showed up barely talking, they got dropped in with the younger ones until they caught up. Siblings mostly stayed together, a quiet attempt to keep the chaos from spilling over. Looking back, some of their choices never made any sense to me.

Free play was the hardest part for me. Too many choices I wasn't ready to make, too much rejection I didn't know how to survive. Norina was the one everyone adored—the prettiest girl in any room, with curious eyes and a confident, friendly air. Kids gravitated toward her, followed her, wanted to protect her. I was proud to be her big sister, officially responsible for scooping her up at the end of the day. She always knew exactly what to play, which table to join. The world seemed to bend around her.

I could never be like Norina, no matter how much I wanted to. Even older, supposed to have more of it together, the freedom to play with anyone felt like being handed everything and nothing at the same time. I'd walk over to join a game, but it was already in motion. No one wanted to start over. I was always too late, and no smile I had could change that. I didn't mind too much. I even found a strange comfort in being alone.

Supposed to be persistent, I knew—but if the other kids made being near them so unwelcoming, why bother? Easier to just drift by myself.

I loved the picture books best. The big ones with oceans that went on forever, fields thick with flowers, rolling hills, cities that reached right up to the sky. Those pictures gave me a quiet kind of hope.

The day I found the shelf with all the best picture books and encyclopaedias, I smacked the back of my hand against it—too quick, misjudged the distance, trying to slide a book back in. My hand went cold for a second, eyes prickling with tears. But as the pain faded, something strange settled in. Relief. Like I didn't have to keep trying so hard anymore. Like I didn't need to fit in at all. Being alone suddenly felt like a choice—and the right one.

That's when I started hitting my hands against solid things—walls, tabletops, the edge of a shelf—whenever I felt cornered or pushed into games I didn't want to play. It was my way of saying no. My way of punishing the moment, the people, maybe even myself. The pain was small but exact, just enough to make sense of what I couldn't say out loud. I'd do it when no one was watching, in busy, noisy rooms where I could disappear into the movement, release the pressure in my chest.

When that stopped working, I found something else. Hitting my head helped too—sometimes even more. I'd do it in bathroom stalls, quiet and contained, where no one could see. But one day, a caretaker started asking about the strange sounds coming from the girls' bathroom. So I found thicker walls, ones that didn't carry sound. I'd press my head—or my whole body—against them.

From spring to autumn, I'd lie flat between the rows of maize, staring up at the sky until my eyes watered. The ringdoves cooed somewhere above, their calls stretching and folding into the sun. I'd search for shapes in the clouds, tapping my head against the ground, trying to find just the right spot. Sometimes, after a few taps, the air inside me would even out again. Other times, I'd stay there for hours, pounding the dirt with my fists, desperate to find the angle that might set something right.

The water overflows. Boiling heat splashes onto my hand, the cup, the floor. I slam the kettle back down and blink at my hand. Red. Burning. But also weirdly cold. The pain is searing and dull all at once, like my nerves can't figure out how to react. My skin throbs, wet and shiny. A cold chill creeps across the burn as air touches it.

I rush to the bathroom and shove both hands under the tap. The icy water makes me gasp, but I don't move.

When Norina and I were first sent to the orphanage, we got there by train. The sound of it felt endless, like it was dragging us into some black hole. The screech of metal, the blur of people's faces through the windows. Our destination, unknown. Our sorrow, complete.

People bumped into me, but I didn't care. I felt like I was floating, powerless, but somehow also filled with power. When I finally stepped into the open air, it was like the world reached for me and I reached back. I was lost, but only I alone could find myself.

I looked up as we passed buildings, apartment blocks with tiny lights in the windows. Little boxes, little lives. Could this be what life was? Could this be mine?

The water numbs my hands, but it doesn't quiet the storm in my chest. I shut it off. The dripping resounds through the room.

I need fresh air. I grab my key card and storm out.

The abduction of Norina and me in front of our family home ended our world before it had even begun. The abduction erased everything the moment they pulled us from that life.

And as much as I wanted to tell the police everything I saw or knew or thought I knew from the little snippets of memories my mind had left me with, I couldn't. The words never came. After that, I stayed silent for a long time.

The authorities just couldn't figure out where we'd come from. No family ever stepped forward. No one responded to news or announcements. It was like we'd always been alone, adrift in a world that didn't want to admit what it had done to us. I kept thinking about the house with the two chestnut trees. I wanted to go back.

I didn't speak a word for months to come. I couldn't make myself try to, not when I didn't have answers. Any answers at all.

A lot of the kids at the orphanage had been

through traumatic things. Some were terrified of men. During adoption visits, it was usually just the woman from the couple who came in to meet us. But there was one man we all trusted. His name was Santa.

On Christmas Day, Santa showed up with a big sack of gifts. He was wearing blue jeans under his red coat, because he came from somewhere freezing. He didn't ask us to sit on his lap or say anything. He just set the gifts down on the floor and stepped back, hands relaxed by his sides. I couldn't see his face under the beard and the hat, but I knew he was smiling.

Kids rushed to him, grabbing their gifts while the carers reminded them to share. I looked at them all for a while. Then I looked at Santa. He was smiling and waving and being merry, but something made me feel like he was more like me. Alone and misplaced. I could feel it, somehow, in his quiet presence. I knew what it was to carry such silence. He and I were the same.

I walked closer. He looked just like the Santa in the picture books, just taller, and a little more human. I took his hand and held it. He was real.

"What's your favourite food?" I spoke for the first time in months. And to this day, I can't remember what he answered.

In the hallway, light spills from under the doors, glowing from rooms I'll never enter. From lives which feel more real than mine. It hits me, the familiar thought: those people probably have something I don't. Something solid. A life that's really theirs. A place that feels like home. The warmth I've always chased from a distance, glimpsed at through windows, but never touched.

I realise I don't know where I'm going. This hallway feels unfamiliar, like I've never walked down it before. Now I'm lost. My eyes drop to the carpet and I notice some mould creeping up the wall where it's peeling away. It's a small thing, but it bothers me. There's too much I'd rather not notice, too much I'd rather not feel.

At the end of the corridor, I spot a metal exit door. I try to push it open, but it's locked. I step back and scan the hallway. Nothing else down here. I turn back and try again. This time I press firmer. The metal gives a dull, solid thud. I let go, hands falling to my side. It's not budging. I get it now.

"That's an emergency exit," a voice says. I turn and see a guy standing there, watching me. "You gotta hit the button on your right. Though, it might not work. This place isn't exactly OSHA-certified or anything."

I blink at him. He looks like Noah, but taller. That reminds me of… oh. That part of my life. It feels like it happened to someone else.

"Elevator's this way. C'mon."

I walk behind him without saying much. Sure enough, there's the lift just ahead. He hits the button for the fifth floor.

"Thanks," I whisper.

"You're good."

We step into the lift. He presses the button for the ground floor, and I feel the shift in my stomach as we drop. The lift hums, then clicks to a stop.

He glances at my left hand, and I instinctively look too. The pain from the burn pulses again.

"I was making tea," I say. My voice comes out quieter than I meant it to.

He looks up at my face, and that's when I see it—the bruise under his eye, raw blue against his skin, puffed just enough to look tender.

"How proper of you," he says, voice dry as paper. The lobby doors slide open behind him and a rush of warm night air curls in, carrying the smell of exhaust and rain-damp concrete.

"Alright," he adds, pointing toward a patch of grass outside, "go wait on that bench out there, okay? That one specifically. Just—trust me."

Without waiting for an answer, he stays in the lift as I step out. I catch a glimpse of him pressing the buttons while the doors close. I head to the bench and sit, watching a family wheel their suitcases into the lobby, their kids clinging to them. They seem so normal. Maybe even happy.

"Hey, you!" Blue-Eye's voice cuts through the night. I look up and see him leaning out of a first-floor window, holding something. "Heads up!"

He tosses an ice pack. I catch it, both hands wrapping around the cold. Then he vanishes back inside. I sit in silence, holding the pack to my burn. It stings less now. The cold dulls the pain, settles the noise in my body.

"Better, right?" he says, jogging over and dropping onto the bench beside me. He's still gathering himself. "Got it from the kitchen. My old man owns the place. I mostly just hang around, run around and pretend I know what I'm doing."

"Pretty sure you're not supposed to put ice on burns, but hey... thanks for running around," I say. "My mind's been running laps lately, too. I think I might be losing it a little."

I don't know why I say it, but it feels right. It feels great to finally say it out loud.

His eyes drift somewhere past me, toward nothing. I can tell he's relieved he's not me—that whatever I'm carrying, he's grateful it isn't his. It's almost sweet, in a twisted way.

"Being twenty is just... confusing," I say.

"You think it stops? I've been twenty-two for, like, seven months. Still just as lost."

I almost ask about his eye, but I don't. He hasn't asked about my hand, so I guess we've made some kind of quiet agreement.

"There's this girl who always shows up at the Costco I hit every Thursday," he says, leaning back against the bench. "She always asks me what to buy. This week it was yoghurt."

I stay quiet, waiting for whatever he's about to say next.

"I just hoped she wouldn't grab the last Greek honey & pecan one." He scratches his head. "Anyway, she kinda reminds me of you. Terrible sense of direction. Always trailing me, trying to find the way out."

"I think she might like you."

"You like me?" His eyes go wide.

"No. I mean the yoghurt girl."

"Oh. Right." He tugs on his earlobe. "I'll see what Reddit thinks. I'm always trying to remember things about myself, like, actual memories, and I can't tell if they're real or not. First instinct is always to Google it, then I realise... I can't exactly Google my own life. *But*, I can Google yoghurt girl."

There's a pause. His eyes glisten a little, and I can tell he's holding something back. A feeling, maybe. A whole mess of them. For a second, sitting out here by the hotel, it feels more like we're outside a mental hospital.

I lift the ice pack and offer it to him. He takes it saying nothing and presses it gently to his eye. The world goes quieter, like it's giving us space. Two strangers with pain we don't know how to carry.

"Sometimes I wonder what life would've been like if I'd actually gotten to live it instead of constantly trying to heal from stuff that wasn't even my fault," he says. "Saw that quote on TikTok the other day, and... I don't know, it stuck with me." He pauses. "When the world loses its mind, the only solace is to find peace within yourself.

This one was TikTok too."

He looks at me with the one eye that isn't bruised, and for a second we just stare at each other.

Then, out of nowhere, we both start laughing. It's quiet at first, then it builds, like neither of us expected it but needed it, anyway.

Chapter Seven
"A Hard Day's Night"

We're in Woodstock, and it's the day of the conference. With a groan, the Kombi doors slam shut behind us. Dead bugs are stuck in the wipers, and the drive has streaked the windscreen with dust. As we step out, the air feels charged.

The town is only just waking. Everything is half-set, half-asleep. Tables are shuffled into place, wires taped across the floor like arteries, banners hoisted with impatient hands. Volunteers argue over where to hang a sign. A woman drifts past carrying a tray of coffee cups.

A large placard near the entrance reads, *"Storytelling in the Age of Social Media."* It's bold and unmissable. Hashtags such as *#FakeNews* and *#IntegrityInJournalism* plaster the screens and posters around the space.

Humphrey pauses just inside the entrance, taking it all in.

"You know, this whole thing with

background checks is a real problem," he says, hands shoved in his jeans pockets. "I heard about this woman who got arrested for pretending to be a court interpreter. She stood up there for months, signing complete gibberish and no one had a damn clue she was faking."

Rosanna rolls her eyes, shifting the strap on her shoulder.

"How does that have anything to do with fake news? That's real news, Humphrey."

"Just let me make conversation for once," he shoots back.

"I feel you try to make conversation all day," Rosanna says, "but you never actually get to the point."

"Ah, give me a break," Humphrey waves her off.

A group of students brushes past us, laughing at something we can't hear. One of them glances at George, then keeps walking like we're exactly where we're supposed to be—out of the way.

Alan, who's been quiet until now, drifts off to explore the venue. His boots squeak on the artificial grass.

Rosanna turns to George. "What are you

even going to say to Christine? What's your pitch?"

George hesitates, his expression tightening like he's rehearsing something in his head.

"I'm going to tell her that what happened to Cornelia was my fault. And that she's the only one who can help me mend my guilty heart, at least to a certain degree."

Rosanna gives him a look. It's somewhere between concern and disbelief.

"Okay," she says carefully, "maybe don't lead with that. Unless your goal is to scare her off in the first ten seconds."

George doesn't respond. He just stands there, eyes locked on some point across the venue, like he's already gone. His jaw tightens and the light drains from him. It reminds me of the way water pulls back before a wave hits.

The silence following is heavier than I expect. I glance at George and something in my chest tightens. I notice how loud everything else is. The conversations, the machines warming up, the chairs scraping across the floor. But right here, between us, it's completely still.

"What happened to Cornelia?" I ask. The words come out quieter than I mean them to. But I can't take them back. I don't want to.

I need to know—for my sake, for everyone's.

Anne leans in a little, eager to catch every word. George stiffens. His whole posture changes. His shoulders pull back and his eyes dart away. It's like a door just quietly shut.

I reach out, resting my hand on his shoulder. A silent plea, asking him not to disappear again. Not into a place where none of us can follow unless he guides us with his words. He's frozen, like he's bracing for impact.

But then, something in him starts to loosen. A flicker of feeling, maybe trust, maybe defeat, moves through him. With a sigh that feels like something breaking open, George turns back to me. And he continues to give us the story I so desperately need.

Summer 1964

It's late afternoon in Woodstock. The heat sits heavy on everything, and the ground smells like damp dirt and grass. The park is wide open, wildflowers scattered everywhere, tall trees throwing long shadows over the crowd. People are everywhere, some with guitars, some barefoot, some in loose shirts or long skirts. A few lean against trees, others sit cross-legged in the grass.

But all of them are watching Terry.

He's standing on a small wooden platform at the edge of the grove. He's maybe thirty, not much older than the rest of them—shaggy brown hair, skinny build. But when he talks, people stop. Like everything he says has already been decided.

"We're the ones who see what's really going on," Terry says, arms out like he's welcoming everyone in. "The ones who know there's more to the world than what they keep telling us. Bobby gets it, doesn't he?"

A few people nod. Some raise their hands. Others mumble *"yeah"* under their breath.

"They want you to think love's something to be ashamed of," he says. "That your body belongs to their rules. But Bobby told us the truth—love is freedom. It's the only point that matters."

A couple of cheers go up. Then more. Soon it turns into a whole wave of noise.

Terry just smiles a little. Not a big grin, just like he expected it. He steps forward and his bare feet are silent on the wood.

"They call us sinners. They call us criminals. But the truth is… we're just free."

The crowd cheers louder. A girl up front clutches her chest, crying quietly. Someone starts playing a tambourine and a few others follow with guitars.

Terry holds up a hand and things settle down. "Tonight, we're doing something they're afraid of. We're showing them what real love looks like. No rules, no guilt, no hiding. If you hold someone tonight, if you kiss them, if you give them your love… that's sacred. That's Bobby's way. That's what we're building here. And they can't take it from us."

"But what if they come for us?" someone says. A boy stands up near the middle. He looks young, maybe seventeen. He's nervous.

Terry doesn't flinch. He looks straight at him. "Then we show them we're not afraid. Love's not a crime. Not even close. And if they try to shut us down, we don't run. We stand together. That's how we stay free."

The boy sits down. He looks a little shaken, but also like something clicked.

Terry steps back again, arms still raised. "Let's begin. Let's pray for our love. Let's show them what Bobby's world looks like."

The tambourine picks back up, louder this time, and people start moving closer together, murmuring words which feel almost like a chant.

George

Someone strums a slow chord, and it spreads from there.

Terry looks out over everyone, and his gaze lands on Cornelia in the back. Their eyes meet. Hers go cold. There's something in her face—anger, maybe disgust.

"This is how it starts," Terry says, still facing the crowd. "This is how we change everything."

George stands beside Cornelia. He doesn't quite understand what's happening. He feels like a bystander to something larger than he can understand.

"These people are dangerous," Cornelia whispers to him. She grabs his hand, like she's trying to pull him back to solid ground.

Terry's gaze shifts to George, and for a second, it's like he's the only person Terry sees. George feels it, like being caught in a spotlight, without knowing why.

"I'll take care of you," Cornelia says. "Promise me you'll do the same."

We're right in the middle of the conference now and the place is buzzing. The quiet from this morning is gone, replaced by voices, footsteps and camera clicks. Some people wander in wide-eyed, as if it's their first time at an event like this, while others move with confidence, like they've done it a hundred times before.

George stands next to me, watching the crowd. But I can tell he's not truly seeing any of it. He's somewhere else. Somewhere with Cornelia.

Journalists move around us, weighed down by gear. Camera crews set up tripods, reporters clutch microphones, producers shout into headsets. A few TV stations have staked out space around the edges.

Locals have taken over the corners, setting up tents and tables with hand-painted signs. They're selling crafts, zines; running workshops about digital storytelling and panels on ethics in journalism. Some have merch—t-shirts, mugs, stickers with hashtags like *#TruthMatters* and *#MediaRevolution*.

But George isn't paying attention to any of it. He's looking for her. The young version of Cornelia he carries in his memory. The Cornelia that only exists in his head now. I can see it in his face, in the way his jaw tightens, the way his eyes flick around the place and land on nothing. He's holding on to a version of her that's long gone. And it kind of feels like she's holding on to him, too.

Then I see her. Not her exactly, but a trace of her. Like she's in the surrounding air. Her memory's everywhere, in the walls, the noise, the people. She's part of this now. She's part of us.

George and I are crammed into the middle of this swirling, spinning circle of strangers, and yet it feels like the world has narrowed to just the two of us and her. I reach for his hand. Maybe to calm him down. Maybe to steady myself. He doesn't let go. He grips it tighter. And together, we move forward into the noise, into the mess, into whatever comes next.

Summer 1964

George and Cornelia drive back to New York City in a heavy, suffocating silence. A silence that clings like damp clothes, impossible to shake off, filling the space between them with weight. It's clear they've just had an argument, though the details of it hang unspoken, too raw to resurface. George stares straight ahead, his hands locked on the steering wheel. He wants to say something, to break the tension, to explain himself, or maybe to accuse her of something he hasn't fully articulated yet. But he doesn't trust his own voice, afraid whatever comes out will be caustic and jagged, cutting deeper into wounds already tender.

"I love you," Cornelia says, her voice soft, like she's throwing him a lifeline. She glances at him, searching his face for a reaction, for acknowledgment, for anything.

George doesn't respond. His foot presses stronger on the gas and the car surges forward. He's driving like he's trying to outrun the conversation, like he's determined to reach their destination before the sting of her words catches up to him. The road ahead blurs into a tunnel of headlights. For a tremor of stillness, it feels like they're the only two people in the world, locked in this moving capsule of unresolved tension.

Cornelia leans forward, her hand hovering over the radio. She presses a button, and the car fills with the jangling chords of The Beatles. It's the middle of "This Boy."

"I might go without you, then," she says, her voice almost casual, but there's an edge to it, penetrating and purposeful.

George's head jerks slightly, his eyes flicking from the road to her face, attempting to gauge her meaning. "Go where?" he asks, his tone more startled than curious.

"To London," she says.

George doesn't respond. His chest rises and falls as he's trying to steady himself. His hands tighten on the wheel, the leather creaking under his grip.

"I don't understand you," he replies.

Cornelia doesn't answer. Instead, she reaches for the volume knob and cranks the music higher. Lyrics pour into the car, filling every corner with what they can't say to each other as if the song itself is mocking their inability to connect.

"You don't have to."

"Okay, gang, I don't think our Christine's here," Humphrey announces, his voice cutting through the noise of the busy conference.

My heart sinks. Around us, the crowd shifts like a restless tide; people hurry between sessions, chatter blending into a dull roar. George paces back and forth, his hands shoved deep into his pockets, trying to stay out of the way but unable to stand still.

Anne reappears, pushing through the throng with a plastic cup of wine in hand. She holds it up like a trophy, a small consolation prize. Rosanna is right behind her. Her cheeks are red, though whether it's from the wine or frustration, it's hard to tell.

"We just talked to Christine's colleague," Rosanna says, her voice almost apologetic. "She's not here today. They've got her working on other stuff now."

Her words hang in the air, hollow and unsatisfying.

"Well, that was useless," Alan mutters, rolling his eyes and throwing up his hands.

No one says a word. The urgency which drove us here fades, leaving behind nothing but a dull sense of defeat.

And just like that, we're back on the road, driving to New York City in the grip of a massive anticlimax. The highway stretches endlessly ahead. The city finally appears on the horizon, but the image doesn't bring the relief it usually does. It feels like we've left something behind, something we came here to find but couldn't quite grasp.

George sits in the passenger seat, staring out the window. He hasn't said a word since we left. He's somewhere far away, and none of us want to pull him back too quickly. Not Humphrey, not Anne, not Rosanna, not Anthony. Even Alan, who's rarely short on opinions, stays quiet. It feels as if the fragile thread holding us all together could snap the moment George utters a single word. And still—he speaks.

Summer 1964

George parks the Kombi a block away from Cornelia's home. The engine rumbles before he turns the key, cutting it off. The music stops, leaving the car in empty silence. Outside, the neighbourhood is still, bathed in the golden hues of a warm evening.

Cornelia steps out first, the door of the Kombi creaking as she pushes it open. George follows suit, the heavy slam of their respective doors echoing in the quiet.

George strides purposefully around the front of the Kombi, his footsteps crunching softly on the gravel as he moves from the road to the pavement where Cornelia waits. She takes a single step towards him, closing the distance. Without a word, they embrace. Their bodies press together as their lips meet. Their love now feels boundless, like it's expanding with every heartbeat, every pulse of connection, every touch.

George pulls back just enough to kiss her forehead, his lips lingering to etch the silence into memory. But as he does, something catches his eye. Across the road, a flicker of movement breaks the stillness.

A young girl in a flowing white dress stands there, barely visible in the dim light. She's motionless at first, her wide eyes fixed on them, her expression unreadable.

Then, as George's gaze locks onto hers, she startles. Her body jolts and she turns on her heel, darting away like a frightened deer. The hem of her dress flutters behind her as she disappears into the night.

George blinks, his arms still around Cornelia. He wonders if she saw it too. But Cornelia's eyes are closed now, her head resting against his chest.

Chapter Eight
"I Feel Fine"

It's just George and me in the Kombi now, the silence stretching out, dense and unmoving. I'm knackered, my hands curling into fists in my lap as I try to focus, to keep it together, to stop myself from slipping back into counting again.

"That was the last time I kissed her," George says. His voice is low and raw now.

I turn to him. "What happened?" I push gently.

"They locked her away," he says, staring straight ahead at the empty road, his hands gripping the steering wheel.

"Who did?"

"Her family. Bobby, her father. His sister saw us that night... Then there was Terry... They both went straight to them. Told them everything."

I wait, letting him go on.

"You see, Bobby had this theory. Called it 'love', though there was nothing loving about it.

'Course, to him, it wasn't nonsense. He was a businessman, sharp as hell. Too sharp. You had to be wicked to make it like he did. He knew exactly what he was doing. Preach chastity and obedience to these... buttoned-up little religious communities—"

He pauses, dragging in a ragged breath through his nose.

"Say all the right things about God, all the things they're desperate to hear. Get them on your side with talk about family and purity. Then, to hook the younger ones who don't buy into all that? Don't bother converting them, just build them their own little fiefdoms. Let them run wild, preaching his message with their own twist. Let them feel special. Terry was one of them. Gave him his own pulpit. Made it feel like his own church. Like a business within a business."

George slaps the heel of his palm against the wheel.

"Don't fight the times. Sculpt them. Be a total bastard in a suit and call yourself a man of bloody God."

My head's spinning trying to keep up.

"I searched for her," he says, softer now. "Everywhere. I thought maybe, just maybe, she'd slipped out. Maybe she was looking for me, too. I checked every place I could think of. Libraries. Record shops. Parks. Cinemas. I walked up and down her street like a lunatic. Knocked on her door more times than I can count. I even tossed pebbles at what I thought was her bedroom window, like some lovesick fool in a movie."

He stops. Breathes out heavily.

"But she was gone. They'd hidden her away. And I... I couldn't do a damn thing about it."

Summer 1964

Cornelia's family live in a semi-detached, multi-family home. The door is dark, glossy wood, a brass angel's head waiting to be knocked. The walls are weathered stone, grey and mossy, with ivy crawling up on one side.

George knocks on the door and tries to peer through the frosted glass, which distorts the interior, making it impossible to see inside. He presses the side of his hand to his forehead and squints through the glass. His bike lies tipped over on the ground behind him, splashed by the heavy rain, which jumps off the pavement in little bursts. The rain hits the tin cover over the front door, creating a loud drumming noise. He drops his hand from the door and glances at the tall church next door. The rain falls so vigorously it turns the building into a flickering blur, like something behind a TV screen, unreal, far away. The entrance is barely visible now behind the downpour.

George leaves his bike behind and runs towards the church, his feet slipping on the now muddy pebbles. He turns the knob, but it's locked. Looking up, he can see long lines of water cascading over his eyes. He knows another way in. He heads towards the back of the church and finds a side door, which opens effortlessly.

He now stands in the church's hallway. The door shuts behind him with a heavy thud. Water drips from his soaked hair and he knows this hallway all too well. It leads to Cornelia's secret hideaway. She could be there. George takes a step and his muddy old shoes squeak on the polished floor.

A tall, crisp-looking young man in a perfectly pressed white shirt steps in front of George. It's David, one of Cornelia's older brothers, the serious one, always watching, always in control. He looks down at George, his expression as imposing and stern as the church looming over the neighbourhood. George isn't particularly tall, but

David's monotone stare makes him feel even smaller. Water drips down George's temple, and he feels his nose running. David grows impatient.

"Can I help you?"

George shifts his weight from one foot to the other. Reflexively, he touches the top of his head with his palm.

"Yeah, uhm..." he trails off. "Yeah. You can."

He was there to talk to them, to reason with them, to show them he wasn't a threat. That he loved Cornelia. As George lowers his hand and lets it dangle limply by his side, he realises that his love for Cornelia is precisely the problem.

"Can I please see her? Can I see Cornelia?"

"I'll have to ask you to leave," David says in a monotone voice, lifting his arm to almost forcefully guide George back to the exit.

George realises he is standing in a puddle of dirt, surrounded by the perfectly cleaned, shiny floor. He sidesteps David's attempt to push him back towards the door.

"Can I talk to her? Just for a minute."

"You have nothing more to say to my sister. She must now cleanse her soul of the sins she has committed."

George presses his back against the door,

blocking the exit to keep himself inside.

"I swear to God, she has done nothing wrong."

"Swearing to God is a sin," David says as he leans forward to shove George out of the way.

George grabs onto David's white shirt in a frantic attempt to grapple him to the floor. He lands a few punches, but David is stronger, bigger. He mounts George with both knees, throwing blows and scratching him. George has been in many school fights before—some he won, others he lost—and he knows exactly what to expect: the wild struggle, the rush of fear and anger pushing him to fight harder. He knows the metallic taste of blood, the adrenaline pumping through his veins, his heart racing, his pulse loud in his ears.

He escapes David's grip and runs towards Cornelia's secret hideout. Then he halts. He cannot go there. He cannot risk exposing her secrets. Cornelia is still a mystery, even to him. But now, more than ever, he knows he must protect her secrets. David catches up to him and throws a wild punch, which George ducks. George tackles David under his armpit and shoves him into the wall. A painting of Jesus falls and shatters at their feet. The sound echoes through the hall.

David opens the door and forces George out. George tumbles into the muddy ground. Rain coats his open wounds, stinging intensely. The door shuts behind him.

Furious, George grabs the nearest stone and hurls it at the door. The glass shatters, jagged shards scattering across the path. Through the broken window, a painting of Paradise stares back at him.

Trying not to slip on the dirty ground, George runs back to his bike. He lifts it from the ground, pushes it into the road, and mounts it to cycle away. He rides past Cornelia's house and the church, knowing she cannot be far. She wouldn't be far.

"Was she carrying your kid? Is this what everyone was on about?" I ask, starting to piece it all together.

George's gaze stays fixed on the windscreen. My question stirs something in him. His eyes darken as he lets go of the steering wheel. His hand trembles in his lap as he slowly shakes his head.

Autumn 1964
George cycles through the upper-class

neighbourhood, where stately brownstones with heavy iron railings line the streets. The houses stand tall and proud, their facades decorated with detailed stonework and large bay windows.

There he sees Cornelia. She's rushing towards the bus station, her long dress clinging to her legs in the wind, almost conspiring to trip her with every step. George presses on and pedals faster. He abandons his bike, letting it clatter to the ground. The sound makes Cornelia glance over her shoulder. Seeing him, her eyes soften with tears, but she quickly looks away. George runs to catch up with her. She presses on, her lips a thin, determined line, holding back words she seems desperate not to speak. He grabs her wrist.

"Talk to me, please. Have I done something wrong?"

Cornelia stops and faces him, bringing a hand to her mouth. She gazes at George, eyes searching his features, wanting to hold on to this moment before reality intrudes. Now, as hope still fills his eyes, unclouded by understanding of their precarious situation.

George holds her gaze. "What's going on?"

Cornelia's gaze shifts, scanning their surroundings with a vigilance honed by necessity.

Across the street, a trio of girls walks by, their giggles subdued as they glance over their shoulders. An elderly couple crosses to the other side, their avoidance deliberate. A young man slows as he passes, his eyes on George in a manner that feels more like appraisal than curiosity.

"Run away with me," Cornelia says, her voice resolute.

She anxiously waits for George's answer.

"Why do you keep saying this?" he leans in closer. He wants to hug her, to hold her close. He should've hugged her. "Why would you run away if you didn't do anything wrong?"

"You don't understand, do you?" She places her palm on his chest, feeling the steady beat of his heart, the pulse of his love flowing into her. "My life is ruined."

"I should've held her hand when she asked me to. I should've taken her to London." George's voice wavers, and he stares down at his hands as though the answers might be etched into the deep lines of his skin. "But I didn't. I was too much of a coward, and I just... stood there. I let them take her. Right in front of me." His shoulders sag, and a quiet sob escapes him. "I didn't do a damn thing. Not one damn thing."

His words hang in the air, heavy and suffocating. I hesitate before speaking, unsure if I should. "Was she seeing someone else?"

George's head snaps up, his watery eyes narrowing. "What kind of question is this?" His voice cracks, a mixture of pain and disbelief.

I shift uncomfortably under his gaze. "Well, she must've had Christine the next year, didn't she?"

His expression hardens, grief twisting into something bitter. "What is it with us people?" he mutters, his voice low and trembling. "Always looking for answers in the wrong places. Always guessing and never listening. She tried to tell us—tried to tell me—but none of us heard her. Not the way we should've."

I close my eyes, struggling to make sense of his words, but all I feel is frustration bubbling up inside me. "Then help me understand," I say, my voice rising despite myself.

I look at George through a pool of tears, and he looks right back at me. Me from my seat in the Kombi, and him from his. He's got decades of pain swimming in his eyes, and I've got my own stuff crashing down at once. I don't know if I feel sorry for him, for everything he's been through, or for myself, for the story that keeps following me every time that tight, anxious feeling creeps back into my chest.

George doesn't reply. Instead, he abruptly shoves open the car door and steps out into the street. I watch him through the windshield as he walks away, his shoulders hunched. Anger flares in my chest and I throw my door open.

"Just tell me what's going on." I shout as I catch up to him.

George stops and spins around, his face lined with a mix of exhaustion and exasperation. "I'm trying!" he snaps. "But you've got to have a little patience."

I halt beside him, glaring. The street is eerily quiet, save for the rustling of a stray cat rummaging through a pile of rubbish bins.

"Patience?" I snap. "I've been following you around like some lost puppy, going from one place to the next, getting nowhere. Christine didn't even bother to show up to that stupid event and *you* won't even call her. What are you afraid of, George?"

His lips tighten, and he looks at me, eyes and face shadowed by regret and shame. "You think this is easy for me?"

"Easy? You're the one dragging me along. You're the one keeping all the answers locked up in your head."

George just stands there, his chest rising and falling as he struggles to find the right words. Finally, he speaks, his voice hollow. "I'll take you to Cornelia now."

"No, you won't." I step in front of him, blocking his path. My heart pounds in my chest. "I can't believe I let you string me along like this. You're a liar, George. Cornelia doesn't even exist, does she? She's not real."

His throat bobs as he swallows. "Fuck you!"

"No, fuck *you*, George."

We stare at each other in stubborn silence. Then, he storms off towards a battered bike leaning against a nearby wall. He grabs it, yanking it upright with a frustrated jerk, and climbs on.

"Wait!" I call after him, but he doesn't stop.

He pedals away, his wiry frame moving with surprising speed. I take off after him, the city coming alive around us. Cars inch forward in a constant rush-hour traffic, their metallic frames glowing in the amber light of the setting sun. Pedestrians weave through the chaos, their faces turned towards their own destinations.

I run, my breath coming in sharp bursts, but George is faster. He stands on the pedals, letting the bike glide before pushing forward again. His white hair stirs in the breeze, and for an instant, I see a glimpse of the man he must've been years ago. He's running towards Cornelia, and away from her. And I'm chasing them both.

Then, the bike wobbles as George hits a patch of gravel. It tips over, sending him sprawling onto the pavement. The bike clatters to the ground, its wheels spinning in the fading light.

I reach him and drop to my knees, the rough asphalt biting into my palms. A kid rolls by on a scooter, perched on its plastic seat like a pint-sized monarch. He's glued to his phone, watching cartoons, while his dad trudges along behind him, pushing the scooter without a glance in our direction.

"Not exactly a graceful getaway, huh?" I say, trying to steady myself.

George lies there, staring up at the sky, his chest heaving. "I'll take you to meet Cornelia," he whispers. "I promise."

Winter 1964

The little brass bell jingles as George pushes open the door to the corner shop. The place smells like old floorboards and oranges, the warmth inside sticky with steam from bundled-up shoppers drifting through narrow aisles. Fluorescent lights buzz faintly overhead. A few people glance up from their baskets and linger on him just a second too long—then look away like they hadn't.

Hands deep in the pockets of his worn winter coat, George heads straight for the counter. He digs through his pockets for change, metal clinking against metal, and drops a few coins onto the scratched-up counter. Without a word, he nods towards a pack of Lucky Strikes.

The shop owner, an older man with sleeves rolled halfway up and a pencil behind his ear, eyes him for a second, then turns and slides the pack across the counter. George takes it. From somewhere back in the store, a low voice rides the quiet.

"She was definitely pregnant," a woman hisses low from behind the canned goods.

George freezes, his blood scorching. The pack of cigarettes crinkles as his fist tightens around it. He turns slightly, glimpsing of two women peering around the end of the aisle—one middle-aged, scarf tight around her head, the other younger with a kid perched on her hip.

"He's the one from that cinema family," the first one murmurs again. "Down by Jackson Heights, right? They show those foreign pictures. Whole family's godless. It's in the blood."

George's stomach twists. His pulse pounds in his ears. His fingers dig into the cigarettes, crushing the box out of shape.

"Poor girl," the other woman adds, shaking her head. "I'd kill myself too."

The air snaps. George storms down the aisle, footsteps slamming across the linoleum. The women barely have time to react before he rounds the corner.

The older woman's eyes go wide. Her little cart slips from her hands and clatters to the floor. George grabs her by both shoulders and slams her back against the shelves with a metallic crash. Cans topple around her as she cries out, collapsing to the ground.

Her friend screams, high and shrill, as she throws one hand over her mouth. Her baby begins to cry. A man from the far end of the aisle rushes in and grabs George by the shoulder, yanking him backward. George barely registers the fist until it connects with his cheek.

He stumbles onto the shelf behind him, but he's already surging forward again. He throws himself at the man.

A fist to the ribs. Elbow to the side of the neck. George's knuckles are already bloodied, and the man staggers. He goes down, and George drops with him, straddling his chest. He punches once. Twice. The man grips George's coat in both hands, trying to hold him back.

The screaming hasn't stopped.

"Enough! Jesus—enough!" the shop owner yells, voice cracking as he scrambles around the counter. He barrels towards them, arms out, helpless to stop the chaos.

But George doesn't stop. His fists keep coming until his vision blurs, swallowed by heat, grief, rage, all of it choking him from the inside out.

"What'd you say?" he mutters, leaning over the man, breath ragged. His voice is raw and low, almost lost in the screaming.

The man underneath him coughs blood, grinning through red-streaked teeth.

"They said they'd kill themselves too... if they were her."

George leans back, one hand on his knee, the other pressed against his temple like he could crack his own skull open and let it all out. The pain is searing and white behind his eyes.

He stumbles away, brushing off the shopkeeper's grip, and pushes out through the front door. The bell jingles again behind him, but softer this time.

His bike waits for him at the curb, its tires rimmed in frost.

George reaches the church, his bike slipping on the icy ground before he lets it fall. The sound of it clattering fades unnoticed. His gaze is fixed ahead, where Cornelia's brothers are carrying her casket across the courtyard. Their faces are pale, their movements slow in the biting cold.

The church looms behind them, its steeple reaching towards the grey sky. Snow drifts lazily, settling on the shoulders of the family gathered nearby. They stand in silence, their white coats and scarves stark against the sombre scene, as if attempting to erase the shame of Cornelia's unmarried, lifeless body. Bobby stands apart, his back to the casket, facing the church doors. His hand moves in small, repetitive motions as he murmurs. George can't make out the words, but the tone is clear, prayers and apologies whispered into the cold.

The casket is placed into the black van waiting at the edge of the driveway. The doors open, swallowing Cornelia's body with a quiet finality. Her mother dabs at her eyes with a handkerchief, her face crumpling briefly before she straightens. The brothers close the van doors with a soft thud.

George's chest tightens. Before he knows it, he's moving forward, his boots slipping slightly on the icy ground. He doesn't stop. Reaching the van, he grabs one of the doors and pulls it open.

And there she is.

Cornelia lies still, her face pale and calm, her expression serene, so peaceful it tightens George's chest. He can't breathe. She looks as though she's merely sleeping, her beauty untouched even in death. The peace on her face strikes him, filling him with an ache so acute it feels like it might split him in two.

David's hand lands heavy on George's shoulder, jerking him back to reality. He removes George's grip from the van with grim determination and slams the door shut, the sound echoing like a gunshot.

"You have no right to be here, child of Satan," David growls.

George stumbles back, his eyes wide as the family members around him blur. Tears well up and spill down his cheeks, stinging in the cold.

Bobby remains turned away, his murmured prayers unbroken, his shoulders hunched as though shielding himself from what's happening. The rest of the family closes in on George, their faces stern and unforgiving.

"Child of Satan, child of Satan," Cornelia's mother mutters, her voice trembling with both grief and fury. The chant spreads, cousins and aunts and uncles taking it up, their voices rising in unison until it becomes a haunting refrain. "Child of Satan."

The words ring in George's ears, louder than his heartbeat, louder than the world around him. He glances back at the van, his vision swimming, a surge of anger rising within him. He wants to scream, to tear through the sea of white surrounding him, but the anger blinds him, then darkens his sight, until the surrounding figures are no longer people but spectres.

The family move closer, their white clothes blending with the snow, their faces a blur of judgement and disdain. All George can see now is the van, growing distant, its black frame prominent against the winter haze.

"I panicked. My heart felt like it was going to burst out of my chest. I grabbed my bike and just... legged it. Didn't know where I was going; I just pedalled like the devil was right on my tail. The city was a blur past me, headlights and street signs mixing. I wasn't thinking, just moving as fast as my legs could carry me. Then my foot slipped. The pedal jerked, and next thing I knew, I was flying off the bike. Everything went dark. When I came to, I was still there, lying on the side of the road. My whole body ached, and the cold felt like it was in my bones. There was this bloke—a homeless fella—standing over me. He was looking to nick my wallet, but the second he saw my eyes open, he bolted. I didn't even care. I just stayed there, staring up at the sky. Don't know how long I stayed like that. Could've been minutes, could've been hours. Time didn't mean a thing. I felt... empty. Like I was disappearing, bit by bit, sinking into the ground. I couldn't move. Couldn't think properly. It was like I'd fallen so deep there was no way back up. I was angry... So angry I thought my chest might burst. My head was spinning. The world was spinning. I wanted to stop it all, to get off this bloody ride and just... float. Somewhere far away. Somewhere I might find Cornelia and tell her—tell her it was all my fault."

"It wasn't your fault," I offer softly, unsure of what else to say. "It wasn't your fault for loving her."

George shakes his head slowly, his hands trembling in his lap. "You don't understand. I was a coward. Her voice—her beautiful, bright voice— that's what got her into trouble. But me? I'm the one who stood by and let it happen. I let her die. Alone." His voice cracks, and he hides his face in his hands. "What kind of man does that? What kind of man lets the person he loves most in the world die alone?"

I feel tears slipping down my cheeks but don't bother wiping them away—Cornelia, sixteen Vasparex pills, her family refusing an autopsy, no priest at her funeral. George mouths all these details to me, but his words blur. I only see his lips moving, the sound fading into silence. She's dead. She's been dead all this time—gone for six decades, lost in silence.

She wasn't pregnant. George was sure of that.

She wasn't unfaithful either—he knew it in the marrow of his bones. He trusted her the way some people trust the sky to hold. She had nothing to be ashamed of. Not then, not now, not wherever her soul is resting. But the rumours moved faster than the truth ever could, and people cared more for the sound of a story than the weight of the facts. They didn't care if it hurt her. They didn't care if it destroyed her. They cared it spread. They talked. They whispered. They judged. Until it became too much for her to carry.

At least, that's what the world said.

That's what the world wanted us to believe. That she gave up. That she chose this ending. That she died by her own hand.

I look at George and try to read between the lines, to see if that's the whole truth. Or if part of this ache in me is just me—refusing to believe she's gone for good. Refusing to believe she would leave like this.

I feel late, like I should have been there to stop her. Like I should have been born sooner to change everything. And now, I can't even begin to understand what's truly stirring inside George's heart.

"I should've protected her." George confesses.

"I should've said something, done something. All the lies they told about her... She knew. She knew what they'd say, and she tried to warn me. But I didn't listen. I didn't believe her. She wasn't pregnant, and I—I doubted her. God help me, I doubted her. And she was... She was the purest, most precious soul I've ever known. And I crushed her under my own stupidity."

I press my hand to my mouth, searching for something, anything, to say.

"I can't forgive myself," George mutters, his voice shaking. "Not for that. I should've believed her. I should've stood by her, no matter what."

"It wasn't your fault," I say, forcing my voice to steady. "It was the way people treated her. That's what took her away."

George shakes his head again, slower this time. "No. What she needed was me. Right then and at that point. And I wasn't there for her."

"She knew you loved her."

"My love wasn't enough," he says, his eyes wet and distant. "I doubted her. Even for a second. And that second... it was enough to break her. To break everything."

"You were young," I say and I reach for his hands, clasping them in mine. "Forgive yourself.

You have to. Cornelia wouldn't want this for you. She wouldn't."

"She was young too," he admits, eyes glistening. His face crumples, and he pulls one hand free to wipe his eyes. "It snowed that day. I remember watching her walk away, her back to me. I knew it was over."

Winter 1964

It's snowing. Heavy, fluffy, dense snowflakes fall relentlessly from the sky. The snow falls with a furious intensity, almost slapping George in the face. He stands there, unsure whether to wipe the wet snowflakes from his eyelids or to reach out and pull Cornelia into a tight embrace.

George's words draw me deeply into their story, into this poignant last scene. I want to hug them both, to offer them the wisdom and comfort I possess now, to assure them everything will be alright. To urge them to hold on to each other and to never let go.

Cornelia, too, yearns to reach out to George but hesitates. Instead, she rubs her palms together to stave off the biting cold. The snow has settled on her long, straight hair, and for a heartbeat, George catches a glimpse of what their future could be if they stayed together. He imagines them living far away, allowing the years to pass, bringing fine lines, wrinkles and white hair like the snow that now blankets them. At this instant, the future feels tangible, possible.

"I never slept with you," George murmurs. "Not in that way. I'm just... a bit confused right now."

"What are you confused about?" Cornelia asks, her voice trembling.

"About this. About us."

Cornelia's eyes shimmer with desperation. "No... George." She clutches the back of his hand seeking to rouse him from a nightmare she herself cannot escape. She waits for an answer, a glimmer of hope in her eyes. But when George's lips part and emit nothing but a faint tremble in the cold, she releases his hand, pulling away as though it has burned her. The fragile smile of hope fades from her lips, replaced by a sorrowful realisation.

She takes a step back, dreading the inevitable.

"Can you give me some time?" George blurts out, his voice raw with urgency.

"I already gave you everything, George. There's nothing more to give." She tears her gaze from his wet eyes, freeing herself from a once solid grip that has now loosened. She turns away, the snow falling on her shoulders, transforming her brown winter coat into a white gown.

As Cornelia walks away, the streetlights shimmer, casting a glow on the dancing snowflakes the wind pushes around. Only Cornelia is on the deserted street. She crosses her arms, holding herself tightly against the stiff wind. Her boots struggle through the wet layers of snow. The road narrows as George watches her depart. His eyelashes grow heavy and frozen, his hands so numb they almost cease to tremble. George squats down, blowing hot air onto his hands, his shoulders hunched as he rocks himself, seeking solace from the pain of his frozen fingers.

Watching this memory unfold before my eyes, I feel an urge to push young George until he falls, just so he might make one last effort to rise. To get up and run after Cornelia. I imagine myself grabbing his winter coat and tearing it off his shoulder.

The world tilts as George collapses, his cheeks brushing against the cold pavement. He watches as Cornelia's footsteps disappear, the fresh snow quickly covering them, leaving the road looking pristine. He feels as though he is mourning

Cornelia even before her eventual departure. He is desperate, ashamed and utterly lost. So he lies there in the snow, curled up on the side of the road, allowing the snow to cover him. Saltwater slips from his eyes, tracing frozen lines down his skin, but his face stays still, grief coiled tight, refusing release.

The tears freeze to his cheeks, the time she gave him suspended in ice, his loss absolute. Snow keeps falling, slow and steady, glowing in the streetlight.

I reach over and tap George's shoulder. It's a gentle nudge—just enough to jolt him, to rouse his older self and help him back to his feet. But George just hunches over his knees, his breath shallow, blowing into his trembling hands.

My chest feels tight, like I'm suffocating on my frustration. George rocks himself back and forth, his shoulders shaking. His lips part, his voice faint:

"Horrible things happen to wonderful people, but—"

"There's no 'but.' Horrible things happen to wonderful people." I pull him into a hug, wrapping my arms around him tightly. His frailty hits me all at once—his thin frame, the way he trembles against me. There's so much I want to say, but I know no words will make a difference. Not now.

He pulls away slightly, curling up on the ground like a wounded animal. His forehead dips towards the pavement, and then he strikes it against the ground with a dull thud. My heart clenches. When he tries to do it again, I catch his head with my hand, holding it steady. He looks at me, then breaks down, a loud sob escaping him. Tears and snot spill as he lets out the guilt he's carried for years.

Around us, the city moves on. People rush by, their faces blank, their lives untouched by the storm crashing down on us.

But here, right now, it's just George and me. Two people caught in the wreckage, holding on to what's left. We know the world doesn't stop for our grief. It never does. But for now, we stay still.

Chapter Nine
"Help!"

The cool New York evening air surrounds us, and everything feels weirdly quiet, like the city has paused for us. We enter Oakwood Cemetery, the old fence rattling softly in the wind behind us. Long smudges of darkness stretch long across the gravel paths, and the rows of tombstones seem to welcome us with a quiet kind of indifference.

George hesitates, his hand resting on the bike's handlebar. His eyes drift to a memory only he can see. I follow his gaze and the cemetery fades into something else—rows of cinema chairs stretching out before him. Their red upholstery is faded, but they hold a strange dignity. George watches as cigarette smoke curls in the projector's beam, twisting and floating like apparitions. Cornelia's brown hair glows softly in the light, her shoulders rising and falling in a rhythm so gentle it feels like the heartbeat of the film itself.

The chairs shift, turning into rows of

gravestones. They stand in solemn alignment, like observing life's theatre, where one story ends and another begins.

The wind picks up, nudging a few wild red roses against the gravestone we've come to see. When it stills, I read the inscription etched into the tombstone: *Cornelia Dean. 1944–1964.*

Just like that, her life boils down to a single, undeniable fact. A story too large for its short and painful ending. In my mind, Cornelia's entire existence seems built on a future which never came to be.

"I brought her to the seat of her own grave," George says, his voice rough, nearly lost in the surrounding quiet.

I glance at him, and I see the reflection of a younger George overlapping the man standing in front of me. It isn't George I'm angry at, I realise— it's me. For daring to wish for a happier ending to a story that was never mine to rewrite. It feels selfish of me to grieve for what could have been when the world had already stolen so much from Cornelia.

George crouches down, his fingers brushing the cold stone. Wild roses sway in the breeze, petals brushing his hand. "What's happened to us, Cornelia?" he says. "What's life gone and done to us? Look at me—old, wrinkled, and always needing a bloody laxative. But you… you're still just as bright in my mind as you ever were. Funny, isn't it? Someone like me, carrying someone like you around in my head all these years, like a film that never stopped playing."

"Why did we come here, George?" I ask, though it sounds wrong the second I say it. "Why put yourself through this?"

He pauses. "Truth is, I've always been a selfish old sod. I couldn't face it on my own. Thought if I kept shoving it to the back of my mind, maybe I could hold reality off a bit longer."

"I'm sorry," I say. It feels like too little, but it's all I have.

"Don't waste your grief on me," he says with a faint smile. "Save it for the ones who never got the chance to live. The ones too bright for this world to bear. If there is a God, well… he's made more cock-ups than I can count. And it's us poor souls left to carry the cost."

He pauses again, his hand lingering on the gravestone. "I loved Hilde. I really did. But I've never been able to love her the way I loved Cornelia."

"Maybe… maybe you didn't know Cornelia

long enough for her to turn mundane?" The words tumble out before I can stop them, and I cringe at my stupidity.

George shakes his head. "No. She was incapable of mundanity."

I understand the guilt gnawing at George's heart. I try to picture the shape of it, and I think I'm doing a decent job of grasping just how heavy it must've been, all these years. To lose someone so dearly, so tragically, so young, so suddenly. To carry that kind of grief in silence, buried deep, like something shameful. And then to simply move on. To live, somehow.

Unspoken sorrow has slowly worn through the fabric of George's soul, and he let it. He surrendered to it. Cornelia wasn't just a tragic story. She was his story, and I can feel the depth of his guilt settle somewhere in me too. I get it.

There's something almost punishing in the way he's walked himself through all of this now, like a live-action version of therapy, played out moment by moment. Late, sure. But maybe still necessary. Still brave.

And yet… something's missing. There's a piece of this puzzle I haven't quite found yet.

I gasp for air. "Excuse my French, George,

but who the hell is Christine Whyler, then?"

He stands, brushing dirt from his knees. "Christine Whyler," he says simply. "I made that up."

My knees give out then, refusing to hold me upright. I crouch down, drained of will, of drive, of the energy to process any of this. I rest my forehead on my knees. I'd scream, if I had it in me.

"Sick bastard," I mutter.

"She's not our daughter," George says, and I glance up as he pulls out his phone. "That much is clear. But she's a journalist. A bloody good one, too. She's reopened the 'Nobody's Children' case."

I force myself upright, eyes locked on the screen. "Bobby's church? That's still a thing?"

"Oh, yes! They're called 'Transcendent Unity' now. And Bobby's still around," he says, his voice grim. "A hundred and four and still kicking. But not for long, if I have my way. Cornelia never gave a toss about rumours. She couldn't have cared less. There's more to this than what people said back then. I knew her—maybe better than I've ever known myself. And by the time I finally understood what she'd been trying to tell me... it was too late."

His voice falters, just for a second. "I carry a

heavy fault. I knew. And still, I did nothing. I was a coward. But I'm not scared anymore."

He straightens a little, steadies his breath. "Before I go, I'm taking him down. That old bastard's not getting away with it. Not this time. Cornelia's story needs to be told—properly. Truthfully. And I need your help to do it."

Winter 1964

The dim light of the old projector flickers across the cramped room, throwing uneven smears of gloom over George. The hum of the film reel and muffled dialogue from the cinema below fill the space, mixing with the stale smell of cigarette smoke curling from the corner of his mouth. He sits cross-legged on the wooden floor, surrounded by a messy pile of cutout newspapers, magazine pages and bits of scripture. Every piece is part of the puzzle he's desperate to put together.

A half-empty beer bottle hangs loosely from his fingers, the glass slick with condensation. He drains it, then tosses it aside, letting it roll across the floor until it hits a stack of old reels. Grabbing another bottle, he takes a long drink, his eyes flicking between passages of the Bible and an article about "Nobody's Children." The projector's beam cuts through the smoky air and the room feels like it's spinning. A whirlwind of words and warnings he can't switch off.

George's pen moves frantically, underlining sentences and scribbling notes in the margins. His hand shakes as he slams an article to the floor. He freezes, staring at Bobby's face, the self-proclaimed prophet whose words are poisoning faith. Bobby's face seems to blur and shift until all George can see is Cornelia's smile. Her curious eyes. The feel of her soft shoulders under his hands in this very room. His chest tightens as he presses his hand over the article, his fingers spreading across Bobby's smug expression. The memory stings and he clings to it like it's the only thing keeping him afloat.

The article under his hand is a rant, Bobby's warning against "unauthorised unions," meant to shame women like Cornelia. Bobby calls his own daughter a divine warning, a message from God to women who step outside their place. George's pulse stutters. He grabs the beer bottle and throws it at the floor. The crash sends shards flying. One cuts his cheek, but he doesn't blink.

He spits out his cigarette and grinds it into Bobby's photo, leaving a dark smudge across the man's face. His anger builds. He stabs his pen into the image again and again, the ink soaking through the paper and into the wood below. Each jab is a useless attempt to tear through Bobby's mind.

George then lies down, curling up on the floor beside the broken glass. His chest rises and falls, and his thoughts drift. The projection room fades, replaced by a memory of the big oak tree from his childhood. He's a boy again, holding tight to the branches while the wind pushes against him, trying to shake him free.

It doesn't take him long to decide where he needs to be next. At the Nobody's Children church, George pushes open the heavy doors. The faint drone of chatter collapses as people turn to look at him. The soft shuffle of feet follows him as he walks down the aisle, the crowd parting like the Red Sea.

His creased shirt and worn-out slacks stand out against the crisp Sunday attire of the congregation. Two of Bobby's men step forward, grabbing his collar. The fabric bunches under their grip as George yanks back, fighting to shake them off. Bobby raises a hand from the stage. The guards pause and then let him go.

George's fists clench as he climbs the steps to

the stage. Bobby stands waiting, his microphone lowered. They lock eyes, and the world seems to shrink to just the space between them. Bobby's face is a mask of composure.

"George," he says.

"Don't say my name." George's voice is low. "Not after everything you've done."

Bobby's jaw shifts. He steps back from the microphone. "You're interrupting my sermon. What do you want?"

George pulls a crumpled piece of paper from his pocket. His hand shakes as he unfolds it and holds it up for everyone to see. The marriage certificate between him and Cornelia Dean, dated 152 days before her death. A wave of murmurs ripples through the crowd. Bobby's expression falters, but he quickly regains control.

George turns to the congregation. "She was my wife. And none of you deserved her."

Behind him, Bobby's voice cuts through. "I never gave my blessing."

George spins around. "Yes, you did. And now you'll fight me over it, you shithead."

Bobby's jaw tightens. He gives a small nod to his guards, who move forward and grab George's arms. The assembly watches in silence as George pulls against them, his gaze fixed on Bobby. Bobby turns back to the microphone, his voice calm again, as the doors close behind George, leaving him standing there with nothing but his anger and the crumpled certificate in his hand.

George takes the now-aged marriage certificate out of his wallet and unfolds it carefully in front of me. The paper is yellowed and creased. I cross my arms and rub my chin with my knuckles, trying to piece together his words.

"Bobby would've blessed his own mother marrying his son if it suited him," George mutters. "But when it came to Cornelia and me? Not a chance."

"What kind of bullshit is this?"

George keeps going like he didn't hear me. "I was already a widower by then. When I married Hilde ten years later, we just... never talked about it. She never asked."

"Where'd you even get this certificate?"

"Cost me fifty bucks. Junior officiant from around the corner signed it. Kid was off his face, couldn't care less what I handed him." He chuckles. "Packed my bags then and left for London. Never went back to New York City. Never said Cornelia's name again."

"The necklace. The one Christine was wearing. You said it was Cornelia's. That wasn't true, was it?"

"I wish I'd given her something. I wanted to. Dreamt of buying her a ring. Of doing it right. But..."

"You think she would've wanted to marry at all?"

George looks off, the breeze picking at his hair. "Truth? I don't know. Maybe I never really knew her after all."

The wind picks up again, rose petals swirling around his hand, brushing against his wrinkled skin.

"George," I say cautiously, "when you said 'fuck you' earlier... did you mean it?"

He looks up. "No."

I nod. "I didn't either."

Petals drift towards me, and for a second, it feels like Cornelia's touching my hand.

George's expression shifts. "Look, I don't know how much time I've got left—"

"Oh, come off it. You're not dying. You're just constipated, remember?"

"Yeah, yeah, but I'll be eighty-one soon," he

says, rolling his eyes. "Let's be real. Not much gas left in the tank."

"Eh, ten, fifteen years? If you cut down on the whisky."

He leans closer. "Listen to me. We have to do this now. We bring the story out. It's waited long enough. Christine's the key. We've got to convince her it's worth telling."

I sit down on the grass beside Cornelia's headstone. "I get Cornelia was failed. That the church twisted her death into a sermon. But what exactly are we exposing here? How is any of this illegal?"

George nods. "There's more. I promise. Someone else can explain it all much better than I can."

Chapter Ten
"Ticket to Ride"

"George, you take all your meds today?" I call out as I shut the door behind me. The latch clicks, and I stand there, staring into the dim hotel room, still smelling of instant coffee and something synthetic.

The shower's running. Steam curls from beneath the bathroom door, carrying the scent of soap and something vaguely medicinal. He's in there, of course. The same time every evening. I made him promise—an evening walk, every night. Good for his heart. Good for his mind. Good for both of us. But we haven't walked in three nights now.

It's been over two weeks since we got to New York City, and for someone who was in such a hurry to dig everything up, George seems... slow. He's plotting something in his own time now. The fire once driving us here is flickering out, or maybe burning deeper, somewhere I can't reach.

"Yeah, yeah," he mutters over the rush of

water. But I don't buy it.

I expel a quiet sigh, dragging my bag across the carpet. I sink into his cracked armchair. It shifts under me, the leather protesting with a soft squeak. As I shift, something jabs at my thigh. I reach under the cushion and pull it out—a record. *Meet The Beatles!* Still in its sleeve, it's pristine. Could be worth something. Probably is.

I slide the vinyl halfway out, just enough to check the label, but a pile of papers tucked behind it spills into my lap. Old clippings, torn and yellowed. Newspaper scraps, photos, headlines— Bobby, Nobody's Children, scandal, miracles, tragedy. Some taped together like he's tried to make sense of them before. Others torn at angles, like they were yanked out of something in anger.

And then, beneath all that, something different.

Loose pages, softer, more fragile. Ripped out of a notebook, maybe a journal. The handwriting is tense and messy, bleeding across the page like it was written in a hurry. I freeze. A chill runs through me and my pulse slows. I glance at the bathroom door. Still the steady rush of water. Still the thin fog under the door.

I shouldn't. I know I shouldn't. But my hands

move anyway. My fingertips hover, then brush the pages. Guilt flares in my chest—quick, familiar—but the pull is stronger. Curiosity overtakes caution, outpaces sense. Everything's too neat, too perfectly arranged, like someone wanted me to find it. Like George wanted me to.

I flip a page. It feels like breaking into someone's dream. Or their nightmare. Like I've peeled back something I wasn't meant to see. And I hate myself for it. But I don't stop.

July 1964

Every day I spend away from him, I swear I love him more. I'm sure of it. I do love him. It happened so fast, so effortlessly… he's just easy to love, in a way I can't totally explain. There's nothing that remarkable about him at first glance. Yeah, he's good-looking and I adore how the skin crinkles under his eyes when he smiles. I love how his ears kind of tip forward when he's talking or telling a story. There's something both boyish and grown-up about him. I can't put my finger on it.

I love the way his chin dips slightly when he's about to tell me something. I love the warmth of his skin when he takes my hand, when he touches my cheek. I've never felt more at peace than when I'm wrapped up in his arms.

I don't really know what love is supposed to feel like, but if this is it… if what I feel for him is love… then I don't think there's anything in this world more real, more complete than this. I haven't known him long, but every second apart from him feels longer than the twenty years I lived without even knowing he existed. Gosh, how I wish I'd never met George. Because now, I couldn't leave him. I just couldn't. And he'd never leave me.

July 1964

He's everything I'll never be again. There's this freshness in his eyes, like he still sees the world brand new. Like he's still got that spark most people lose after they're born. I really believe that no matter what life throws at him, he'll figure it out. He's kind in this way that makes you want to believe in people again. And I really, really hope nobody breaks that in him. Gosh, he deserves more than what this world's gonna give him.

But I envy him. I envy how he sees things. To him, everything just is. If it's blue, it's blue. If it's round, it's round. No second-guessing. No spiral of thoughts. He sees things for what they are… clear and simple. I don't know if I'll ever be able to do that.

Mostly, I envy how he can just be. When he holds my hand, I feel like I'm grounded… like I'm this twisted root, buried too deep in my own ideas, my own fears. I'm stuck in the dirt, hanging on for dear life, but he... he's calm. He pulls me back from the edge just by being near. And for a second, I think maybe I don't have to worry so much. Maybe it's not all that complicated. Maybe I just overthink everything.

But still, I worry. I worry about him. He's so honest, so open, and I wonder... what if the world changes him? What happens then? I hope I get to be the one to hold him when that day comes. I hope I can be the one to bring him back to himself if he ever starts to fall.

July 1964

George and I spent the whole day in my secret room. We danced and danced and laughed and hugged and kissed and kissed. I think that was the moment I started to really fall for him. Deeply. Like, really fall. He felt like mine. Completely mine. And while we danced, I let my mind wander... I let myself drift off a little. And weirdly, even though George was right there with me, I think I went somewhere else. Somewhere inside me.

Professor Leslie's still waiting on my answer. Still assuming I'll say yes. I'm spending the summer telling people I was gonna be a teacher. Or maybe an artist. A traveller. Anything but that. And parts of that were true. But the thing I haven't admitted to anyone, not even to *myself, is that I was about to become Professor Leslie's wife.*

Wife. The word makes me sick.

He promised me a seat beside him, teaching together. But that was just another way of saying I'd belong to him. I'd be his. And the thought of it... being someone's possession, someone's little pet... makes my skin crawl. Every second I think about it, I feel like I'm going to burst with hate.

He's my father's friend. A close friend. Not bad looking, I guess. Put together, for a man his age. But his age. Gosh, he's older than my father. And now that I really sit with it... it's disgusting. It's unbearable. They can't force me. I won't let them.

And George... George, dragging on that cigarette, beaming like he's got the whole world figured out... I want that. I want to be that sure, that untouchable. I want to be drunk. I want to be high. But I already am. Drunkenly in love. Stupidly, helplessly, recklessly in love with him. I want to run off with him. I want us to disappear. To be no one. To be free.

July 1964

Driving with George, I feel like we're these two runaway twins, lost somewhere between earth and sky. Somewhere far away from home, from all the things people expect from us. It's like we've slipped through a crack in the world... no labels, no roles, no rules. Just music and wind and the road stretching out forever.

With him, I'm not just me... I'm more. I'm someone untamed, like a wild child with no past, no chains, no fear. It's freedom. It's escape. It's everything I was told I could never be. And when I'm with him, I feel like nothing can touch me. Not the past. Not the rules. Not whatever's chasing me. It won't catch me. Not now. Not ever.

July 1964

What breaks me about George is that he thinks everything's gonna last forever. But it's not. It's really not. I'm running out of time. Out of choices. Something has to give. If I don't act soon, I'll be stuck. Trapped.

And still... I can't stay mad at him. I try, but I can't. He won't let me. And then he pulls me into him and I just melt. I forget the ticking clock. I forget the fear.

July 1964

I'm home. Professor Leslie is marrying Sammy. Poor, sweet Sammy.

She's not even sixteen. She doesn't know. She doesn't get what they're doing to her. And I feel... Gosh, I feel so relieved. And I feel disgusted for feeling that way. I hate myself for it.

My father knows about George now. Someone told him. Doesn't matter. I'm not ashamed. I've got nothing to hide. I told him I was leaving. He threw a fork at me. It hit my cheek. Left a mark.

My mum just stood there. Just... stood. Didn't move, didn't speak. Was she scared? Did she care? I don't know. I don't know. I've never felt this alone.

August 1964

What a terrible, sick thing... to twist something once so pure, something people used to believe in, and turn it into something cruel. Something selfish and ugly, just to get what you want. How do they do that? How can they stand to do that?

Sometimes I wonder if my anger towards God has more to do with my father than with faith. Maybe I can't believe in anything anymore because of him. And honestly, the world's not exactly making it easy to believe in much right now.

What happened to him? What happened to the man I used to call "Dad"? The one who held my hand? I'm ashamed of him now. And that shame runs so deep, I wonder if just having his blood in me makes me part of what's wrong.

If I could drain that blood out of me... cut the

tie… I would. No hesitation.

Those poor kids. They're scarred for life, and I don't know how to fix that. What could I possibly give them that would make any of this better? Nothing. There's nothing I can do.

I went to the police this week. The guy, Harold, I think, looked at me like I was some little girl telling stories. I gave him everything. Every piece of truth I had. And still, he looked right through me.

I know what I know. I know what I saw. But nothing matters. Not even God can save us now.

They're still out there. Walking through fields. Picking daffodils. Snipping them down with these old, rusty scissors, one by one. And I feel it. I feel the despair like a weight on my chest. And worse than that… I feel shame. Shame that I'm tied to this family. This family that's turned into something I don't even recognise.

I wish I'd been born in a different city. In a different body. In a different world, where being free didn't come at a price.

And the worst part? I know. I know too much. I can't un-know any of it. And all I can do is try to run. But if I can, if I can somehow pull myself together, get strong, get loud, maybe I can stop them. Maybe I can make my voice louder than theirs.

But I'm weak. Gosh, I'm so weak.

August 1964

Today, I told my father that I knew. I told him I wasn't going to let them keep hurting innocent people. He didn't say a word. He slapped me.

I don't feel like a person anymore. Not to him. Not to anyone. My words mean nothing. My thoughts, my feelings... they don't exist. I don't exist.

And yet, I've never felt more human. More alive. Because I said it. I said it out loud. And now I'm trapped with the truth.

August 1964

The Beatles are everywhere and I wish I could see them. I wish I could scream into their faces, let them know how happy they make me. How free I feel when I hear their music.

It's like they take me somewhere far away. Somewhere I've never been, but somehow feels like home.

Their music lifts the stone from my chest. For just a little while, the heaviness fades... and I feel alive. Nothing else matters then. Just me, their music and the sunshine in my mind.

Oh, how I wish that could last forever.

September 1964

If God exists, I wonder what He thinks about crime.

George

I've read all the biblical explanations, the justifications for punishment, for the afterlife. I've memorised them all.

But I still need to know: what does He think about injustice? About the innocent who suffer while He watches? Why does He let it happen? Why does He sit back when He has the power to stop it?

Is there really no other way to balance good and evil? Must the innocent be cut down to make sense of the world? Why?

Sometimes, I feel like I might be God. All I do is write and write and cry… but nothing changes.

September 1964

I wish I could be born again. Born a boy. Born stronger. I wish I had the power to fix every broken rule in this world. To give girls voices that are heard in a way they can never be silenced again. To give women better choices. Real choices. I wish I could save Sammy. I feel heavy. My eyes… my body. But my mind is light. Clear.

September 1964

I wish my brothers didn't resemble our father so much. They walk like him. Talk like him. Eat like him. It's as if they learnt everything from him, and no one else.

Sometimes I wish I had been born a boy too.

Maybe then I could've been different. Acted differently. Maybe I wouldn't have to watch them follow him.

I try to remember my father from when I was little. When he held my hand. Took me to the movies. Walked with me through Central Park. When we'd eat ice cream and I was just his little girl. And he was just my father. That was enough then. He wasn't perfect... but he was real. He was humble. And that was enough. But now... I don't know him.

Now he's lost in this new world. This new religion. This new way of thinking. He was always charming. Always clever. But now I hate how he uses those gifts. And I hate that my mother followed him into it... without question, without hesitation.

I hate that she never questions anything. Never speaks her mind. She just follows. And I wonder... was she always like this? Was there ever more to her than obedience? I wonder if I'll become her.

These thoughts scare me. I'm afraid of myself.

October 1964

Father has been meeting with all these men lately. They come and go, shaking hands, nodding, making deals. They are to take over their own branches of the church. A business model, I guess. A business. That's what it is to him now. He plans to oversee it all, to step away from preaching himself. To manage... To control... I think he is becoming something else, something colder, something harder. Or maybe I never knew him at all.

The house is never quiet. Their voices fill the halls, laughing, talking, planning. Always planning. I hear them from the dining room, gathered like kings. And I am afraid. Afraid of what they are building. Of what they are plotting. Afraid of what men like them can do. Some of them have already been preaching under his name. But this... this is something else. Expansion.... Conquering... That's the word that comes to mind. He wants to conquer. I don't recognise him anymore.

I tried to speak to David yesterday. I thought maybe I could reach him. Maybe through him, I could reach Father. But he's changed. He's not my sweet brother anymore. He's something else now. A stranger. A monster. And Mum... she's gone. Not physically, but in every other way. She's lost to this house. To him. To them.

I have no real proof. No evidence. Just this feeling. This terrible knowing that fills my bones. But it will never be enough. It will never be enough to stop any of this.

October 1964
Found some of Father's notes... family meetings,

strange gatherings. Names I recognise. Girls from town. Still in school. Too young. Why would their parents allow this?

Then I found the insurance papers. Not just for the church, but personal ones too. All with Father listed as the beneficiary. Sums so large they made my stomach turn. Some claims already filed... for fires, for thefts... things that never happened.

Is he planning something? Staging it? It's bigger than I thought. A scheme. A terrible one. He's twisting faith into profit, and I feel sick.

There's more... I know there is. But the closer I get, the more I fear what I'll find.

How can one man wear God's name and hide so much behind it?

December 1964

I dreamt of George last night.

We were at the cinema, sitting side by side like strangers... Strangers who have known each other forever. It was like meeting for the first time all over again. I remember looking at him from the corner of my eye. He looked funny to me... familiar and unfamiliar all at once. I think he thought the same of me.

We just sat there, watching the screen. I don't even remember the movie. It didn't matter. Nothing mattered except that he was there. That he was by my side. That I could feel him near me. We said hello. And then... we just were. Side by side. No words. No explanations. I wanted to stay there forever. Just a little longer. Just a little more time.

Gosh, if I could sell everything... everything... I would. Just to go back to that moment. To sit at his side again. We wouldn't have to speak. We wouldn't have to do anything. Just... be. It was so vivid. So clear. More real than the world I wake up to.

I love him. I love him so dearly, as dearly as I love life itself.

And now, his love —

I will carry it with me.

Always.

Chapter Eleven
"Yesterday"

"Are you fucking nuts, Dad?"

Well, so much for a nice evening walk.

Jesse's voice explodes through George's phone speaker, loud enough for half the hotel parking lot to hear. George always cranks the volume up too high, whether it's a call, a voicemail, or one of those YouTube history documentaries he falls asleep to.

"Please, just give me one—one—sane reason why flying to America by yourself, without telling a single soul, was a good idea."

"I'm not alone," George says, glancing sideways at me. He lifts the phone slightly in my direction, as though it's a physical burden he's trying to offload. "I'm with Julia. She's right here. Want to talk to her?"

"You're nothing but selfish, Dad."

George pulls the phone back to his ear. His expression shifts, his mouth pressing into a tired, weathered line, his eyes staring at something far away. I've seen this look before. It's the face of a man aching for closeness, for understanding, but knowing he won't get it. It's the same expression creeping onto his face whenever he remembers Cornelia is gone.

"You always do this," Jesse continues, his words clipped. "You've always done this. Everything is about you. The rest of us—we just revolve around your choices like we don't have lives of our own. Do you have any idea how stupid and disrespectful this is? Especially to Mum?"

"Hey, don't bring your mother into this."

"Oh, I am. Because you never cared about her. Or me. Or any of us. And you're still pulling this selfish bullshit."

The call ends with a dull beep.

George releases a quiet puff of air before lowering himself onto a bench. He watches a few travellers wrestle their luggage through the hotel's sliding doors. They open. They close. They open again.

1981

Jesse wobbles on his tiny legs, then bursts into a run, his laughter spilling out across the front garden of Bluebell Cottage. He looks just like George—round, rosy cheeks, as if flower petals had been pressed to his skin. He toddles forward with the unsteady eagerness of a boy who hasn't yet learnt how much the world can hurt. George, thirty-seven and seven years into marriage, watches him with quiet amusement.

Hilde is there, camera in hand, her blonde curls bouncing as she chases after their son, snapping a picture every time he giggles. She is spirited, strong, a woman who moves like she was born to run. Jesse got that from her.

She places a plastic ball on the stone path, nudging it towards Jesse. He lets out a squeal and lunges forward, wrapping his arms around the ball as he tumbles onto the grass. Silence for half a second, then laughter again, high and pure. George is already moving, scooping Jesse up and tossing him into the air. The boy stretches his arms wide, reaching for the sky, his delight lighting up the afternoon.

I feel it all like I am there, like I've slipped once again between time's fingers and fallen into the memory with him. The warmth of the sun on my skin, the sound of Jesse's laughter, the scent of fresh grass. I forget this isn't my past to step into. It belongs to George, and I am only borrowing it.

"Are you okay?" I ask as I sit beside George on the bench. He's hunched forward, elbows on his knees, staring at the ground like it holds the answer to something he's been searching for. When he finally nods and straightens, he props himself up with a palm against his thigh.

"My boy never quite saw how much I worked for what we had," George says, voice low now, almost like he's talking to himself. "Some families go without, you know. We weren't rich, but we got by. I made sure of that. Did what needed doing to keep things steady, keep us safe. Out early every morning, never sat still long. Always working. It wasn't easy, starting over in a new place. Had no guide, no plan—just took one job after another till I found my footing. Made it work, somehow."

He exhales through his nose, shaking his head. "Jesse never had to scrub floors or wash dishes in the back of some greasy café. I did that, so he wouldn't have to. That's what you do, isn't it? When you're a parent. You carry the weight, so they don't have to feel it."

I watch him as he speaks, rubbing the sides

of my shoes together. I don't remember much about George's family. I think Jesse visited once, last year, with his teenage son. They were in and out so fast I barely registered them. I do remember the boy had a limp. I never asked George about it.

What I realise the more I know George is he's not an enigma. He's just a man, carrying the strain of all the years that came before.

"Christine W-h-y-l-e-r," Humphrey mutters as he types on his laptop keyboard, pressing enter to search.

I lean back in my hotel lobby seat and notice everyone's still here—Rosanna, Alan, Anne, Humphrey and Anthony—all gathered around George, giving him reassuring pats on the back while Humphrey scrolls through the first page of Google.

"I thought you guys had moved on?" I ask.

"Why would we?" Rosanna waves a dismissive hand. "You think we'd leave you and George to deal with this alone?"

"We're just as invested," Alan chimes in.

Humphrey leans in close to the screen, squinting as he reads aloud, "*Underground, secretive, and elusive—'Transcendent Unity' church: fraud, multi-level marketing, and tax evasion—or just a misunderstanding? Founder and CEO, former pastor of 'Nobody's Children', Jeffrey "Bobby" Dean, now potentially facing charges."*

Anne shifts in her leather seat. "Does anyone want a drink?"

"Not now, honey," Humphrey replies without looking up.

"That sounds great, actually," Alan says. "Double, no ice."

Anne heads to the bar, leaving us in silence as Humphrey keeps scanning the article.

"This," George says, nodding at the screen, "this is exactly why we need Christine. She's onto something."

"There's not much else on it, though," Anthony points out. "Nobody's child has been taken to court yet—haha, pun intended. Sorry."

"Not yet," George says. "But this is our chance. If we can get Christine on our side, we can bring the truth to light."

"I don't mean to sound pessimistic, George," Rosanna says carefully, "but if this is all Christine has, what more can we do? Unless you're planning on illegally digging into Bobby's private business tax records."

"No," George shakes his head, "but I can share Cornelia's truth with the world."

I rub my eyes, exhaling. "I feel like this is escalating and I don't even know how or why anymore."

Anne returns, holding a glass of wine in one hand and a whisky in the other. Her smile fades slightly as she nears the table, sensing the shift in the air.

"Child abuse," George says, his voice firm but low. It cuts through all of us. "Forced, arranged marriages. Child trafficking. Emotional manipulation. Fraud. An empire built on a facade of love for a higher power which doesn't exist."

Anne sinks back into the booth, and silence falls over the group. The lobby around us vibrates with unnoticed collisions, a current of movement; yet we remain locked in place, stuck in our own bubble, stuck with the truth.

"Cornelia tried to warn the world," George adds. "She tried to tell me and I didn't listen. She saw what was starting to take root in that godforsaken church, and they silenced her."

"They spread the rumour about the fake pregnancy," I speak, barely able to get the words out. "Made it look like she couldn't cope with the gossip and took her own life."

I want George to stop skirting around it and just say it. Plainly. I want him to mention Cornelia's diary, so I don't have to. So I don't have to be the one to admit I've already read them. Pages he kept hidden for years, only now choosing to share.

Cornelia was seen with George. People talked. Whispers turned to rumours. Someone came up with the idea of a fake pregnancy and soon enough, everyone believed it. The story they told, the one the world saw, was that Cornelia couldn't bear the shame, the pressure. That she took her own life. And Bobby, of course, used the narrative for his church. Turned it into some tragic parable to pull people in.

But that's not all of it.

Cornelia knew too much. And someone made sure she never got the chance to tell anyone. They silenced her. And George, he knew. Maybe not everything, not right away. But enough. He was close. He was piecing it all together. And instead of staying, instead of fighting, he ran. He knew, and he ran.

And now, after all these years, he brings it all back. These journals, these memories, this pain. But why? Why now?

I want him to say it out loud. To stop treating me like a child. To stop acting like he's hiding something or protecting me or plotting whatever this is in secret. I want him to let me in. Because how am I supposed to stand beside him if I don't even know what I'm standing in?

"She was stronger than that," George says, finishing my thought. His eyes are dark and heavy now. "And she wasn't going to be quiet."

"No, no, no, no—I can't do it." George pushes the phone back towards Humphrey like it might electrocute him. "One of you folks has to do it."

"Come on." Alan nudges him. "That's exactly why they have this number—so you can call, complain, make suggestions—"

George squints like he's just been asked to wrestle a bear. "Can we not maybe just send an email instead?"

"Nobody reads emails anymore, trust me. Picking up the phone works best," Alan insists.

"I'm not so sure about that." George crosses his arms. "People ignore unknown numbers these days, especially on smartphones. That's the youth of today. Just ask Julia." He gestures vaguely at me.

"That's not really—" Alan talks right over everyone.

"But just ask her!" Rosanna chimes in, dragging me into the middle of it. "Come on, Julia, tell them. Would you pick up?"

I glance around at the expectant faces.

"Well, Christine isn't exactly young. She's what, sixty? She plays by your rules."

"Can one of you kindhearted people please just make the call for me?" George's voice cuts through the noise, exasperated.

"George, I think this one's yours." I fold my arms.

"Alright. Fine." He throws both hands in the air. "Fine! I'll admit. I'm scared of cold calls, okay? There it is."

Silence.

"There you have it, folks," he adds, flustered. "I can do a lot of things in person, but this? I can't do it."

"Ohh, George…" Rosanna coos, patting him like a nervous pet. "That's okay, we're all scared of something." Then, without missing a beat, she straightens up. "Give me that phone."

Alan presses dial.

Rosanna rolls her shoulders, shakes out her

arms like she's warming up for a heavyweight match, then picks up the call.

It rings twice.

"New York Tribute." The receptionist tries to be upbeat, but sounds rather bored.

"Oh, hello, sweetheart," Rosanna says, her voice sugary. "I'm calling about one of your articles."

A pause. "Uh-huh."

"It's about the 'Transcendent Unity' church piece."

The group instinctively leans in.

"Complaints can be submitted through our online form," the receptionist recites mechanically.

"Yeah, well, I was hoping you could put me through to the writer?"

"We don't do that, ma'am, but we have a general inbox where you can reach the team. Someone will get back to you. Or... you could try reaching Ms Whyler on X."

"What's an X?"

A hesitation. "Twitter?"

Rosanna pulls a face. "Ahh, X that." She waves a dismissive hand. "Look, honey, this is crucial. Bigger than the X! I have something important to report about that article."

"I understand, ma'am, but Ms Whyler isn't taking any unsolicited material, and she has a full writing schedule. As I said, you're welcome to submit something to our tip box."

"Yeah, sure, I'll do that." Rosanna sighs and hangs up.

"Oh, scrap that." Alan snatches the phone from her hand.

Unfazed, Anthony takes another sip of his bourbon. Alan redials.

"New York Tribute," the receptionist answers, now with a forced politeness.

"Hello, this is Barack Obama," Alan says, dropping into a terrible impression. "And I'd like to speak to one of your journalists."

Rosanna swipes the phone from him. "Are you not with it?"

"What?! Everybody loves Obama!" Alan protests, throwing his hands up. "If I were the receptionist and Obama called, I'd put him through."

George groans, dragging his hands down his face like he's physically pulling his headache out. He leans forward, staring at the hotel barista, who's pressing down on the steaming espresso machine handle.

His eyes gleam.

"I've got an idea."

Chapter Twelve
"We Can Work It Out"

I can't believe we're actually doing this—we're stalking Christine Whyler.

She works at The New York Tribute, a towering glass fortress of journalism reflecting the city skyline like a polished mirror. The entrance is a flurry of movement; reporters, editors and media professionals rush in and out, clutching coffees, briefcases and folded-up commuter bikes. The revolving doors spin like clockwork, sucking people into the heart of the newsroom and spitting them back out into the chaos of the city.

We sit on the edge of a sleek marble ledge just outside, pretending we have some legitimate reason to be here. I glance at my reflection in the building's pristine surface, questioning my life choices. This might be the dumbest thing I've done since taking that job at Fred's gym. But, as they say, *"Good things come to those who wait"* or whatever. So, here we are, testing that theory.

"How do we know when she's coming out?" I ask, shifting my weight uncomfortably.

"She will. She takes a coffee break," George says with absolute certainty.

"How do you know that?" I squint at him. "It's 11:45 right now. She could come out at any time between now and—"

George smacks my shoulder in rapid succession, nearly knocking me off the ledge.

"She's here, she's here, she's here," he blurts frantically.

He jumps up, smoothing his clothes with the urgency of a man about to meet royalty, then hesitates, realising he has no actual plan, before awkwardly lowering himself back down.

I yank him back down before he draws too much attention to us.

Christine walks right past, oblivious, heading away from the building with a sharp, decisive stride.

We scramble to our feet and follow her discreetly, or at least as discreetly as two amateurs can manage. She heads into a small corner café, a place with handwritten chalkboard menus and the smell of ground beans hanging thick in the air.

Trying to blend in, I grab a laminated menu

from a stand by the entrance and nod along as I read out the different types of cold brew to myself.

We settle at the back of the café, sinking into the wooden benches, doing our best to look casual. A fluffy brown cat hops onto the back of our seat, flicking its bushy tail right in front of George's face, like it's conspiring to give him a fake moustache for his disguise. George nudges the cat aside, his focus locked on Christine. I look at the clock on the wall as time goes by.

Christine massages her forehead with her knuckles, battling a migraine. She finally takes one last, long sip of her coffee and sets the cup down, not on the little saucer it came with, but on the wooden table. Then, pushing her chair back, she stands. And walks. Walks right towards us. No way. She's coming to our table. I don't know whether to be thrilled or terrified. Both, probably. George and I fumble, pretending to be busy with anything but blatantly stalking her. We're pathetic.

"Okay, what do you two want?" Her voice is curt, no-nonsense. "You've clearly been following me all the way from work. This isn't a coincidence."

George and I scramble to our feet.

"It's a pleasure," George says, reaching out to

shake her hand. She doesn't take it. He hesitates, then awkwardly pats his trousers as if brushing away imaginary crumbs. "I'm George and this is Julia."

Christine's eyes flick between us. "Well, George and Julia—I don't know who you are or what you want, but—" Her expression shifts. She narrows her gaze. "Wait a minute. Are you the ones who called my office earlier today?"

"Yes, ma'am." George's smile is full of hope, like a kid meeting his hero.

"Ah, Jesus Christ," she says to herself, staring into the middle distance. "Please excuse the unintended pun—and my future swearing—but what the fuck?" She turns on her heel, striding back towards her table to grab her handbag.

George rushes after her. "Ms Whyler, please, just give us a moment."

"I'm sorry, but I'm busy."

"Just listen."

She lets out a sharp exhalation, gripping her bag tighter. "Look, I get this is important to you, but it's off my plate. I wrote that article months ago, and I've moved on. It was a nightmare to get published, let alone noticed. The higher-ups don't want this stuff out there." She shakes her head.

"Nobody in the industry wants to go after churches with deep pockets. It's bad business."

"There's more to this than financial fraud," George says.

Christine pauses, observing him. "Go on."

"There are generations of abuse. Illegal activity."

She scoffs. "Like every other corrupt institution." She tightens her grip on her bag, stepping around us. "Now, if you'll excuse me—"

"What would you do, Ms Whyler," George then says, his voice raw, "if the person you loved most died, taking a secret with them? If *you* also knew something wasn't right, but ran from the truth? And years later, you had the chance to make it right?"

Christine stops. She turns. Her eyes narrow with skepticism as they lock onto George. He's standing tall, but I can see the slight tremble in his hands.

"Can you bring evidence?" she asks.

I glance at George. He nods, slow and sure.

Christine lets out a soft huff, adjusting the strap of her bag. "Alright. Call me when you're ready. You have my number." With that, she walks out of the café.

Without a word, George bolts for the door. I hurry after him, just in time to see him stagger onto the side of the pavement and retch into the gutter beside a rusted-out mailbox.

I watch him, pale and swaying, steadying himself against the brick wall of the coffee shop. It annoys me to see him like this—this fragile, exhausted version of himself. Jesse was right. He doesn't know when to stop. He's so fixated on this he's tearing himself away from reality. I feel pressure building in my mind, like a solid rock growing heavier in my brain. My jaw tightens, and I rub my fingers together, trying to stop myself from counting.

"Sorry," George mutters, pressing a hand to his forehead. "The anticipation got to me. All of this... I've bottled all of this up inside me for years. I guess it finally decided to break free." He digs in his pocket for a tissue, wipes his mouth, and tucks it away again. "I suppose the laxatives are working, too. Thought they were supposed to go the other way."

I let out a sigh. "Maybe we should stop."

George straightens, wiping his forehead. "Stop? This is only just the beginning."

I cross my arms, gripping them tight, bracing

myself. "You're chasing a ghost, George. Cornelia's gone."

He looks at me, and his eyes, tired and worn, soften into something almost like a smile. "Oh, she's here," he says quietly. "She's always been."

I want to argue. I should argue. But I don't. Because George has a way of pulling me along, and maybe, just maybe, I want to be pulled. Because I believe in him. Because even if he's chasing ghosts, I can't let him do it alone.

"What now?" I ask.

"Facebook," he says. "We're going back to Facebook."

I scratch my head, trying to catch up. "How did you know she'd come out of that office at lunchtime?"

George grins, tapping the side of his nose like he's revealing some great secret. "I sent her a voucher."

I blink. "A voucher?"

"Yeah, you know, one of those email deals for a free coffee. But I made it specific—only today, only between 12:00 and 12:45."

I squeeze my eyes shut, pressing my fingers against my temples, willing my brain to work faster. "Where the hell did you even get that voucher?"

Before I get an answer, George grabs my wrist with surprising urgency. "I'll explain later— let's go!"

George fishes the pair of chopsticks from his front pocket, cradling them in his palm like a fragile little bird. His thumb glides along the smooth wood, tracing old, invisible patterns. His gaze turns glassy, bright with something distant. Once again, he's not here with me anymore.

I know that look. I used to see it in Auntie at the gym. When her mind drifted somewhere deep in the past, leaving only a husk behind. It's the kind of gaze which tunnels so far back, it almost forgets to return.

Whenever it happens, I know George and Auntie are somewhere else, with the people who once meant the most, in places that once held everything.

And yet, even when they're not always with us, the people we've lost remain in different ways. We carry them in our habits, in the way we eat, the rhythm of our steps, the cadence of our laughter. Nothing about us is wholly original. I wonder how much of George is Cornelia. How much of Cornelia lingers in George's children. And maybe, just maybe, how much of George and therefore Cornelia, I have absorbed along the way.

We stand outside Cyber Dusk, an internet café with a neon-lit sign humming above the entrance. Two cosplayers push past us, slipping inside. The door swings open, revealing a pulse of blue and pink lights, then clicks shut behind them. George hesitates.

"Has Halloween moved?"

He doesn't wait for an answer before stepping in. Inside, the air vibrates with a remixed chiptune track, layered over lo-fi beats. A host jumps in front of us, beaming.

"Hey, guys! Care for a map?"

George clutches his chest, like the kid just shaved five years off his life. We're handed brochures, each filled with details on events, best practices, and where to find what.

"Looking for anything specific?" the host asks.

"Oh, we're meeting some kids. Her age." George jerks a thumb towards me.

The host's gaze flicks at me. "Oh."

"Oh," I echo.

We step inside, plunged into the blinking

chaos of arcade machines. The air smells of fried snacks and too many people packed into one place. The music shifts into something heavier, a synthwave track with deep bass rattling in my chest.

George nudges my arm and nods towards the host. "Why was she wearing a fox tail if it's not Halloween?"

"They might be a furry."

"A what now?"

"They're called *furries*. People who like to dress up as animals. It's… a thing."

George stares at me, then at the crowd. "And we all just… act like this is normal?"

"Oh, George," I sigh.

George's eyes catch a spark, and in a blink, he rushes towards an arcade cabinet. The screen flickers, displaying the Street Fighter logo. His fingers hover over the buttons, tracing them the way he always does with his chopsticks.

"Jesse and I—" He stops, his voice turning rough. "I used to take Jesse to play one of these. He loved Street Fighter II." He shakes his head, a soft laugh catching in his throat. "I liked the first one better. That was when he still let me sit with him when he played. He was little then. I taught him how. He was so eager, so full of life. I was proud of him."

George drops into the chair, palms spreading over the console. He pats his pockets, searching. I step closer and slip a coin into the slot. The game hums to life. The screen blinks, and for a fraction of a second, George hesitates, then instinct kicks in. Ryu bounces into action against Zangief. A well-timed punch. A duck. A spinning kick. George's muscle memory takes over and years collapse into a heartbeat.

1988

George wrestles with his tie, muttering under his breath. The knot is too loose, then too tight, then, somehow, both. He huffs, yanking it straight, and studies himself in the mirror.

He throws his jacket over his shoulders, rolling them back so it settles properly, and heads downstairs in a practiced rush. The house is still waking. Pale light spills across the banister; the radio in the kitchen mumbles the news in flat, morning tones.

He grabs his coat from the hook, pulls it on—one arm, then the other—bends to pick up his briefcase; and then, pain. A sharp, bright whack to his foot, the scrape of plastic skidding wild across tile. A small red toy car wobbles to a stop beside his shoe.

From upstairs, Hilde's voice cuts through the morning haze. "Jesse, no battlefields by the front door! One day, your father's going to break his neck, and then what? You'll have to push him to work in a wheelchair, and we'll have to move to a house without stairs."

A scrabble of movement follows, and then Jesse, all elbows and wild electricity, comes tearing into the hallway. He throws himself onto his knees, slides across the tiles like a stuntman, snatches the car into his fist, and springs up again, grinning.

"Jesse won!" he announces, fists raised.

George crouches to tie his laces. The second he does, tiny fists pummel his back.

"Jesse won the fight over enemy!"

George groans, shaking him off. "The enemy has a meeting in twenty minutes. We'll have to call this one a draw." He straightens up, unlocking the door.

"Round two starts now, Dad! Get ready—fight!"

George steps outside, shaking his head. "We'll play later, yeah?"

Jesse catches the door with both hands, feet braced against the tile. His chest rises and falls, his grin faltering.

George is already in the car. He rolls the window down as he starts the engine, glancing back just once to wave. Jesse is still in the doorway, turning the toy car over in his hands.

"King of the Hill." His lips move, just barely, like he doesn't expect anyone to hear.

George's hands tremble on the controls.

"*You Lose,*" the game announces, and George deflates. He's now hunched over the controls, like he's intending to hug the machine.

"George?" I try to bring him back, away from the story clinging to him, pulling him towards the widening gap between what could've been and the distance grown between him and his son.

"George?" a voice then calls from behind us. We both turn around.

A tall teenage girl stands in front of us. Her wavy, silver hair shimmers with a soft pink tint under the neon light, looking almost electric. She lifts a hand in greeting and smiles. I look at George for an explanation.

"Alice." George stands up, smoothing down

his jacket. He walks over to my side. Initially, he smiles at me, raises a hand, but nothing follows. Taking a deep breath, he tries again. "This is Alice. From Facebook."

I smile at Alice and nod in acknowledgment, then look at George for further clarification.

"Alice is going to help us," George says. "And we're going to help Alice." He smiles with renewed enthusiasm.

"You use Facebook?" I laugh, squinting.

"We use whatever takes us further," Alice says. "Whatever helps us understand things other people can't."

"It's nice to meet you." I stretch out my hand.

"Likewise." She shakes mine.

Out of the corner of my eye, I see George as we shake hands, a small, almost fatherly smile on his lips.

Alice leads us to a quieter corner, where low cushions are strewn across the floor. The arcade's noise dims into a distant hum. When the group seated there notices us, they rise, shuffling in anticipation.

"Here's everyone else." Alice gestures. "We're so glad you're here."

I flick my gaze between George and the kids.

Then back again.

"These are my Facebook friends," George announces again before picking a spot to sit. He looks drained.

He struggles to lower himself onto a cushion, joints creaking in protest. With a grunt, he props his back against the wall. I hesitate before sitting beside him.

The girl next to me extends a hand. She looks younger than Alice, maybe fifteen.

"Emma," she says.

I shake her hand. Next to her is a slender teenage boy, wearing a jacket too big for him, sleeves dangling past his wrists. His hair flops into his eyes when he nods in greeting.

"Daniel," he says, offering a quiet wave.

I smile back. I then glance at George.

"Alice, Emma and Daniel are my friends from Facebook," he repeats.

"I got that." I nod.

"They've also been part of Transcendent Unity."

The three teens exchange glances before Alice speaks again.

"We heard about Cornelia," she says, looking at me. My expression must still be confused. "And we all agree—it has to stop. All of it."

Emma flips open a sketchbook on her lap. The neon light from a nearby machine casts shifting colours across her face as she sketches.

"We thought long and hard," Alice continues. Daniel nods beside her. "We're ready to speak."

George's shoulders relax just a little. Alice sips from her avocado smoothie and I feel like I've stumbled into a secret society. Daniel laces his fingers together and rests them on top of his head, staring at the ceiling like he's trying to focus. Emma darkens the last lines of a Daruma doll she's just drawn, its left eye defined in ink.

"God isn't love," she murmurs, still drawing. "I can't imagine a God that's pure love and nothing else. If love exists, there shouldn't be suffering. If suffering remains, then there is no God." She dots the final mark, not looking up. "You make a wish when you draw the Daruma's first eye, you know."

She tilts the book towards us. "When your wish comes true, you fill in the other eye."

Chapter Thirteen
"In My Life"

Christine drops the papers onto her desk with a soft thud, finally revealing her face. It's only five or six sheets, but the way she had been holding them made it look like a mountain. She removes her glasses and places them atop the papers before rubbing her eyes with her fingertips.

George and I sit across from her, separated only by the small office table. My breathing is all wrong, like my reflexes have shut down. I force myself to take deep, steady breaths before I pass out from the lack of oxygen. Behind Christine, her goldfish makes a tiny blub, releasing bubbles as it watches us before flicking its tail and swimming away.

"I'll piece this together for you, okay?" Christine says. "I'll write the story."

Relief softens George's chest, carrying him back down into the padded chair.

"But—" Christine adds, pressing her

fingertips to her temples. "Not so fast." She straightens, pushing the papers back towards us. George watches them slide across the desk, burdened with the silent gravity of everything unsaid. "Before anything else, you need to go to the police." She leans forward. "These are minors we're talking about."

I already know what's in these papers. Alice, Daniel and Emma told us what happened to them. Not just in words, but in every broken expression, every cautious glance. They explained how the Church of Transcendent Unity exploited and mistreated them, forcing them into near-unpaid labour for its youth team and making them work illegal hours for little compensation. They documented their observations, what they were told to ignore, what they were coerced into saying, and what they were compelled to keep secret. Worst of all, they wrote about the abuse—horrific allegations against youth group leaders and higher-ups. Some kids we haven't even met yet sent in their own testimonies. I spread the pages out with my fingers, staring at the inked words.

"They tried," George says. "They did go to the police. Nobody listened."

"Well, they better try again," Christine

replies flatly.

"They didn't have enough evidence to make a case."

"If that's the situation, I can't help either. I need real, solid documentation before I can run this."

"But you do!" George's voice rises as he gestures at the papers. "Both you and I know this is real. You've speculated yourself something's not right with this church."

Christine lifts an eyebrow. "Tax fraud. That's what I speculated—based on an actual ongoing court case. The founder and main decision-maker—" she pauses, tilting her head, "or whatever we're calling him—has been stacking cash away. Nowhere have I mentioned exploited kids, forced labour, or marriages with minors. If you can get me proof that this so-called leader isn't just a scam artist but the architect of a deeply rooted chain of abuse? Fantastic. Bring it. The police will love it too." She taps a nail against the desk. "But as it stands, these are just handwritten testimonies. And more importantly, these are minors. Where are their families? Their guardians? What do they have to say?"

"Some of these kids have parents who are

knee-deep in the church," I say. "It's not that easy."

"If I don't have reliable sources, I won't get this approved, and your buddy Bobby and his pyramid scheme will keep dancing around the law." Christine leans back in her chair. "Nothing personal, George. Just doing my job."

George shoots up from his chair, making the table and papers rattle. His voice hardens. "It is personal." His hands grip the edge of the desk. "I lost someone because of that absolute scum of a church, and I will never forgive myself for not stopping it. Cornelia is dead and nothing will bring her back. That old bastard has been wrecking lives for decades and no one has done a damn thing. Nobody deserves this." His voice trembles as he lets the air drain from his lungs. "I will not sit back and watch it continue for the rest of my days without taking action."

George stares down at the papers. His shoulders sag, spine curving inward. I can see it— the man clawing at what's already gone, reaching for memories sifting away like dust between his fingers.

I place my hand over his, gently squeezing his icy fingers. "Stay with us," I whisper.

Christine presses her lips together in a faint,

compassionate smile. "I'm sorry for your loss, George. I really am." She stands up. "I'll leave you two for a bit. I need coffee. If you want one, let me know." With that, she steps out of the office.

George sinks back into his chair, drained. I stare at my shoes, letting silence settle between us before kicking the tips together, trying to jolt myself into speaking again.

"Was it Alice, Emma and Daniel who gave you the coffee voucher?" I ask.

George nods.

"How did you even know Christine would use it?"

"No matter who you are, there's an eight out of ten chance you'll take a free offer when it comes with urgency."

"Who said that?"

George turns to me. "Look, sometimes shit works out because you're lucky." His voice tightens. "So whether it's luck or sheer flipping determination, we're going to help these kids build a case. And we're taking it to the police.

"This is Detective Davis." he extends his hand, but only halfway—more a gesture than an invitation, a handshake he clearly has no interest in finishing. "I hear you've been giving my desk sergeant a hard time with some story about a corrupt church."

George and I turn towards the front desk, where the sergeant sits on his high stool behind a partition of scratched-up plexiglass. His expression is frozen somewhere between boredom and contempt. He keeps his eyes on the paperwork in front of him, his jaw working in slow, exaggerated shifts as if he's chewing on the effort it takes not to roll his eyes. Aware that we're watching, he pointedly shuffles his papers to one side. He then leans back just enough to suggest he's warding us off by sheer theatrical willpower.

I look back at Davis, taking him in. He's built like a guy who's spent his whole life chasing trouble. His face is worn, like a city street after too many winters. His eyes, though, hold something steadier. Heavy, not careless. He looks exactly like the detectives on TV, except real. Just someone who's seen too much and keeps going anyway.

It isn't the first time George and I have been here in the past couple of weeks. Not even close. I can still see us at the counter, papers clutched in our hands. Each time the sergeant flipped through them, shook his head, slid them back. Not enough. Not for us. Not today. Over and over, heads shaking, doors closing, our words left hanging in the stale air. I lost count of how many times we walked out of here empty-handed, promising each other we'd try again tomorrow.

I blink and pull myself back into the moment. Davis hasn't moved.

"Listen," he says. "You're not the first people to come in here with claims like this."

"We know you're busy," George cuts in with confidence, though I can tell he's bracing himself. He shifts slightly, almost like he's ready to block Davis if he tries to walk off. "But this is bigger than tax fraud. We have testimonies from minors—forced labour, abuse, arranged marriages."

Davis pushes out a soft huff. "I know these kids and their situation all too well."

"And yet here we are," George replies.

Davis's mouth pulls into something halfway between a smirk and a wince. His gaze skims the floor for a second, jaw tightening before he lifts his eyes again. "Look, testimonies alone don't cut it. We need documentation—bank records, emails, anything that ties it to a federal charge. You think I haven't heard these stories before? I've written half the damn reports myself. They just end up gathering dust. As I said, we need proper testimonies."

"And the team has that," I reply.

His eyes flick to me. "They do, huh?"

"Yes. If you'd just listen to them."

George puts a hand on my arm. Davis shifts as if to leave, angling his body towards the hallway. George is faster, stepping into his path; not aggressive, but immovable, like a doorframe you don't notice until you walk into it. He then steps closer to Davis, toe-to-toe with him. "Detective Davis, I've not come all this way for you to act like this isn't worth looking into."

Davis doesn't flinch. He doesn't back down either. He shifts his weight, folds his arms across his chest. "If there's proof of coercion, especially with minors, then we're talking federal. That means the Trafficking Victims Protection Act. But talk won't cut it. I need corroboration—financial irregularities, witnesses willing to go on record. Otherwise, it dies the same way it always does. In a file cabinet no one opens."

"We have people willing to talk. What more do you need?" My words come out sharper than I intend, but I don't pull them back.

For the first time, Davis really looks at me. Not the quick, cursory glance, but a long stare.

"You think this is the only nightmare on my desk? I, for one, don't like wasting hours chasing ghosts. You want me to risk my job, my neck? I need more than faith."

He makes another move to brush past. George shifts with him, calm but unyielding. The room tightens, the sergeant pretending not to notice though his pen has stopped moving.

George's voice drops. "These kids trust me. They've told me things they haven't told anyone else. They'll sit down with you, Detective—but not if you walk away now."

A flicker passes over Davis's face, but he presses his lips together. "That's not the point."

"It is," George insists, softer now, like he's offering less an argument than a truth Davis already knows. "You don't have to believe me. Just give them the chance to tell it themselves."

Davis's fingers twitch against his sleeve. Silence stretches. George steps back just enough, to give the detective room to choose. Davis rubs his forehead with his palm. "You get me someone who was inside—someone who'll sit across from me and talk—and I'll see what I can do. Surveillance, maybe. But it better be solid. Because if I stick my neck out, I can't afford to have it cut off."

He adjusts his jacket. "And don't mistake me showing you anything down the line for friendship. I've got bosses breathing down my neck, and a dozen other cases waiting."

24 hours later, Detective Davis barely slows his stride as he all but shoves George and me into a dimly lit records room. Christine follows in a rush. Davis swings the door shut behind us and nudges a couple of chairs towards us with the sole of his foot. George and I take our seats while Christine remains standing, arms crossed. Davis doesn't press her. Instead, he takes the last chair, lowering himself into it with a deliberate ease, placing his tablet on the table between us.

He stares at his locked tablet, his eyes pendling ever so slightly from left to right, weighing something invisible to us. The silence stretches, heavy enough that I can almost hear the hum of the lights overhead. He leans back in his chair, pulls out a passport photo, and slaps it down on the table. It's a slightly older coloured photograph of a man in his twenties.

"This is Frankie," Davis says. Before I can even focus on the face, his hand covers it, palm flat like he's stamping something out, and then the photo is gone again, whisked back into his pocket. "My baby brother."

I glance at George to see if he's as thrown as I am.

Davis lets out a low sound—not quite a laugh, not quite a sigh. A short, dry humph that carries a sting of irony, as if he's impressed in spite of himself, and irritated that he is. The corner of his mouth twitches, but it doesn't turn into a smile.

"You and these kids are something else. They told you I work here, huh? Yeah, they're clever. Good kids."

His tone shifts. A grit building in it, like gravel underfoot.

"Frankie joined Transcendent Unity fifteen years ago. And right around then, I stopped hearing from him. Ten years of nothing. Calls unanswered. Doors shut. Then, one day—" he taps his pocket where the photo rests, the gesture sharp, controlled— "a letter in my inbox, five years back. Says he's gone. Drug overdose. No call. No explanation. Just gone."

He goes still for a moment, a pulse showing in his temple. There's no outburst, but the hate is there, thinly veiled, simmering.

"Ten years," he says again, quieter this time.

"They scooped him away from me. From us all. I know all too well who these Transcendent Unity people are. It's not my first rodeo. God, I wish it was. I did it for Frankie back then, but I was led by fury. Couldn't see straight. I even quit my job for a while. Came back when I was more use. Still couldn't build a strong enough case."

He flicks a look at George, something measuring in his eyes.

"Well, what am I saying? You probably know more than I do by now. You've found yourself a hell of a team to go at this with."

George looks him back in the eye without saying a word.

"You didn't get this from me, understand? Officially, you were never here." Davis slides his tablet forward and presses play.

The screen flickers to life, and Emma appears—hunched, arms wrapped tightly around herself like she's holding herself together. Her posture's rawness speaks louder than any sound, despite the muted video. Davis pushes the volume up.

"I, uhm... I was in Transcendent Unity from the day I was born until I got out at the end of last year." Emma's words stumble at first, like she's tasting them for the first time, the reality of them settling in her bones. "They made me marry when I was fifteen. The guy was, like, twice my age. I had to work in the office, signing people up, filling out forms, answering calls. I was also sent out to talk to new people, bring them in, kind of sell them on the church. I was the first person they met before all the... ceremonies." Her voice trembles, but she pushes on. "I stayed married for a year and two months. I didn't see any of the papers they used—it came from somewhere overseas, I don't know. He kept my paychecks. All of us girls gave our paychecks to our husbands. That was just the rule. And I... I couldn't take it anymore. So I left." Her voice falters.

Davis leans forward slightly, eyes calculating, gauging every flicker of her expression. He doesn't react to her pain, not outwardly. Instead, he lets the silence stretch, making her words settle in the air before he speaks.

"Ms Garcia, I need you to understand what you're saying here." His voice is calm, measured. "You were forced into marriage as a minor. You were financially controlled and exploited for labour. And you were expected to submit, physically, emotionally, completely?"

Emma blinks rapidly, trying to hold back tears. Her hands clench into fists in her lap. "Yes," she whispers. "They told me my body didn't belong to me, it belonged to the church. That I had to serve them no matter what. Even now, it's like I'm still there. Like I can't breathe."

Davis taps his pen against the table—precise, rhythmic. Emma flinches slightly at the sound, and he catches it, setting the pen down and leaning back, putting distance between them.

Back in the room with us, Davis shifts his focus to the next video, swiping the screen with the casual ease of flipping through case files.

"Mr Taylor," he says in the video, voice even. "You mentioned you were forced into relationships with older church leaders. Explain that to me."

Daniel has his fingers laced tightly together, his knuckles white, and his jaw muscle twitching. He stares at the table.

"They gave me these... 'spiritual partners' after I turned seventeen. They were all way older. Old enough to be my parents. They told me it was to help me grow up, to prepare me for turning eighteen—like some big test. They kept saying I was chosen, that it was my destiny. That saying no would shame my family, the church, even God." He releases a tense sigh, unclasping his fingers, only to press his palms flat against the table. "But it wasn't about teaching me anything. They didn't give, they just took. And when I tried to fight back, they locked me up until I couldn't fight anymore."

Davis watches him closely. "So you're telling me," he says, "that you were systematically groomed. That they manipulated you into believing this was your purpose. And when you pushed back, they isolated you. Punished you."

Daniel lifts his gaze for the first time, locking eyes with Davis. "Yes. They made me believe I owed them everything. That if I spoke up, I'd lose everyone and everything. It took everything I had to leave. And now I'm here. Because someone has to hear this. Someone has to stop it."

Back in the room with us, Detective Davis doesn't look away from the screen. He gives the smallest of nods, then swipes to the next video.

"Your foster family took you in when you were little, Ms Price?"

Alice straightens, lifting her chin. "Yes,

Detective," she says. "They're devout church members, born and raised in Brooklyn. They never had kids of their own. There were three of us. I was the oldest. My brothers are still with them. I left right after my sixteenth birthday."

Davis scribbles something in his notepad. "Why?"

She hesitates, but only for a second. "Because I saw stuff I wasn't supposed to."

Davis looks up. "Like what?"

Alice's fingers tap against her knee. "Money. A lot of it. I was good with numbers, so when I was fourteen, my foster dad let me help with church money stuff. I ended up doing most of it for him because I was faster. I signed his name on things. I saw cash go missing, numbers that didn't add up, money going places it shouldn't. When I asked questions, they told me to shut up. Said the church had its own truth, and I didn't need to understand."

Davis tilts his head to check his notes. "So you're telling me you witnessed financial fraud? That your foster parents, church believers through and through, were actively involved in what appears to be financial fraud?"

"Yes. I kept some of the cheques. I ran away

because I knew if I didn't, something bad was going to happen to me."

Back in the room with us, Davis switches off the tablet.

"We're placing the three of them under protective custody until we summon Child Protective Services." He then looks at George. "You found these kids how?"

"Facebook," George says. "Searched the church's name. Wasn't hard."

Davis narrows his eyes. "And why were you searching?"

George's hands tremble as he folds them on the table. "Because in 1964, I was in a romantic relationship with the founder's daughter."

Davis straightens. "What was her involvement?"

"She uncovered corruption. Documented everything. She mailed it to me in secret."

Davis studies him. "Did she ever go to the authorities?"

George shakes his head. "No. As in, not successfully. She died in 1964." He pulls out his *Meet The Beatles!* album from his briefcase, opening it to reveal the letters and clipped newspaper articles. "But she's still willing to speak."

Davis flips through the letters, one by one, the pages whispering against each other. He finally nods. "We'll be in touch." He pinches the letter from December 1964 aside and sets it back on top of the album cover, then slides both the album and the journal letter across the table towards us. "This one, you can keep." He rises to his feet. "And Mr George?"

George looks up.

"You better get a lawyer. In case shit hits the fan." He looks at Christine. "You too. I expect nothing but a great deal of collaboration from your part, Ms Whyler."

And with that, Davis steps towards the door, pauses, then turns back. "You flew all the way to New York for this?"

George nods.

Davis considers that for a moment. Then he gives the smallest of smiles before stepping into the light and closing the door behind him.

"I will be running Cornelia's story." Christine's fingers tap against the laptop keys, the sound clicking decisively in the quiet room. Then, with a decisive snap, she shuts the lid. "It's what we can prove right now. We're not printing allegations that won't hold up in court. Because if I do, they'll sue me into the ground, and no one will ever hear the rest of the story."

George shifts in his chair. His gaze drifts past Christine, settling on the fish tank bubbling behind her. Christine straightens her posture, adjusting her glasses, and continues.

"Once there's more progress on the financial fraud and the rest of the allegations, we'll dig into it. This could be big-time news. For now, we have to be patient."

George finally pulls his attention from the fish tank and looks Christine in the eye. "Do you have any kids, Ms Whyler?"

"No kids, no husband, sir."

He nods, filing the information away. His fingers find a dried-out crumb on the table—maybe old food, maybe something else—and picks at it with his nail until it flakes off.

"My daughter refuses to speak to me, and my son thinks I'm a big-time arsehole," George says. His voice is even, but there's a weight to it, like stones settling in deep water. "I've done a lot of things wrong in my life. I've gathered so much knowledge, yet I don't know how to make this better. I wish my wife Hilde was here. She was a splendid mother, a brilliant wife. I was a mediocre husband at best and a terrible, terrible father." He pauses, his chest rising before he releases the tiredness pressing down on him. "At least, that's what my son says." His shoulders droop. "It is what it is. I can't change the past."

Christine folds her hands on the table, watching him. "I plan to retire soon."

George blinks, thrown by the change of topic.

"This job has been fun and games," she continues. "Don't get me wrong, I love it. But at this age? I think I'm ready to just let it be. Enjoy a cocktail on the coast of Spain. There are so many young, talented reporters coming up. It wouldn't hurt me or them if I stepped aside." She waves a hand, brushing the thought away. "But I digress. I do want to write this for you, George. This is all a bit surreal—you two coming all the way from England with this massively loaded story from the '60s. It's both deeply personal and, at the same time, affects so many others. I think you're here at the right time." She gives George a small, approving nod. "Great detective skills. It's never too late for a career change."

I settle into my chair, watching George. I

know the drill by now, but this is the first time I hear him telling Cornelia's story to someone else, start to finish. Not in snippets, not in casual remarks, but in one full, unbroken piece, rich with journalistic detail. I admire George for his tenacity. It takes more than just courage. It takes an unyielding, almost reckless determination.

George pulls the *Meet The Beatles!* record from his bag, running his palms over the cover. Christine flips her laptop open again and meets his gaze with a reassuring smile.

"Thanks for trusting me with this," she says. "Now take your time. Let's start from the very beginning."

And so, George begins.

Chapter Fourteen
"Penny Lane"

The sun is setting a little earlier than the night before. Even though it's still summer, I can feel it slipping away like water running through my cupped hands.

George and I stroll through the streets of New York City. The pavement is still warm underneath our feet, the air thick with the smell of food carts and distant traffic.

"I shouted at my old man when he turned up at my graduation," George starts to chat. "Drove up in a battered old Plymouth, bless him—ugliest bloody car you ever saw, made a racket too. And he parked it smack out front, where everyone could see." He lets out a small chuckle, but there's no genuine humour in it. "We'd just lost my mother, and both of us were angry at the world. But I was angrier at him than I had any right to be. Reckon we were both grieving in our own way, but he... he took it better than I did. Handled it with grace, you know? Dignity. Never made a fuss. He'd known hardship long before I even knew the meaning of the word."

George nods to himself, running a hand down his shirt, smoothing out creases which aren't even there. "He walked in, tried to be part of it all, bless him, but it wasn't his world. I looked at the empty seat next to him, the one which should've been my mother's, and instead of sitting by him, instead of standing with him, I sent him away. Like he was an embarrassment, standing there alone, looking so small. He just nodded when I told him to go home. Didn't argue. Just pressed a small box into my hand and said, 'This is for you, son.'"

George pushes out a weary sigh, his eyes locked on the pavement ahead of us. "He'd made me a tie himself, out of old cinema reels and scraps of film stock. Funny, isn't it? But I—I never said thank you. Never said sorry. And he never held it against me. The thing about him was, he never let my anger touch him. I was his son, even when I didn't deserve it."

The road stretches endlessly ahead of us, swallowed by the glow of streetlights flickering on one by one.

"Bit late now, ain't it? Me blathering about it.

Bit useless now."

"It's never useless to speak from the heart, George."

He hums in agreement. "Bought him and my sister a house back here, round the time Hilde and I got our place in London. Things were good then, new job, money coming in. Told him he didn't have to work the cinema anymore. His hands were too shaky, eyesight going, and those old projectors were beasts. Place was dying anyway. Folk didn't care about the past anymore, not in the eighties. Everything had to be new, shiny, faster."

We stop at an ice cream cart and George pulls out his wallet. The vendor hands him change, and he folds the notes neatly between his fingers, tucking them away like it's second nature.

"He passed a year after he shut the cinema." George hands me a cone and takes a bite of his own. "Never asked me about my work, my success. Used to get right under my skin. But now? I see it. He'd lost and started again so many times, he learnt not to hold on too tight. Being an immigrant was like living in a world that was never quite yours."

We take a seat on a bench, watching the sunset glint off the windows of a high-rise across the street. George finishes his cone and stares at the wrapping for a long moment.

"When Isla was born in '85, Hilde and I went to Parliament Hill. I ran up that hill with her in my arms, and Jesse was chasing us, laughing his bloody head off. Got to the top in no time. I felt... brand new. Like the entire world was ours."

I glance at George. I'm watching how his mind flits from one memory to another, skipping like a stone over water.

"After Cornelia died, they read her name out at the church," he says. "Declared she was no longer part of Nobody's Children. They had all these rules, where God's in all of us, rock music's the devil, the world's hurtling towards the end of days. Right load of rubbish, really. But back then... it felt like the days were slipping away faster than I could hold onto them."

He chuckles, but it's hollow, and he wipes the sweat from his forehead. "Bobby used to rant about how the world needed to stay divided. Purpose, or some such rot. Can't even recall half of it now. But Cornelia—she squeezed my hand and said, 'I'm losing my mind, let's get out of here.' And heaven help me, I felt the same."

His movements grow more strained. He

wipes his forehead again, his face is pale.

"Do you want to head back?" I ask, gripping his arm.

"No, no." He waves me off. "This is lovely." He gestures around, taking in the golden light spilling across the buildings. "Very nice."

Then he turns to me, studying my face. "Ah, I've been talking too much. All day, every day…" he mutters, almost to himself.

"I love your stories, George."

He smiles, eyes crinkling at the corners. "You ever gonna tell me one of yours?"

I sit up, caught off guard. Before I can answer, he waves his hand dismissively. "Maybe one day then."

He shifts to stand up, but his legs give out. He collapses to the side, his body folding in on itself before he props himself up and vomits into the grass behind the bench. I scramble for tissues, but he beats me to it, pulling out his own with shaking hands.

"Oh dear," he wheezes, laughing weakly. "Old age gives you everything but a decent stomach for dairy."

I help him back onto the bench, but before I can say anything, he pushes himself up again.

"No more ice cream for me." He dusts himself off, straightens his shirt. "Shall we make our way back?"

"Faith, Fear and the tragic end of a young life: The Story of Cornelia Dean"

The article is out, circulating online, printed in black-and-white, spreading across every outlet. I scroll through the words on my phone, absorbing Christine's compelling, careful writing. She's captured George perfectly—the way he talks about Cornelia, the way he feels about this whole situation. The article recounts his memories, his past, what he saw and heard while he knew her. It pieces together the rumours, suggesting what might have really happened.

It covers everything: the cruel gossip claiming Cornelia was carrying a bastard child. The unsettling truth that her death had nothing to do with a pregnancy at all. That she knew something dangerous about the church, something that could've destroyed her father's business. That maybe she was too strong to buckle under pressure. That maybe something else—something darker— was behind her death.

I stop scrolling and fix my gaze on George's

black-and-white photo in the article. An old picture, one he still keeps in his wallet. It completes the story. Shows who he was back then. Next to it, is a small, passport-like photograph of Cornelia, taken from the local archives. And for the first time, I see her face.

Up until now, I'd only ever pictured her in my mind. But somehow, she looks just as I imagined.

Beside me, George grips his phone tight, his fingers pressing firmly into the edges. His shoulders stiffen. I see it before he even speaks, the glassy sheen of unshed tears in his eyes.

"Her eyes," he speaks. "Just like I remember. It's been so long since I've seen her, but I never forgot her face." He swallows, tapping his screen. "She looked just like this. Even more beautiful in real life."

And then, just as he points at the photo, his phone rings.

"It's Christine Whyler." He barely glances at the screen before answering. I don't need him to put the volume up, because the voice on the other end is already filling the room.

"Alright, what do you think?"

"Thank you," George mutters.

"Well, yeah, but this is an investigation-in-progress. Thank me when these bastards are behind bars." A pause. "On a different but similar note—have you seen the other news this morning?"

George shakes his head. "No. Why?" He glances at me, making sure I'm following along. Christine hums softly, half to herself. "Someone egged the Transcendent Unity headquarters. Not much, maybe a dozen eggs, maybe a couple of packs. Small group, they're saying. Irrelevant. Point is—this article's been out for what, a few hours? And already, something's moving. Stay alert, alright?"

Chapter Fifteen
"Strawberry Fields Forever"

The carers at our orphanage came from all over. We used to joke that each of us picked up the accents of the ones we clung to most, like tiny nations forming dialects of their own. It felt like we were building small territories, not ruled by borders but by voices. The caretakers in my little corner always wafted with hairspray—the thick kind that froze everything into place, and left their hair stiff and frizzy. Somehow, I found that comforting. It smelt like control, or the idea of it.

I grip the rough branch of the walnut tree, fingers digging into its grooves, and pull myself up. My shoes press against the trunk as I push my body higher, hooking my legs over a sturdy branch. The movement shakes loose a scatter of bark dust, dry flakes that fall into my eyes. I wince, rubbing at the sudden sting. For a heartbeat, the whole world shrinks to that sting.

I drop back down, and panic tightens in my

chest. The trees, the entrance—they all look the same. I can't tell if this is the way into my old orphanage or the way home. The edges blur, overlap. The images trade places like they're testing me, one swallowing the other. I turn in circles, the world tilting, spinning. I don't know if my childhood home was ever real, or if it's only a patchwork of borrowed stories stitched into me by someone else's memory.

A knock. Not a door—wood. My head snaps up.

Norina is at the gate, knocking to come in. But the gate's locked, and she's already standing inside the garden.

I jolt awake. The knocking continues.

George is still snoring in his armchair, head tipped back, unbothered. The room is dim, washed in the soft amber glow of the bedside lamp spilling over old papers and half-empty glasses. My heart hammers as I move towards the door. Another knock—measured, steady, like it knows it'll be answered.

I check the peephole. A man stands outside; early forties maybe, with short dark hair gone grey at the edges. His suit is plain but fits like it was made for him. His hand holds up a badge. His face gives nothing away.

He must see the shift of light behind the door, because his voice follows—calm, level, used to being obeyed.

"This is Special Agent Sato, FBI."

I hesitate. My hand rests on the chain. There's something in his tone—not pushy, not threatening, just... final. I wait there longer than I should, thinking of nothing and everything at once, until my hand moves on its own. I slide the chain off and crack the door open.

"Can I come in?" he asks, polite but direct, already scanning past me.

Before I can even think about waking George, the floorboards creak behind me. He's already there, standing beside me. He looks at Sato with a heavy, unreadable stare, then gives a small nod.

I open the door wider.

The air changes, as if the space itself is deciding whether to trust him. Sato takes everything in with one sweep—the cluttered coffee table, my phone charging in the corner, George's worn slippers by the radiator. Then he nods, once, like he's catalogued it all.

"Mr Stan," he says first, and then, turning to me, "Ms Lane."

He pulls out a small notepad and flips it open with a flick of his thumb. "Just want to make sure I've got the right people before we begin."

George nods once. "That's us."

"Appreciate it." Sato gestures towards the sofa. "May I?"

When George nods, Sato sits—posture straight, but not rigid. From inside his coat, he draws out a slim folder, the edges soft from being opened and closed too many times.

"I'll need your cooperation," he says. "We've been keeping tabs on the Church of Transcendent Unity for some time. I just have a few questions."

I perch on the edge of the armchair. George stays standing, arms crossed. Sato opens the folder and slides a photograph onto the coffee table. It's Emma.

"You know this young woman?"

George barely glances at the image before he answers. "Yes." Then his eyes lift, tense, expectant, braced for impact.

Sato studies him for half a beat, then says, quietly, "She died this morning. Suicide."

Something in me stalls. The words land, but don't sink. I'm aware only of my fingers, the way they tighten against the chair. The words hang there, like ash falling through the air. My pulse starts pounding somewhere in my skull, in my hands. A distant buzzing fills my ears. The whole room feels like it's tilting. George turns and looks at me, his face drained of colour.

Sato waits. He doesn't fill the silence. When he finally speaks, his tone is careful, almost too careful. "If you know anything—conversations you had with her, things she said, anyone she mentioned—now's the time."

George's hands curl into fists. When he speaks, his voice is rough. "You're telling me a kid who spoke out ended up dead, and now you want us to piece it together for you?"

Sato doesn't flinch. "I want to make sure she didn't die for nothing."

George stares him down, then his shoulders slump, his gaze dropping to the floor.

"She was scared," George says. "Didn't trust the system to help her. Seems like she was right."

Sato's expression doesn't change. He leans forward, elbows on his knees. "I won't argue with you on that," he says quietly. "I've been trying to get authorisation to move on that group for months. My boss thinks it's all smoke. But when kids start dying, it's not smoke anymore."

I glance at him. That's the first crack, a glimpse of the man under the badge.

Sato straightens up again. "I can't promise justice, but I can promise attention. If either of you knows something that can help me make that case—emails, names, times, anything—I'll make sure it gets looked at. I don't care who I have to upset to do it."

George studies him. "So you're not here to close this down."

Sato shakes his head. "No. I'm here to find a way to open it back up."

The silence that follows isn't empty anymore. It feels like something beginning to take shape.

He turns to me. "Ms Lane?"

I open my mouth, but nothing comes out. I glance at George's trembling hands, at the folder on the table, at Emma's face staring up at us. Finally, I manage, "Could you give us a minute?"

Sato holds my gaze for a beat, then closes the folder.

"Take your time," he says, and props one palm on his knee to stand.

He wanders a few feet away, busying himself with the hotel décor—his eyes drifting over the half-empty bookshelves, and the mess George and

I have made in the days we've been here. He doesn't touch anything, just looks, taking quiet mental notes.

I turn to George. His eyes are red, though no tears fall. He looks at me, and for a long while, we say nothing. My throat tightens. I hate the world, and I want to give George a big hug.

"She came to us twice," Sato speaks from a corner of the room. "Your Emma. Tried to file a statement last winter. Then again in May. Both times, she withdrew. Said she was scared."

He looks at George. "You were the one she trusted, weren't you?"

George blinks, caught off guard. "She didn't trust systems," he says. "Not anymore. Maybe she thought I'd do better than the rest of you."

"Then she wasn't wrong."

George studies Sato. "You've got kids, Agent Sato?"

"No," he replies. "Didn't work out that way. But I see enough of them. Usually when it's already too late."

The sound of the city filters in faintly through the glass—a siren, a car horn, the hum of something distant and alive.

Sato reaches into his coat and pulls out his

notepad again. "Tell me everything you can remember. Every name, every location, every little thing that didn't sit right. I'll cross-check it myself."

The room is hollow and still by the time the door closes behind Agent Sato. George doesn't move, but the silence does—thickening, pressing in. The chair takes it for him—his boot hits it once, a dull thud against wood, the sound of something giving way. The chair skids, its legs dragging across the floor. He buries his hands in his hair. His shoulders shake. I jump to my feet and step towards him.

His phone lights up then—Christine's name flashing across the screen. The phone rings and rings until it stops.

George sinks into the armchair and pulls out a half-hidden bottle of whisky. He pours some into the glass he used earlier for his tablets.

"Where did you get that?" I ask, but I don't try to take it away. I know it's hurting him, but I can't bring myself to rip away one of the few things he's got left.

He takes a sip, closing his eyes as he tries to steady himself.

"I need to make a call," he says, his voice cracking as silent tears roll down his cheeks.

He dials Jesse's number. It rings. And rings. And rings. Then voicemail. George freezes when he hears his son's voice. When the beep sounds, he pulls the phone away for a second to wipe his face, then lifts it back up.

"I'm sorry," he says into the silence. "I'm so sorry, son."

He ends the call and lets the phone drop beside him. Then takes another slow sip of whisky.

"You shouldn't be drinking," I say.

He gives a tired little laugh. "Plenty of things shouldn't've happened."

He gets up, bracing himself like he's shaking something heavy off, then gestures towards the table.

"The day I heard about Cornelia's funeral, that Beatles record turned up at the cinema. My dad picked it up. *Wasting money on these stupid records again, are you?*'" George mimics his dad's gruff voice with a soft fondness. "I didn't say a word. Just ran off with it. Opened it up in the toilets."

He looks away, seeing the memory clear as day.

"Pages fell out. Cornelia's handwriting. Pages of it." He tilts his head back, asking the ceiling for answers. "Could've just taken it straight to the police."

His throat bobs as he swallows. He laughs under his breath, bitter.

"I didn't. I'm just as bad."

"Don't say that."

Before I can stop him, he picks up the *Meet the Beatles!* record and hurls it to the floor. The sleeve tears open, releasing Cornelia's letter from December 1964. A black-and-white photo of young George drifts after it, settling in the wreckage. He watches it land, chest heaving, as though he's been waiting years for something to break finally.

"Bobby's giving a speech tomorrow night."

I blink. "What?"

"Big Unity event. Live TV, music. The complete show." He glances at me. "The kids from Facebook got us a couple of tickets."

"Can't we just leave this to Christine? Or the FBI?"

"No."

"Why not?" I demand. "What's the point?"

"Because I haven't done my part. Not yet."

I try to stay calm. "Can't it wait?"

"It can't."

He leans down, picking up the record sleeve

from the floor, but leaving the photo behind. He walks back to the armchair and drains his whisky.

"Stop drinking that," I snap. "You're killing yourself."

He laughs, but it sounds like breaking glass.

"I'm dying anyway," he says, louder now, raw. "Got a bloody party of bowel cancer brewing in there."

His words hit like a slap. My vision blurs as I stare at him, at the way he stands there, glass in hand. I shake my head no. George shakes his head yes.

"When were you going to tell me?"

"Today. Plenty of time to prepare. Kids are sending me the event details any second."

"No, George." My throat tightens. "About you. About dying."

"Well." His smile falters, then widens, wet with unshed tears. "I'm telling you now."

He lifts an arm. I don't hesitate. I run into it, wrapping myself around him, holding on as tightly as I can.

People make you like them less before they leave. Maybe that's just my theory—or maybe it's the universe's way of softening the blow. I can't say I hate George. I hate the way he keeps things to himself, how he shuts down at the worst possible times. But hate him? Never.

I never thought I'd be indulging one of his last wishes like this. Yet here we are. George is very ill, and all I can think—selfishly, terribly—is what I'm going to do without him.

We're at the Beacon Theatre, a grand old beast of a place that looks like it could host an ABBA reunion and a resurrection right after. The entrance is a sea of people, a tide of faces lit by the spotlights. Barricades and neon tape dictate the flow, corralling their excitement into lines and queues. Security staff in matching headsets bark orders, while the crowd thrums with a fervour you'd expect at a pop concert.

But we're not going through the front.

A heavy metal door yawns open at the back of the building, leading in from the car park. A tall young guy in a suit stands waiting, his expression still. He gives George a brief, knowing nod and motions us forward with a flick of his hand.

We step inside, and before I can process where we're being led, another man slips lanyards around our necks. The badges are glossy, official-looking, and warm from someone else's hand. The suited dude is already moving again, gesturing for us to follow. We do.

It's all motion, corridors folding into more corridors, each one narrower and brighter than the last. Crew members rush past us with clipboards and coffee cups, voices leaking through headset mics in bursts of static. The air smells of sawdust and sweat. From somewhere distant comes the clatter of wheels over concrete, a piano note held mid-tune, a woman's laughter swallowed by feedback. Someone brushes past me in a blur, adjusting their earpiece, too focused to even notice us.

My phone vibrates in my hand. Christine. She must be calling because George hasn't answered. I look down at the screen glowing in my palm but don't answer either. The call fades, and my screen goes dark again.

Ahead of me, George moves with that old, deliberate calm. His posture is upright, his steps sure—like he's walked this path before, maybe many times, in secret.

And that's when it hits me. George has been orchestrating this for longer than I realised. He's built connections, webs within webs—people who move when he calls, who open doors that should stay locked. It unsettles me, how much he's kept to himself. How much he's already decided without me.

I reach out, instinctively, to clutch the fabric of his shirt for reassurance, but something stops me.

In the low backstage light, George isn't an old man. Not anymore.

For a fleeting second, I see him as he must have been at twenty—raw and bright with purpose, eyes burning with a need that could have saved or ruined him, depending on the hour. I watch him like a ghost watching another ghost. His memories walk beside him: Cornelia's laughter, that terrible purity of their love under the weight of faith; the rain-soaked bicycle rides; the endless clippings and letters spread like offerings across the floor. A man building a truth no one asked for.

His pace doesn't falter, but mine slows. When I blink, the vision dissolves. The air smells of lilies and old paint. The present resumes. We've stopped. A door ahead of us opens, spilling warm light across the hallway. George steps through first, and I follow.

Inside, it's quieter. The air is cooler, the thrum of the theatre replaced by the low static of waiting. A small lounge stretches out before us, lined with varnished doors. The young man in the suit strides ahead, stopping at one marked VIP. He knocks once, opens it without waiting, and gestures us inside.

As we cross the threshold, I notice the tiny bulge of an earpiece under his hair and the quick glance he gives George. These people are not theatre security any longer. They're George's men now. The guy locks the door behind us. The shift is immediate.

Our footsteps sink into the carpet, swallowed whole. The air smells faintly of lilies—too sweet, almost spoiled from being trapped indoors too long. Fresh bouquets line the walls like an audience. In the corner, a vanity glows under a ring of warm bulbs, a halo made of cheap electricity. Scattered across its surface: a comb, a few makeup bits, a half-drunk bottle of water. Nearby, a rack of garment bags hangs like ghosts in waiting.

Someone sits in the middle of it all, back turned.

He flinches, his shoulders tightening as if he's bracing for weather. When he swivels the chair around, it's stiff, mechanical.

"Excuse me?" he snaps.

And then we see him. It's Bobby. What's left

of him.

He's folded in on himself, hands trembling on the armrests. His skin looks thin enough to tear, veins threading through it like blue ink bleeding across paper.

I glance at George. His fists open and close at his sides. When I look back, Bobby's face flickers, and for an instant I don't see a frail old man. I see the preacher—that preacher—eyes sharp and silver, smile lacquered into place for the pulpit.

Bobby grips his walking stick and hauls himself upright. The effort makes him smaller somehow.

"What's all this?" His voice is papery but still aiming for authority. His eyes flick to the door, calculating. Always calculating.

George takes a step forward. His stare fixes on Bobby like he's seeing something risen from a grave.

Bobby's chin lifts a fraction, a ghost of irritation skimming across his features.

"How can I help you, sir?" he says, brittle.

"Been keeping up with the news?" George asks.

"I don't read the news."

"'Course you don't," George says. "But I bet

you keep an eye on your own headlines."

Bobby's fingers whiten around the cane. His eyes search George's face like a puzzle he's almost solved.

"Who are you?"

George closes the gap between them until their breath mingles. His voice scrapes low, almost tender.

"The freaking devil," he says. "And I came to collect."

Bobby jerks, looks towards the door. "Security?" he calls, louder.

Silence. Something in him changes. His face smooths over like wet clay.

"Oh," he says, a smirk stirring. "I see. I see what this is."

George doesn't blink.

"Didn't think I'd ever see *you* again," Bobby murmurs. "I must say, I'm pleasantly surprised."

"There's nothing pleasant about the two of us standing in the same room," George replies. "There never was. There never will be."

Bobby nods slowly, like a doctor diagnosing an old wound. "You still sound like a troubled young man. But you must know by now—God loves you."

"And I don't love him back," George says evenly. "And he should respect that."

Bobby clears his throat. "What can I do for you, George?"

George lifts a hand, unsteady but certain, and points at Bobby's chest.

"I want you to pay for everything. Everything you walked away from. The lives you played God with. Cornelia, who you murdered. And my life—" his voice cracks but steadies, "the one you twisted into knots."

"Oh," Bobby hums softly. "So that's what this is about. You."

"Don't gaslight me, you moron." George's voice lashes the air. "God might love you no matter what, but I'm not God."

Bobby breathes in—long, sanctimonious. "God is in all of us, George. The Living God, the creator of life—not some idle ghost whispering in the dark. Jesus was a reflection, a shadow. But the Father—" He raises his chin. "The Father is the architect of the universe."

"If he made this world," George mutters, "then he's as sick as you are."

That lands. Bobby's expression flickers—barely—but George sees it.

"He's evil," George continues. "He needs help. Because he made *you*."

Bobby smiles, slow and mirthless, and slams his cane against the floor. The sound cracks through the room like thunder, but George doesn't move.

"Listen, Moses," George says. "You took faith and forged it into a weapon. You turned salvation into a choke chain. It took a lifetime of ruin to understand that. To stand here, with nothing left to lose. But you—" He leans in. "You're about to watch your world collapse the way mine did when Cornelia died."

For the first time, Bobby has no sermon ready. His hands grip the cane's head, white-knuckled, as silence spills between them.

Then George moves—sudden, wild. His hands clutch Bobby's collar, the fabric twisting in his fists. The old man teeters, caught between falling and being held upright. His cane clatters to the floor. His mouth opens, no sound, only the stark fear that turns him human again.

George tightens his grip, brings him close enough that their foreheads nearly touch. And then—something fractures.

George remembers the years that broke him

and rebuilt him into something unrecognisable. The shame, the grief, the strange alchemy of survival. And in that brief, burning second, he knows he's not here to become Bobby. He's here to end the version of himself that needed revenge.

He releases him. Bobby staggers, blinking, and George's hand curls into a fist that doesn't swing.

"Well, George," Bobby croaks, smoothing his collar. "I hope you've saved up all these years. You'll be hearing from my lawyers."

George lets the words hang like smoke. "I hope you live long enough," he says quietly, "to see the true horror of being you."

George turns, walks towards the exit and knocks once on the door. The lock clicks open.

"Who's out there?" Bobby barks, twisting towards the sound as we step into the hall.

The guy in the black suit waits, expression blank. He guides us away, his stride brisk. Two younger men—part of whatever network George's built in the shadows—clap him on the shoulder as we pass.

I glance back one last time. Bobby is just a figure now, framed by the warm vanity bulbs, shrinking into the glow. Then I turn forward, quicken my pace to match George. My phone buzzes again. It's Christine.

Hours have folded in on themselves—day into night, night into something else—and still, the world keeps calling. Christine's name keeps flashing on our screens, her calls and messages flooding in as the protests take hold. She feeds us the pulse of the city—news, videos, briefings in all-caps. People spill into the streets, their voices swelling in both organised and chaotic waves across New York.

Now the city screams Cornelia's name.

They demand answers. *Tax the churches. Open their books. Hold them accountable.* The chants roll through avenues like thunder, ricocheting off glass towers and stone cathedrals.

And then I see it—what George has done.

He's used their own playbook against them. Built his own movement, his own congregation, his own believers. At the heart of it, his own goddess—Cornelia. Their tactics, turned in on themselves. The faint stain of darkness, now on Bobby.

But Bobby stays silent.

Somehow, he keeps low, slipping through

the cracks, refusing to speak. Still, his followers cling to him as if silence were holiness.

Christine's voice crackles through the phone. "You didn't hear this from me, okay? But the FBI raided two Transcendent branches. Arrested the leaders."

I blink. "On what charges?"

"No idea yet," she says. "It's small moves for now, little pieces shifting. But we're getting somewhere. I guess we'll see them in court soon."

I lower my phone and glance at George. He's sunk into his armchair, thumb tapping lazily at his screen.

"George?" I call. He doesn't look up. "George?" I try again, but my voice falls flat. I can't even summon anger.

He straightens and holds up his phone instead. "Did you know," he says, "that if you use liquid detergent, you're supposed to put the cap inside the tray? Otherwise it just runs straight into the drum." His eyebrows lift. "Maybe that's why my clothes smell weird."

"Your clothes smell just fine."

"Well, sometimes they're stinky." He shrugs. "Hilde had her way of making sure everything came out clean. I never figured it out."

I nod. "More protests are on the way."

His expression shifts—barely. Then a small, crooked smile. "That's great, isn't it?"

"It is." I smile back. "I saw placards with Cornelia's name. The world's starting to learn the truth. Soon everyone will know she was the first victim of Bobby's teachings."

George's face hardens.

"She's not a victim," he says, and his voice catches fire. "She's not a goddamn victim." His eyes flash. "She's a hero. She was born to make this hell a better place."

Tears burn my eyes right away, blurring the room into fog. But through it, I see him— unyielding, defiant, almost young again. Calling him impatient would be cruel. He's waited his whole life for this moment. I wouldn't dare take that from him.

But soon, the world might take him from me. And that, too, feels like punishment.

"How long have you known, George?" My voice is steady, but only just. "That you're dying?"

He shrugs. "A few months now."

I nod, anger rising, hot and sharp. "And how much time did they give you?"

He hesitates. "A few months."

We just stare, caught in that impossible space where love and resentment live side by side.

Somewhere, the TV shifts to a car insurance ad—too bright, too loud.

I hear myself say, "Well, you're lucky then, with this terminal death sentence. A few months is quite something…" The words land like glass. I hate myself for them immediately.

His eyes darken, then soften. Beneath all that exhaustion, I still see it—home. That steady, unshakable place I can always find in him.

Then, the hotel phone rings. I wipe my cheeks and answer.

"A family member named Jesse is at reception," the clerk says. "He's waiting for you."

I glance at George, then back at the receiver. "Please, send him up."

Minutes later, the door rattles with a hard knock. I cross the room and open it.

Jesse stands there, his teenage son beside him, two heavy suitcases at their feet. Jesse's backpack slips off his shoulder, thudding to the carpet. His eyes sweep past me and fix on George.

George lights up. "Jesse! Alex! You know Julia from next door, right?" He wipes his face, forcing a healthy smile.

Jesse nods, eyes still locked on him. "Yeah, I know Julia from next door." Then, to me—"Hey, Julia from next door."

They step inside, the air thick with something old and unsaid.

"How are you two?" George asks, opening his arms.

Jesse shifts, placing his backpack between them instead. George's hands fall.

"Your oncologist called, Dad."

George flinches.

Jesse tilts his head, voice cool. "Didn't even know you had an oncologist. But here we are."

Something flickers in George—recognition, guilt, love. His gaze slides to Alex. "Nice shirt," he says. "Still looks pressed after a long flight. Six, seven hours?" He inhales. "I was just telling Julia I finally figured out how to keep my clothes from smelling musty."

He sighs, smiles again, brittle.

"The oncologist called because he thought you were dead," Jesse snaps. "No sign of you. The clinic's panicking. And guess what I had to tell them? That my father flew to freaking New York to throw himself into a goddamn church scandal over a girlfriend no one's ever heard of." He laughs once, sharp. "Do you know how insane that is? That I didn't even have to explain it to the doctor, because he'd already seen you on the news?"

The TV's cheerful jingle swells behind him. Jesse snatches the remote, hits the button. Nothing. He presses harder, jaw tight.

"Why have you never told me about Cornelia?" His voice drops.

George doesn't answer.

"Did Mum know?"

Something in George fractures. He looks past Jesse, past all of it. "There's time left," he mutters. "There's time. I can fix this." His fingers start twitching.

Jesse watches him, unreadable, the remote still in his hand. A decision lands in his eyes. He presses off. The screen goes black. Silence blooms.

"Of course you can," Jesse murmurs. "Because this is, once again, all about you."

George freezes. Their eyes meet.

"Your grandson is going through with the surgery," Jesse says flatly.

Something else passes over George's face— grief, confusion. He glances at Alex.

"The bone-shortening surgery, Dad. He finally made it up the NHS list."

George steps forward. "Jesse, you never mentioned this."

"Because you don't care." Jesse's voice cracks. "You never listened. You were never there for Alex. You were never there for Mum. You don't care about us. You never did."

George's fists tremble at his sides. "I worked for you. Day and night. I built opportunities. I made sure you had everything."

Jesse laughs, low and hollow. "Your life, not mine." He points at the floor between them. "The degree. The house. The choices you made for me." His voice wavers, then steadies. "I fucking hate that house."

Alex shifts on the sofa, arms folded. "Man, I wish someone paid my student loan."

George exhales, empty. He starts to speak, but the words won't come.

Jesse shakes his head. "This was a mistake." His voice is tired now. "I thought—" He stops. "I thought maybe you'd changed."

He turns to Alex, lifting one suitcase. "Let's go."

Alex hesitates, then stands. He glances at George. "Bye, Grandpa." His voice is careful. Then, to me: "Bye."

I nod, barely. The door closes behind them. Silence.

George stands there, hollow-eyed. "Nothing is where it should be," he says. "Nothing's in place."

"That's just life, George."

He rocks gently, back and forth. "I don't know what I'm supposed to do now. With any of it." His gaze drifts. "I failed. As a husband. A father. A human being. I should've held it in. I say things I don't mean. I do things I regret. I was never—will never be—a nice person. I had this one last chance. And now, I have nothing left to hold onto."

I take a step closer. "You don't always have to hold onto something. Maybe you're just… finally coming to terms. Maybe that's the point."

I don't wait for an answer. I grab the room key and rush out, heart thudding.

The lift's already on its way down. I press the button anyway, tapping my foot until the doors open. When they do, I step inside and will it to move faster.

When I reach the lobby, I push through the doors into the night. The air is sharp, electric against my skin. People drift in and out of the hotel—talking, scrolling, living—and then I see them.

Jesse and Alex stand by the curb, luggage at their feet. Alex keeps throwing his arm up for passing taxis, but every cab is already full.

"Wait!" I shout, feet hammering against the pavement. My voice sounds more desperate than I intended.

Jesse looks up, a sigh slipping through his teeth.

"Please," I gasp. "Just stay for a second."

He studies me, wary.

"George loves you," I say. "Both of you. He always talks about you."

Jesse gives a short, dry laugh. "I bet he does."

"He cares," I insist. "He worries about you. He looks after you."

Jesse's mouth twists into something brittle. "He worries so much, he makes it all about himself. He's a selfish old bastard, Julia. Don't get blinded."

He rubs his temple. "I studied what he wanted. Bought a house I can't afford, drive a car I hate to a job I despise more every passing bloody day." His fingers come together in a tight little gesture, a kind of punctuation. "Was this what 'looking after me' was supposed to mean?"

He jabs a finger towards Alex. "And when I told him his grandson wanted to study Postcolonial Neo-Maritime Trade Policies—" he rolls the words like stones in his mouth—"instead of saying '*Nice. Great idea, Alex,*' my father puts on his all-knowing voice and goes, '*What does that even mean? What's he going to do with that degree?*'"

Alex shrugs. "He's got a point, Dad."

Jesse sighs, but the tension slips a little, like a knot giving way.

He turns back to me, voice quieter now. "I appreciate you looking after my father, I really do. But you don't know his dark sides. You don't know him. The man *you* see—the friendly old guy who played Santa, who handed out gifts every Christmas, who sponsored your teenage years, helped you land your first job—that's *your* George." He shakes his head. "But you and I don't know the same man."

A shiver runs through me. And then I feel it—something shifts in the air behind me, a subtle pressure, a presence. I turn.

George stands there. Hands trembling at his sides.

The pieces slide together too fast, too cleanly, and I hate myself for not seeing it sooner.

My mind drags me back—to that December at the orphanage. Children tearing open presents, laughter ricocheting off the walls, wrapping paper snowing to the floor. I remember gripping Santa's hand and feeling safe. Seen.

I remember asking, "What's your favourite food?"—just to keep him there longer, just to make him talk.

And his laughter, warm and unguarded:

"I eat anything, as long as I can eat it with my favourite pair of chopsticks."

For the first time in years, I hear that voice again, echoing inside me. I see him—not the costume, but the man in jeans beneath the red suit. His hands. Those same hands trembling now.

The image overlaps—memory and present, red and grey—and my breath stutters. I press my knuckles against my mouth.

"Stop living all these double lives, Dad," Jesse says. "It's exhausting."

I stand between them, drowning in the past: Norina's disappearance, the panic, the loss, the constant ache of being unwanted. My fingers curl into a fist. I start counting under my breath.

George notices. A soft, steadying smile ghosts across his face.

"When Hilde fell ill for the first time, and my kids stopped speaking to me—you held my hand," he says.

I meet his eyes.

"It was Christmas, 2011," he continues. "Doctors had just diagnosed my dear wife Hilde with stage four cancer." He exhales slowly. "Jesse moved her into his apartment, convinced he could care for her better than I ever would. And he was right."

Jesse presses his lips together, his eyes wet.

"During Hilde's treatments, he and his sister spoke to me less and less. By the time she passed, my own children were strangers to me." His voice thins, a fragile thread. "I was furious—at them, at myself, at life. I rewrote my will. Started drinking again. Gambled away more than I want to admit."

He looks at me, eyes flickering with something between shame and remembrance. "Remember the little maize garden near your orphanage?"

"You mean the big maize field?"

A small, wistful smile pulls at his mouth. "Yeah. That one." He pauses, breathing through the memory. "I was stumbling home one afternoon after a week of losing at the casino. Had LSD in my pocket, bought off some neighbourhood kids. I was a joke of a man by then. A washed-up, soon-to-be-retired fool. But then…" He trails off. "As I walked by that garden and the wind swept the maize leaves aside, I saw a little girl lying on the ground, hitting her head against the earth as if punishing herself—"

"For not remembering the way home," I whisper.

George nods, eyes glistening. "You did absolutely nothing wrong, child."

I wipe at my eyes.

"That day, I stopped drinking," he says. "I tried to learn how to give instead of destroy. I visited hospitals, orphanages. Tried to fill the hole left by losing Hilde, by losing my children's nearness."

"No one ever adopted me," I murmur. "But a charity paid my way through school. I was given an allowance. Affordable rent." I say it half to him, half to myself. "All I had to do was check in on my neighbour. Make sure he took his meds."

I meet George's eyes. The recognition between us is like an old key clicking into its lock.

Alex sits down on one of the suitcases, obediently surrendering to the scene.

"How will I ever repay you?" I mouth. The sound barely makes it out.

George smiles. "You don't owe anyone anything."

He turns to Jesse. "I've messed up before, and I'll probably mess up again until the day I die." His tone is firm now, steady, the voice of someone making peace with his own ghosts. "But until I take my last breath, you need to know—I have no time left to be anything but grateful that you are my son. And I am proud of you."

For a second, everything pauses: the traffic, the air, even the light... as if the world's caught between blinks.

Then, to break the stillness, a gust of wind kicks up. A piece of paper skitters between them, curling at Jesse's feet. He stoops to grab it, just to have something to do with his hands.

"I stole from you," Jesse blurts out suddenly. "I stole from you, Dad."

George lets out a noise halfway between a laugh and a sob. He nods, almost relieved.

"Every Friday night," Jesse continues, voice trembling, "I took money from your wallet so I could go out with the boys."

George laughs, full-bodied now. "I know."

"You knew?"

"It's why I always left my wallet in my coat by the door. And why I made sure there was extra change in my pockets too." His eyes glint. "Because I knew you'd be looking."

Jesse presses a palm to his forehead, massaging his scalp.

George steps closer, placing both hands on Jesse's shoulders. "I'm sorry," he says. "For not seeing your needs sooner. Those broken, dirty shoes you brought into my office that day—how angry I was about it—" His voice softens. "I was unfair. And I'm sorry."

Jesse shakes his head. "I don't even remember that, Dad."

"Then you must have the worst memory in the world. You take after me." His smile turns wistful. "Your sister got Hilde's brains and beauty. You, on the other hand, got stuck with my traits. I'm sorry, son."

Jesse snorts. "I've seen worse."

A passerby bumps into Alex's suitcase, making him jolt. The second one wobbles, then rolls itself neatly against the curb, like it's decided on its own to stay.

Some things just have a way of falling into

place. Like this luggage. Like this small, impossible moment.

The man strides towards the hotel entrance. "Are you going in or out?" he calls over his shoulder.

George and Jesse exchange a look, and in perfect sync, turn to the guy. "None of your fucking business, arsehole."

Chapter Sixteen
"Lucy in the Sky with Diamonds"

The courtroom is silent, except for the occasional creak of wooden benches as someone shifts in their seat. At the front, the judge sits behind a broad mahogany desk, raised just enough to assert authority. The air carries the dry tang of paper, dust, and something faintly chemical, like the ghost of old polish. The jury remain still, their faces unreadable. We're all here for Alice and Daniel. George, Christine, Jesse, Alex and I sit towards the back. Alan, Anne, Anthony, Rosanna, and Humphrey have also all come for support, a patient, meaningful force behind the two.

Alice has just turned eighteen—barely—and the number sits on her like new skin, still stiff at the edges. Her hair is brown now, freshly dyed. A quiet rebellion dressed as compliance. I suddenly have the urge to reach out—to smooth a strand behind her ear, to hold her close, to shield her somehow—even though she doesn't need me to.

Nothing can dull her voice because she's strong, and I'm rooting for her.

Just behind the line of supporters, half in shadow, I spot Detective Davis. He's leaning against the far wall, hands in his pockets. When I glance back, his eyes are already on me. I smile.

At the front, Darnell Malcolm, the defence attorney, adjusts his tie with a slow tug. He paces a little in front of the jury box, his shoes clicking against the worn floorboards.

"Ms Price," he begins, "you said you were adopted into a family tied to the Church of Transcendent Unity. Is that right?"

"Yes." Alice's voice is steady, but her fingers are tightly interlocked in her lap.

"And you ran away from that home. Why?"

Alice shifts in her seat before speaking. "Because they forced me to work for the church. I wasn't allowed to say no."

Malcolm tilts his head, easing one hand into his pocket. "You weren't allowed? Or you just didn't like it? There's a difference."

"I didn't have a choice."

"Right, but ain't it true that thousands of kids all over the world help out at home, do chores, volunteer at church? That doesn't make it abuse, now, does it?"

"Objection, Your Honour. Argumentative." the prosecutor, Sophia Leung, interjects.

"Sustained," the judge says, barely looking up from her notes. "Mr Malcolm, move on."

Malcolm offers a polite nod. "Of course, Your Honour." He smooths his tie again, a gesture both habitual and theatrical, before stepping closer to the witness stand. "Let's talk about these 'financial records' you claim you saw. You're how old now?"

"Eighteen."

"Eighteen. And yet, you're telling this court that you, a teenager, were somehow handling church financial records? Does this not sound a little funny to you?"

"They made me sort documents. I saw tax returns. I saw money being moved in ways which didn't make sense."

"Or maybe you just didn't understand what you were looking at?"

"I know what I saw."

Malcolm chuckles low, shaking his head just once. "Oh, you know, huh? 'Cause I got an affidavit right here—from their current accountant—saying everything's squeaky clean. Are you telling me you know better than a trained professional, Ms Price?"

"Objection, facts not in evidence," Sophia says quickly.

"Sustained," the judge replies. "Counsel will confine himself to the record."

Malcolm gives a small bow. "Apologies, Your Honour."

The silence that follows is taut, like a string about to snap. Alice steadies herself. "I know they're hiding money. And I know they forced kids like me to work for free while they pocketed millions."

Malcolm turns back to the jury, throwing his hands up. "Ladies and gentlemen, we got ourselves a runaway teen, mad at her family, claiming she uncovered fraud. But somehow, no papers, no receipts. Funny, isn't it?"

"Objection! Mischaracterising the witness's testimony," Sophia Leung speaks, rising to her feet.

"Sustained. Move on, Mr Malcolm."

The judge's pen scratches the page; the sound is surgical. Someone in the back coughs. The tension resets but doesn't ease—it just changes shape.

I glance at Alice. Her whole body is trembling—not from fear, but from the effort of staying still. Next to me, Christine scribbles notes into her agenda, then looks up and gives me a reassuring smile.

The trial moves forward, and before I know it, Daniel is being prepared to speak. A quiet dread unfurls in my chest, slow and steady, like ink in water. This isn't going in our favour.

Malcolm turns to Daniel, his expression cool. He shifts his weight onto one leg, hands clasped easily behind his back.

"Mr Taylor, you stated that church leaders 'forced' you into dating certain men. Can you clarify what you mean by 'forced'?"

Daniel meets his gaze without flinching. "They assigned me a mentor. A much older man. They said I had to spend time with him, do what he said. It wasn't dating, it was—"

Malcolm raises a brow. "And yet you stayed. You didn't leave. Why's that?"

"Because I didn't know I could."

Alice's hand is shaking over her knee. Without thinking, I place mine over hers and squeeze.

Malcolm scoffs. "You were seventeen, not seven. You knew what a bad situation was, didn't you?"

"Objection. Argumentative."

"Sustained."

Malcolm exhales, feigning patience. "Mr Taylor, did you believe you had the freedom to say no?"

Daniel's silence stretches on, suffocating the space we're all sharing. Then he finally speaks. "Do you know what it's like to be told your whole life that disobeying means eternal damnation? That your family will throw you out? That you'll have nowhere to go?"

Malcolm's expression stays even. "Mr Taylor, have you got proof this mentor of yours did anything illegal?"

Daniel's voice wavers slightly. "Just my word."

"No pictures? No texts? No witnesses?"

"He knew better than to leave proof."

"Objection, speculation," Sophia says, rising.

"Sustained," the judge replies.

Malcolm smiles faintly. "Withdrawn. No further questions on that point."

The hearing continues, with brief recesses breaking up the tension. Each break feels like surfacing from water that's colder every time you go under.

Then, it's George's turn.

Darnell Malcolm walks towards George's stand, slower now. He clasps his hands lightly in front of him, tilting his head slightly, almost like sizing George up.

"Mr Stan, let's start with something simple. Where did you meet Ms Cornelia Dean?"

"She came into our cinema. My father used to run a little theatre back in the '50s, all throughout the '60s, '70s and '80s... We played all kinds of films—French New Wave, old noir pictures. Cornelia came in one evening, sat in the back."

A few quiet shuffles in the courtroom, even a soft chuckle from someone.

"And very quickly, you became close," Malcolm prompts.

George nods. "We started seeing one another. Spent time together. She confided in me."

"Ah. Young love," Malcolm muses, his tone light but pointed. "This was, what, sixty years ago?"

"Yes."

"Sixty years." Malcolm pauses, letting the number hang in the air. "And you say she confided in you. Told you secrets."

"Yes," George says. "She trusted me. She let

me in. She told me about her father's church, about the money, about the girls—"

Malcolm raises a hand. "One thing at a time, Mr Stan. Let's not get ahead of ourselves." He adjusts his stance. "You said 'her father's church.' Ever attended a service there yourself?"

"Yes."

"And what was your impression?"

George shifts slightly. "Crowds gathered. It felt... strange. And Cornelia—she didn't like it when I was in there. Like she was afraid I might get pulled into her father's stories. She was always trying to get away."

"But you never personally saw anything criminal happen?"

George looks down, rubbing his palms together. "No." He hesitates, then his brow furrows. "But something wasn't right. Cornelia warned me. She said they made fake insurance claims. Girls were being married off too young. It had become a business, not a church."

Malcolm clicks his tongue. "And she told you this directly?"

"Yes."

Malcolm raises an eyebrow. "She used those exact words?"

"She implied it."

Malcolm's expression stiffens. "Implied. But she never came out and said it, pointing at real evidence."

"She didn't need to."

"So all this was Ms Dean's suspicions. No solid proof." Malcolm shakes his head. "Alright. Let's back up. This all happened in what year?"

"1964."

Malcolm nods slowly. "So it's been sixty years. Sixty. And you only decide to come forward now. Why?"

"Because I was afraid."

"Afraid." Malcolm folds his arms. "Afraid of what, exactly?"

George stares at the table.

Malcolm presses on. "And tell me, Mr Stan— what exactly did you do about this fear? Did you go to the police? Speak to a journalist? Warn anyone?"

"No."

"No," Malcolm echoes, nodding. "Instead, you packed up and crossed the Atlantic."

Silence. A faint shuffle from the gallery.

"So, let me get this straight." Malcolm gestures. "A young woman that you're deeply in love with confides in you. Says she's afraid. That something terrible might happen to her. And your response is to pack up and move to a new country?"

George doesn't answer.

Malcolm leans in slightly. "Mr Stan. Did Ms Cornelia Dean ever explicitly say, 'I am in danger'? Did she ever write, 'My father will have me killed'?"

George's jaw tightens. "She didn't need to."

"But she never said it."

"She was scared. She couldn't say it out loud. That's why she wrote in her diary. She made sure I'd read it."

Malcolm shrugs. "People get scared all the time, Mr Stan. It doesn't mean there's a conspiracy." He glances at the jury, then back at George. "Now, about those letters. You claim she wrote to you."

"She did."

"And where are those letters now?"

"They were submitted to investigators. They're in FBI custody now."

A faint murmur ripples through the gallery. Malcolm blinks once, his expression unreadable.

"Custody," he repeats. "That's quite the

word, Mr Stan. You turn them over voluntarily?"

"Yes, I did."

It's a week earlier. The memory opens like a film reel. We're tucked into a dimly lit coffee shop on the Lower East Side, the air heavy with the scent of burnt espresso and rain-soaked pavement. Special Agent Sato sits across from us, looking like he hasn't slept in days, his jaw rough with stubble, dark circles sinking under his eyes, his coffee untouched.

"And you're saying," Sato mutters, stirring his cup but never drinking, "that you left New York City after Cornelia Dean's death in '64 and didn't tell a single soul you even knew her?"

George drums his fingers against the side of his mug, staring into the dark liquid like it holds the answer. "Correct."

Sato leans back in his chair, arms crossed, his face unreadable. The silence stretches until George shifts, hands twitching against the table. He clears his throat and speaks again.

"They killed her. She wasn't the sort to simply surrender. Her father and his people, they made sure she never left alive."

Sato flips his folder open, scans a page. His

eyes move slower than his hand, which taps the table once, twice. "These letters are… poetic. Fragments. Nothing overtly criminal."

"She couldn't write it outright," George says, voice sharpening. "She was being watched. You can see it in the phrasing—the hesitations, the breaks."

"Or maybe you're seeing what you want to see."

The rain outside grows harder, louder. Somewhere, a car horn blares and fades. George looks down at his coffee, and for a moment, I can see the ghost of Cornelia's face reflected in the liquid.

"You don't believe me," George says.

"I believe you believe it," Sato replies. He slides the folder back into his briefcase and snaps it shut with a soft click that sounds louder than it should. "And maybe that's enough for a jury to feel something. But feelings don't win cases."

"Then what does?"

"Paper trails. People willing to burn for the truth." Sato's smile is small, humourless. "You never said a word back then. Why?"

George lifts his gaze. His voice is calm. "Because folk didn't listen back then." A beat.

"They do now."

Back in the courtroom, Malcolm props his hands on the edge of the witness stand, leaning in just enough to crowd the space.

"Do those letters contain any concrete evidence, Mr Stan? Any names, dates, specific claims?"

George tightens his fists in his lap. "No. Only her fear."

Malcolm straightens up slowly, smoothing his tie, then turns to the jury.

"No further questions."

The air outside the courthouse feels different—thinner, rinsed clean but fragile.

"Hey, do you like ice cream?" Alice asks while watching people trickle onto the street in slow, tired streams.

"Sure."

We glance over at George. The colour is coming back to his face, but he still looks worn down. I can't help but worry.

"You two go on," he says, waving a hand. "I need a bit of a sit-down."

"Are you sure? I can come back with you."

He chuckles, the sound thin but warm. "Don't fuss over me. I'll grab a taxi." He glances skyward, squinting against the thick clouds. "Bit cloudy for cycling today."

He steps off the curb, lifting a hand to stop a cab. Jesse, who's been lingering nearby, crosses over to him and pauses by a rusted old lamppost, offering me a brief, grateful smile.

Taxis sweep past; a few slow, then one pulls up. George turns back towards me. There's something tender and irreversible in his look.

I offer him a small smile, careful not to overdo it. Push too hard, and I'll cry. "You did well today, George," I say. "I'm proud of you."

He nods once, his eyes softening. I follow him a few steps towards the waiting cab, feeling the heaviness in his frame, the way he leans just a little more into each stride. For the first time, it strikes me. He's old. Properly, heartbreakingly old.

"Are you sure you guys will be okay?"

"Just fine." George gestures at the line of yellow cabs. Jesse reaches to open the door for him, but George insists on doing it himself, ushering Alex in ahead of him.

Before he gets in, George turns once more to look at me.

"I'm proud of *you*, Julia."

I nod, throat tight. Jesse, Alex and George settle into the cab, and the doors thud closed. The window rolls down; George's hand lifts once, steady as ever, before the cab merges into the traffic and vanishes.

"I think it's really cool, what you and George are doing," Alice says, stepping closer.

"Me too," I admit, surprising myself with how much I mean it. For the first time in what feels like forever, I feel it—a flicker of pride, small but real.

"I mean, you left everything back in London to be here. To help us."

I think about what I left behind. About what I'm still carrying. Maybe it's time to let go of some of it.

I look at Alice. "You're helping George more than you know," I say. "And I appreciate you."

We stand there, just looking at each other, the city thrumming around us.

"And then they stared at each other and thought, 'We're the bravest ladies alive in New York City today,'" Alice declares dramatically, throwing her arms out and breaking into laughter. There's a wild kind of light in her eyes, defiant, stubborn, alive. "I sometimes narrate over my own life," she admits, grinning. "Makes me feel less small." She tilts her head, waiting for me to say something back, then nudges me with her shoulder. "Right, come on! Ice cream. Best in the city, I swear."

She grabs my arm and tugs me forward.

Christine steps off the court steps behind us, weaving through the slow-moving crowd. She waves, not from afar, but close enough to catch my eye. I mouth a thank you. She responds with a bright okay gesture before clicking away on her small, sensible heels, her hair bouncing in the autumn breeze.

The VW Kombi gang spill out next, offering quiet but spirited encouragement: a few claps, a thumbs-up, an earnest "Keep going!" hitting deeper than they'd ever know. They know this wasn't a victory yet, but it felt like the beginning of one.

"Hold up! Where are you two going without me?" Daniel's voice rings out behind us, his sneakers slapping against the pavement as he bounds down the steps.

Alice glances back. "Thought you weren't coming."

"I said I was going to the bathroom, not that I didn't want the best ice cream in town," he huffs, jogging to catch up.

"Well, hurry up then," Alice calls back. "This city doesn't wait for anyone."

We fall into an easy rhythm, heading towards the busy streets. It feels like a beginning, somehow.

"You know," I say, surprising myself again, "I'm thinking of starting a YouTube channel."

"What about?" Alice asks.

"That's the thing. I don't know yet."

"I know this guy," Daniel says. "Spent a thousand bucks on all the gear to start out—now he's making ten grand a month."

"He's totally selling weed on the side," Alice deadpans.

"Yeah, but think about the return on investment," Daniel grins, nudging her.

We keep walking, our footsteps light against the endless city. And for once, the future doesn't feel quite so heavy.

"Breaking the Silence: Survivors Speak Out Against the Church of Transcendent Unity
For decades, the Church of Transcendent Unity

presented itself as just another faith community—a place of worship, guidance and belonging. But behind closed doors, former members say, it was something else entirely.

Founded by Jeffrey *Bobby* Dean in 1961, the church has grown into more than just a religious institution. It operates businesses, owns real estate and wields influence stretching far beyond Sunday services. Critics have long questioned where the money goes and whether members are truly free to leave.

Alice Price, 18, has been adopted into a family devoted to the church. She was raised to obey, to work without pay, and to never ask questions. *I was sorting their financial records before I even knew what taxes were,* she says. *I saw the money coming in. I saw where it was going. And it wasn't to charity.*

Daniel Taylor, 19, was targeted by male church leaders at 17. *They told me it was a blessing. That I was chosen. I thought I had to do it. If I didn't, I'd lose my family forever.*

Emma Garcia, who has since tragically passed (read more *here*), was forced into a child marriage, compelled to work illegal hours without pay, and subjected to abuse that caused lifelong trauma and ultimately contributed to her premature death.

Now, the FBI has launched an investigation into the church's finances, citing potential tax fraud and money laundering. Former members continue to come forward, describing a system built on psychological control, forced labour and secrecy.

Jeffrey *Bobby* Dean has denied all allegations. But evidence is piling up.

What happens next will depend on whether justice can catch up with faith."

Chapter Seventeen
"Hey Jude"

I press two fingers against the blinds, pulling them apart just enough to peek outside. The world beyond the glass feels both familiar and foreign, like a place I once knew but can no longer recognise. People walk past our hotel, wrapped in their own lives, their own worries. Outside, it's just another day. Inside, everything feels different.

While the city moves on, article after article floods the internet, dissecting the credibility and the unravelling state of the Church of Transcendent Unity. I scroll through Reddit threads, conspiracy theories, leaked testimonies, arguments from former members and comments from spectators, treating it all like some unfolding drama, popcorn in hand.

Cornelia's name is everywhere, painted across protest signs, chanted in the streets, printed in headlines. Half the signs scream her name in anger, in grief, in demand for justice. The other half cry out for God, for faith, for whatever they believe this church should represent. Women march, voices raw, refusing to be silenced. The government is being pushed, pulled, forced to reckon with its own complacency—the church, the state, the power they've held together for too long.

"We'll be outside the federal courthouse if nothing changes," a protester tells the news.

I switch my phone off and glance at George. He hasn't moved from the old armchair he claimed as his when we got here. On TV, Tom chases Jerry with a hammer, the chaos flickering in blues and yellows across the room. George looks smaller today. Smaller and older.

A few thin lines of light stretch across the wall above a painting I haven't paid attention to before. I stare at it, feeling a strange sense of presence, like I've seen it before but never truly noticed. It reminds me of sitting cross-legged in our room like this when I was little, just watching the afternoon light shift. I didn't need to understand it then. I just watched, knowing there was time to figure everything out.

And now, despite everything, I feel it again— hope. Not the kind demanding answers. Just the type letting you believe there's still time.

George takes a sip from the small bottle of whisky, thinking I haven't noticed. I glance at his shirt pocket, at the worn chopsticks always sticking out like two pens. All this time, the answer's been right there in plain sight.

A few weeks ago, before Christine's first article went live, I asked George why he was so anxious.

"At your age, you must've seen it all a million times."

It was a stupid thing to say, and I knew it the second the words left my mouth. But George didn't scold me.

"I've seen plenty," he said. "It's why I know all the ways this could go wrong."

And yet, despite knowing exactly how bad it could get, he came back. He stood up and fought for someone he lost decades ago, as if Cornelia had never been lost at all. Like she wasn't trapped in the past, but just waiting, somewhere, for someone to find her.

Autumn has settled in now, but all I can think about is summer. What a summer we had, gone forever. I catch myself longing for it, the limbo of not knowing what was next. Before things became real. Before the weight of truth settled on our shoulders. It feels almost unreal now, how good that summer was.

Jesse and Alex are asleep on the sofa, snoring in unison, father and son, perfectly alike. I look at Jesse and see a version of all of us. A generation always chasing something higher, something better. Ever climbing, never arriving. Everyone working towards their highest self, yet no one feeling like they've reached it. The goalpost moves, the chase begins again, and no one dares admit they're tired.

I think about what George said in court. About staying silent for decades. About how his heart must have shattered a thousand times, only to patch itself up enough to keep going. I think about his father, a man who left Eastern Europe with nothing but pride in his homeland. His world.

But for George, New York City was his world. Until it wasn't. He left, built a life in London, but he never really let go.

"I felt anger," George told me, when I asked why he helped me all these years. "Anger at my son for pointing out my flaws. Pride in him, too. But sorrow, deep sorrow, for having let him down in so many ways. And then I saw you children. Who felt neither pride nor shame nor anger. Children who felt nothing at all."

And I wish he was wrong. But he isn't. Because I don't feel it either. Not pride, not belonging, not direction. I exist between what was and what is, but never in the space of what could have been. That space is too big. Too dangerous.

"They're just using Cornelia," George had said when I showed him the growing protests. His words stick in my mind.

My phone vibrates. It's Christine.

I step closer to the window and pick up without saying anything.

"They raided one of the central compounds," she says, voice tight with urgency. She speaks with the calm certainty of someone who's seen enough to know when it counts.

"The FBI came in full force. Burst through the doors. Full search warrants. Armed agents moving through the halls, pulling files, seizing everything they could grab. They arrested half a dozen people on the spot. It was something else, kid. I watched from across the street."

"When?"

"This morning."

I fight the instinct to rub my fingers together. My mind flashes back. The sound of a door bursting open. Silence before the exploding movement of men in body armour, shouting, storming into the room where Norina and I had been. Light slicing through the dark. Commands fired in every direction. I clench my fists, pulling myself back.

"How did you get in there?"

I can tell Christine smiles. "You know one person, then another, and before you know it, you're standing somewhere you're not supposed to be. It's how this business works."

I nod.

"This guy, Bobby, though—he's still out there. They might get him soon. They're hitting him hard for financial crimes. Money laundering, tax fraud. I want to see just how guilty he really is."

"They're pushing their own truth."

"Who is?"

"The protesters." I say. "The church. Bobby. They're all pushing their own versions of reality. And in the eyes of the law... he might not be guilty at all."

Christine pauses.

"You're smart, kid. That's exactly the problem."

A beat of silence. Then her voice softens.

"Listen, you hang tight, okay? You got this. Just hold onto George. You're both going to be alright."

The call ends.

I lean against the cold radiator, watching Jesse shift in his sleep. The blue light from the TV flickers across George's face.

I'm going to miss him when he's gone. When that time comes, it's going to split my world open.

"George?" I whisper.

He lifts a finger and points at the screen.

"This one's my favourite episode."

Summer 1964

"Evil music... has reached our shores," Bobby declares, his voice oily-smooth at first, almost sorrowful, before swelling into something theatrical.

He unclips the microphone from its stand with an almost ceremonial gesture, like he's unsheathing a blade and paces the length of the former sock factory turned sanctuary. Sunlight slants through the dusty high windows behind him, catching in the floating air like flecks of gold. Holy light, if you asked him. Industrial decay, if you knew better.

A factory once built for work, now repurposed for worship. Or maybe for something else entirely. A factory of lies. A factory of power. A factory of sin and self-interest dressed up in scripture.

Bobby raises his free hand, palm out.

"Jesus," he says, "Jesus taught us exactly what to do when temptation slithers in... when sin tries to worm its way inside our very bodies."

He closes his eyes, shaking his head slowly and mournfully.

"And this music... these beats... they are not innocent. Those aren't works of art. They are not expression. Someone tuned them—yes, tuned them—to wavelengths mimicking the chants of ancient ritual. They mimic the very pulse of rebellion against God."

His voice rises, preening, theatrical.

"They do not lead us closer to Christ... but away. Away into confusion. Into chaos. Into a life without guidance, without grace. A life tuned not to Heaven's frequency... but to Hell's static."

He stops pacing.

"I have seen it with my own eyes," Bobby says now, lowering his voice to a hush that somehow carries even louder. "I have seen little girls lining up at dawn! Just to get their hands on this."

And with that, he lifts the object high. The *Meet The Beatles!* vinyl record. The sleeve catches the light just so, particles of dust shimmering around it like tiny lost souls. For a second, it almost looks holy. But the way Bobby holds it, like evidence in a trial, turns that shimmer sour.

George's body reacts before his brain does. A sharp jolt upward from the pew, like every bone in him wants to launch him forward. He catches himself, locks his knees, and drops back into the seat with a thud.

He's seen that record before. Cornelia has the record. On her dresser, next to her mirror, next to her world, within her secret room.

Bobby turns, holding the record aloft like a curse.

"They queue for this. They push. They shove. They claw for a ticket to this... altar of filth. What does this tell us about our children? About their future? About their souls?"

He points a finger skyward.

"A future where no child—I said no child— should ever stand in line for the devil's music."

He turns, pacing again.

"The Bible is clear," Bobby says, voice sinking deeper, darker. "'Thou shalt not make unto thee any graven image, or any likeness of anything that is in Heaven above, or that is in the Earth beneath, or that is in the water under the Earth.'" He inhales. "And yet here we are, watching our children worship men with guitars and matching haircuts like golden calves!"

His voice peaks.

"We have to stand in line for one thing only—the gates of Heaven. And not by ticket. Not by idol. But by prayer. And by love. Our love for Christ... and our love for each other."

George is staring. He hates him. He knows it. And yet, there's something about Bobby that pulls him in every time, like staring at a car wreck. Like slowing down on the highway to watch the wounded, even though you know you shouldn't. Morbid fascination. Or maybe it's worse than fascination. Maybe it's attraction. Not the good kind. The kind living in the stomach. The kind you feel when you pass a house with the curtains drawn and wonder what is happening inside. This church isn't a home for lost souls. It's an accident scene. And George can't stop looking.

Until.

Until she touches the back of his hand. Gentle, steady and real. He blinks, the trance breaking, and looks at Cornelia. Without a word, they slip out the side aisle.

Outside, the grass is dry and patchy. George's bike lies where he left it, tipped onto its side like it too was hoping to escape the sermon. He stoops, grabs the handlebars, and with a single practiced motion, swings one leg over, landing on the seat in a clean hop. Before he can even plant both feet on the pedals, Cornelia is already moving. She's stepping in front of him, hands bracing on his shoulders, before tucking herself sideways onto the top bar of the frame, just ahead of the handlebars. The metal creaks faintly beneath their combined weight.

George wobbles, just for a second, his heart jumping as the balance shifts beneath him. Then the back wheel catches. The tires grip grass, then gravel, then dirt. Friction, traction, movement. And they are gliding forward, slowly at first, then faster, the wheels spinning heavier. Cornelia leans back against him, just slightly.

George presses his lips together. "That was your record. You're not gonna get it back?"

Cornelia turns her head, just enough to catch

his eye over her shoulder.

"Of course I will." She says it like a threat. Like a promise. And then she smiles wider.

The truth of Cornelia's death is anyone's guess. Did they take her life? Did they push her past the point of no return? Did the weight of exposing her own father finally crush her? She died while speaking her truth—this much is certain. But how it actually happened… we'll never know. It's a truth buried too deep to ever dig up. And maybe we don't need to.

Because what Cornelia did achieve—is already enough. It's been enough all along. And now George can finally breathe, knowing he's spoken his piece. Told the part of the story that belonged to him. What he's done now—maybe it's everything Cornelia ever hoped someone would do for her. Maybe it's all any of us can do in a lifetime.

George and Cornelia… they made a good team. Even after six decades apart, they somehow managed to stay on the same path, fighting the same quiet war. Strange, isn't it? After everything, they still found a way to walk each other home.

Couple goals, I suppose.

The two ride on, down the road, away from

George

Bobby and his poisonous words.
George pedals.
And pedals.
And pedals.

Chapter Eighteen
"While My Guitar Gently Weeps"

George sits in his chair at Alan and Anne's rooftop bar. Only tonight do I realise the two are the owners of an upstairs loft. By day, it's a coffee shop; by night, a bar.

Rosanna isn't some wellness guru or meditation coach, like I'd assumed. She's a freelance architect. Most of the bar—the rough timber beams, the soft, amber lighting—bears her stamp. Humphrey's retired, finally, after decades as a vet. Anthony runs his own construction company.

Maybe people don't become so mundane once you know them. Maybe they just become human. Maybe life begins here—when the story slips from glossy veneer to unpolished, wounded truth. And maybe I've been holding myself back all along, craving connection but never daring to ask for it.

Daniel sits at the edge of the rooftop, legs

swinging over the city, sketching on a sheet in his lap. It's Emma's face he's drawing, so alive it almost feels like she's here with us tonight. And maybe she is.

The bar is closed tonight. This is George's farewell. Jesse insisted on taking him back to London. No one can blame him. The cancer that started in George's bowel has spread to his liver. End-stage now. For real. He needs to slow down. It wrecks me to see him like this. My invincible George. My rock. My best friend. Dying.

I take a sip from Anne's wine and watch him. He isn't doing anything dramatic, nothing grand. He's just… here. Doing what so many of the old caretakers from the orphanage did when their time came—they slowed, they softened, and eventually, they left us. That's what old people do, isn't it? They leave.

All the Georges I've loved, imagined, chased across the jagged streets of New York… they are old now. Even in my mind, time has caught up. Time didn't forget George. But neither have we. He carries every story, every lesson, every fragment of the past, bundled up and ready to pass on.

Tonight I learnt that Alex was born with one leg slightly longer than the other—congenital limb length discrepancy. Doctors had given him the option: lengthen the shorter leg or shorten the longer one. The family chose the latter, for safer, fewer complications.

Jesse, meanwhile, is planning to quit accounting. Wants to start over. His wife is all in.

George sits in his chair, watching the city lights flicker on and off like stars being born and dying all at once. And for the first time in a long while, I feel him fully here. Not trapped in memory, not lost in some unreachable past, but here. With us.

I know George is dying. I know that now. But George has made sure his story won't die with him.

They say failure binds people tighter than success ever could. And maybe it's true. Maybe it doesn't matter that Cornelia left a mystery unsolved, or that George didn't "figure out life" until it was too late. Maybe the win was simply enduring. Showing up. Telling the truth, after all.

And maybe life isn't all that cruel if I let myself believe I don't need all the answers. Maybe not knowing is part of finding my way back to myself.

The lawsuit rages on. Arrests. Investigations. Headlines. Bobby, somehow, is gliding through it all, landing on his feet like someone in that Reddit thread said—like a cat. No matter how you throw them, they land square.

And I wonder: did people like us ever stand a chance? When you stripped it all down, threadbare truth and all, did we ever hold any real power against a system built to swallow us whole?

"When I die, son," George says, fishing out his chopsticks from his front pocket, "please don't bury me with these."

Jesse chuckles, but he's listening.

"When that day comes, I want you to say: *'You old bastard, held onto the past like there was no future.'* And then let me go. Because none of this stuff really matters in the end. Where there was love, there was truth. And that's all that stays."

I love George for letting the world settle around him. Jesse pushes George's hand back. "Nah, Dad. Be proud of what you love. Hold on to the things that matter to you. Don't let me or anyone else tell you different."

George smiles faintly. Then, carefully, he gets up. Jesse moves to help him, but George waves him off. He walks over to a trailing, tired-looking jasmine plant near the railing. He pushes the chopsticks into the soil beside it.

"Alan," he calls, nodding towards the plant, "tie it up with some thread. It's going to hang in there. Rise tall. Sometimes we all just need a little extra support."

He turns back, a glint still in his eyes.

In the middle of this whole mess, we all forgot. George's eighty-first birthday.

How everything had come full circle—from me once thinking George had it all, to life proving there's always a little more space for a little more.

"George," I call. I pull the folded letter from my pocket and hand it to him.

He looks at it for a second, holding it carefully between his fingers.

"Happy belated birthday," I say.

George doesn't hesitate; he rushes to unfold the letter and stares at it. We've all written him a poem each, some shorter, some longer, but all straight from the heart.

"There's a blank space there for you to write something too," I tell him. "It doesn't have to be a poem."

George looks at me, then at everyone around, and his eyes fill up with tears.

"When I die," Alice chuckles. "I want to come back as one of those Cornish pasties you Brits love so much," she smiles. "Useful. Warm. Filling."

I look at Alice, wonder what's in her heart. I wonder what's in all our hearts, really, the ones who had to grow up too soon, fighting battles no kid should have to.

And somewhere, maybe in memory, maybe in real life, I swear I hear a ringdove sing. And just like that, it smells like maize fields again. Smells like home. Not the kind you live in, but the kind you heal in.

George pulls up a little stool beside the jasmine. I realise it's just us here now—George, Alice, and me—away from the others, near the plant and the edge of the city.

"Listen to me," George says, locking eyes with me. His voice is soft but certain. "There's something I need you to know."

He takes Alice's hand too.

In a perfect world, maybe we would've taken Bobby down like heroes from an epic tale. We'd have cut the hydra's many heads off, sword raised high. But this isn't fiction. This is real life. And maybe, in the end, what we've done—surviving, holding each other—matters even more.

The ringdove coos in my heart as George speaks, but I resist, not wanting to hear the truth, although it is everything I've ever yearned for.

"No." I whisper.

George places Alice's palm over mine. And for the first time in forever, my hand doesn't shake.

"I'm sorry it took me this long," he says. "Here's your Norina, Julia."

He tilts his head towards Alice. I look at her too, and everything just stills. The air forgets how to move. Even the city noise draws back, quiet. Something under my ribs stirs, as though it remembers how to breathe for real again. I look at her the way you look at something you lost before you knew how much it mattered.

I'd spent years chasing the memory of her, sprinting through summer fields, desperate to find the real-life Monet I used to dream about. Soft edges, impossible colours. Something I believed would disappear if I got too close.

And now she's here, standing right in front of me. But I can't touch the moment. Not yet. It feels too delicate, as if breathing too loudly might ruin it.

Her dyed brown hair and those eyes. I beat myself for it—silently, with a sting. For not seeing her sooner. For clinging so tightly to the image of little Norina—forever three years old in my mind—that I missed the truth growing up right in front of me.

She watches me with the eyes of a child, sensing something's missing but not sure what it's supposed to be. The bleeding truth stands right in front of me. And once again, I don't know what to do with it. I want to reach for her. Rest my hand on the crown of her head, just like I used to. I want time to loosen, to let me catch up.

I stay still. She's here now, but also somewhere else entirely. In the before. In the years we lost. And I don't know if I've earned the right to cross that space.

Still, I hope. Wordlessly, stubbornly. That something in her remembers too, even if she doesn't have the words for it. I try not to cry. But the tears come anyway. Good ones, honest ones. Tears for my sister. For a stranger who once held my whole world in her tiny hands.

And maybe that's the part no one ever warns you about. That finding someone again means mourning, too. Not because they aren't here... but because of all the life that passed while you were looking.

I don't know what comes next and I don't know how to start. But I'm standing here now and so is she. And that has to count for something.

"Wow," Alice's eyes twinkle, her voice small. "Never thought I'd live to see something like this."

I turn to George. "Why didn't you tell me sooner?"

"I wanted you two to meet with no expectations. Blood's not thicker than water. Better to be safe."

He leans back, breath rough around the edges. But content. Settled.

"You never looked for me?" Alice asks, and it cracks me wide open because she's right.

I was lost in my own grief for so long I forgot to look beyond it.

"You remember me?"

"Of course, dummy," she smiles. "I was three. You were my world."

And now I know. I see it. In her eyes. In her smile. In everything about her. Norina, who lived in every inch of my memories, now stands in front of me. I pull her into a hug and never want to let go. She doesn't smell like my baby sister anymore. But she feels like her. And I think, just maybe, she will one day forgive me.

"What language do you dream in?" she asks against my shoulder.

"My dreams?" I wonder. "In whatever language I understand, I guess."

"Yeah," she says, pulling back to look at me, "'Cause when they adopted me, they told me I had an accent. An accent they couldn't quite place."

"Must've been the carers," I say. "They spoke all sorts of languages to us." I wipe my face with the back of my hand.

"They smelt like nail polish remover."

"And hairspray."

She wipes her tears, and for a second, I feel like the luckiest person alive just sitting here with her.

"You sound like a real New Yorker now."

"Because I am." She smiles and I can't unsee it now, how unevenly this world has bent the two of us.

I glance over at George. His smile is small, worn, but real. He takes a deep, rattling breath. Illness sits on him heavily today; the creases on his face are deeper, his body thinner. It's like the years have stretched him too far, leaving behind nothing but kindness and stubbornness holding him up. Despite this, there's relief in his eyes.

I realise, this entire journey was a little more personal to me than George ever wanted to admit.

Maybe I'd been part of this plan of his all along. And I no longer blame him for his secrets. He didn't owe me explanations. He gifted me my world back.

"How did you even do this?"

"A bit of Facebook." George shrugs, wiggling his head like a magician admitting to a cheap trick. "A bit of bribing. A bit of flirting my way through the records at the Child Protective Services and the New York State Adoption Information Registry."

I shake my head in disbelief.

"My middle name's Norina," she says, and I turn back to her. "They just changed it to Alice when I got here. Made it my first name like it was easier to pronounce or something."

I stare at my sister, Norina, and for a second, I forget how to breathe.

"You can call me Norina," she smiles, soft and certain. "You're the only one who deserves to."

Then she laughs, nervous, teary, brave. "You can call me whatever the hell you want, honestly. Just... please don't let anyone ever take me away from you again."

My throat tightens. All the pain—hers and mine—sits right there between us, raw and electric.

"I'm sorry," I cry.

She shakes her head. "Don't. It's not your fault."

And I believe her. I honestly do. I let her words settle inside me like something I've waited to hear my whole life.

"Alice is a *sheeday*," George pipes up proudly, like he's just solved a puzzle.

"George!" I wipe at my eyes.

"What? She has those pronouns," George says, gesturing vaguely in the air with two fingers like he's sketching out some imaginary quotation marks. "Right there on her Facebook profile. I know what I'm talking about."

I can't help but laugh now, wiping the last of my tears away.

"George, stop." I turn to Norina. "I'm so sorry about him. He's... not usually like this."

She straightens up, playful defiance flickering in her eyes.

"I must disappoint you, sir," she says, raising an eyebrow at George. "My pronouns are she/her—which probably makes me more of a *sheeherina*."

George lets out a delighted snort, like he's just learnt a new word no one else knows.

The city around us shifts and sighs, as it's settling down for the night. Lights bathe the streets in gold, the occasional plane droning overhead like a reminder of how far we've all come.

Later, I'll learn the truth about our biological parents. That it was them, not fate, not poverty, not some twist of bad luck, but them, who sold us away. Who closed the gate to their garden and handed us over like we were nothing but problems to be solved.

I no longer blame myself for forgetting the way home. For only remembering the faces of carers who smelt like nail polish remover and hairspray. For loving the places that held me better than the place that should've.

I no longer waste breath wondering about the people who should've never been parents. I don't know where they are, or if they even still are, and I don't care to know. I've stopped feeling sick over the 'what ifs'. I don't chase the past anymore.

All I want is to reach for Norina's hand and hold it tight. Not just because I want to keep her next to me, but because I hope she'll want to hold mine just as tightly back.

Right now, I don't want to know anything except the love I have sitting right here with me.

George

The kind of love I'll carry for the rest of my life—
for the people who belong in it, like maize belongs
in my maize field; bending in the wind without
permission, without apology, just as it should.

Chapter Nineteen
"Come Together"

"There's going to be an evidentiary hearing," Christine says to George over the phone. We're all listening in.

"We'll be there," George replies simply, before hanging up.

Jesse's already moving, stepping closer to George, circling him like he might physically block him from leaving.

"Dad, what's going on?"

"They want us in court. First thing in the morning."

"No, they don't," Jesse fires back, desperate. He glances at me, eyes urgent, pleading for backup.

George doesn't answer right away. He's moving around the room, pulling a shirt from the wardrobe—something old, carefully pressed—and lays it on a hanger prepared to iron.

"Dad." Jesse watches him like he's watching someone gear up for war. "What are you doing?"

"There's a new witness coming forward," George says without looking up. "They're calling everyone in."

"You don't have to go," Jesse insists, shaking his head like a kid again. "Dad, we're flying out tomorrow."

"Change the tickets. I'll cover it."

"No," Jesse's voice cracks. "Dad, you've done everything. You fought. Enough. Please. Just come home with us."

Jesse looks at me again. Almost begging now. "Help me out here."

I'm caught between them, with absolutely nothing to offer except silence. Alex rubs the back of his neck, uncomfortable.

Jesse inhales, cheeks puffed full of air, before releasing it in a slow, deflated stream. "Oh, for fuck's sake."

When we arrive at the court, it's like walking into history being written.

Everyone from our side is here—Christine, Norina, Daniel, Jesse, Alex and our VW Kombi team. But beyond that, there's also a crowd. A real one. Protesters, supporters, people holding handwritten signs, banners, pieces of cardboard scrawled with messages like "Justice for Cornelia" and "We Believe George".

Humphrey's car pulls up to the kerb. George steps out slower than usual, but with a kind of last-reserve dignity. He's wearing his Sunday best—a brown suit with wide lapels, a little loose on his smaller frame now, but neat. Intentional. Almost defiant. Today, I don't just see the young, bruised man from the past. I see George—whole, tired, but standing on his own terms. Jesse looks out at the crowd and pushes out a breath. We walk towards the steps. The crowd parts in a strange, reverent way, people moving aside but never taking their eyes off us.

"Mr George!" someone calls out.

A younger guy points back at the group. "We read your story. All of us. We can't tell you what it means, for you to come forward like this. Thank you. Thank you to Cornelia. For everything."

George nods, humbled past words.

Another voice from the side, a woman now, calls out, "Stay strong, Mr George!"

And then she steps forward, impulsively, pulling George into a hug. Others follow, too quickly, too eagerly, bodies crowding in, hands reaching.

Jesse's arm snaps out protectively in front of George.

"Don't. Please, don't touch him. Jesus Christ…" He mumbles. "Actually, not even that guy."

Norina clamps down on my hand as we push towards the doors.

Inside, the air is taut. There's murmuring, the low rustle of bodies settling. The gallery is full to bursting. A video camera blinks from a discreet corner.

We sit. I hold the back of George's hand and Alex clasps the other. Across the aisle, attorney Sophia Leung stands poised, her suit still too new, her files arranged in sharp military order.

"All rise."

We all stand as the judge enters, robes whispering across the floor.

"Be seated."

The formalities pass in a blur, names read into the record, the judge establishing order.

"Ms Leung, you may proceed. You indicated a new witness?"

"Yes, Your Honour. The State calls Jacob Miller."

The heavy doors creak open.

The sound slices clean through the quiet, and when the witness steps in, my chest tightens. Tall. Lanky. Mid-twenties, maybe. And painfully familiar. My stomach knots before my mind even catches up.

"Catch!" I hear Blue-Eye say in my memories, and the image of a melting ice bag flashes through my mind.

It's him. The strange guy from the hotel. Only now, he's in a suit and walking towards the stand.

He takes his oath and sits, glancing briefly at Leung, then scanning the room with a restless flicker. I squeeze Norina's hand until my knuckles ache.

"Please state your full name for the record."

"Jacob Alexander Miller."

Sophia Leung barely looks up from her notes. "And your relation to Jack Miller, the founder of Miller Hospitality Group?"

"He's my father."

"And are you familiar with the Church of Transcendent Unity?"

"Yes. My family and I are members."

Leung gives a short nod. "And how would you describe your family's relationship with Jeffrey

'Bobby' Dean?"

Jacob's jaw flexes. "Close. My father saw Bobby as a mentor, a business partner and a spiritual guide."

"Objection, Your Honour. Relevance." Malcolm raises an arm.

"Overruled. Proceed."

"Mr Miller, did that relationship influence your family's business dealings?" Leung continues.

"Yes. Dean's church directed where the money went. And who benefited."

"Objection—calls for speculation."

"Sustained. Keep it to what you personally observed, Mr Miller."

Jacob shifts in his seat. "I personally witnessed Dean dictating financial decisions to my father."

Leung nods—eyes flicking up to Jacob, a subtle accord passing between them.

"Mr Miller, you mentioned in your statement that you received what was called 'training.' Could you explain what that meant?"

"It meant punishment." He pauses. "Your Honour, may I show the court what that training entailed?"

"You may," the judge nods.

Jacob's fingers fidget in his lap, then still. Slowly, he unbuttons his cuff and rolls up his left sleeve.

Gasps ripple through the courtroom. Bruises. Faded, some still purple, others pale and waxy. Jesse shifts beside me. I can feel the tension radiating from him, the disbelief, the pity.

The room feels smaller. I can hear the blood in my ears. For a moment, everything in me aches for him—for all of them—for the versions of ourselves that learnt too early to survive by obedience.

Flat sharing, odd jobs, poor family backgrounds—or maybe just the weight of where we come from—rich ones too, childhoods we're still trying to make sense of, the urge to break free from whatever current prison we find ourselves in. That never-ending wheel we're all still spinning, whether it's in London, in New York, or in some far-off corner of the world. We're all so wildly different, yet somehow running in the same direction.

A warm tear slips down my cheek for Jacob.

Malcolm's tone hardens, dragging us back to formality. "Objection! Prejudicial and irrelevant character evidence."

"Overruled. The Court will take note of the witness's condition for the record."

Jacob looks down at his arm. "When I questioned Dean—or refused to sign documents I knew were wrong—this was my lesson."

He rolls up the other sleeve. More bruises, more silence.

"Mr Miller, do you have any corroborating evidence for these allegations?"

"Yes. My counsel has filed supporting documents with the clerk."

Sophia Leung turns to the judge. "Your Honour, we move to admit Exhibits 24 through 30—internal ledgers, correspondence, and transfer records between Jeffrey 'Bobby' Dean, Jack Miller, and senior members of the Church of Transcendent Unity."

"Mr Malcolm?" the judge calls.

"No objection to authenticity, Your Honour, but we reserve argument on relevance."

"So noted. Exhibits 24 through 30 are admitted."

Leung opens the top folder, scanning its contents before speaking again. Her tone softens almost imperceptibly.

"Mr Miller... these documents also reference

charitable accounts. Can you tell the court what you discovered?"

The courtroom stills again. Leung continues to stare at the pile and a tiny smile escapes her lips before she looks up again.

Jacob lifts his gaze, steady now. "Fraudulent donations. Money laundering. And lists of participants—including sitting board members."

Whispers flare through the gallery like brushfire. Blue-Eye—Jacob—looks straight at George. Then at me. His eyes are clearer than I remember. I give him the smallest of nods.

George leans in, muttering from the corner of his mouth, "Did we accidentally stay at the arsehole's hotel?"

I almost choke.
"I'm going to complain," George adds under his breath. "Place was ugly as hell and dirty."

Chapter Twenty
"Let It Be"

Bobby is arrested on a bright, almost too-beautiful autumn morning. Handcuffs, TV crews, flashing cameras—the whole circus. He pleads not guilty.

The charges read like the closing credits of a monster movie.

- *Money Laundering in the First Degree*
- *Criminal Tax Fraud in the Second Degree*
- *Endangering the Welfare of a Child*
- *Coercion in the First Degree*
- *Criminal Facilitation in the Second Degree (in connection with a Murder-for-Hire)*
- *Conspiracy to Commit Murder in the Second Degree*

Bobby is held without bail at Rikers Island Correctional Facility, pending trial.

I carry the little foldable stool under my arm the whole way, careful not to bump it against my leg. The cemetery is still, an honesty cities never manage. The silence here feels earned. At

Cornelia's grave, I open the stool and set it down beside me.

George sits slowly, knees stiff, back aching, but his hands are gentle when he leans forward and lays a single rose across Cornelia's name.

I look at him and think of last night—the phone call. How it came with a quiet, creeping certainty of something inevitable.

Yesterday, George's phone had rung late in the evening, a number from Rikers Island Correctional Facility flashing on the screen.

For a moment, we both just stared at it—that small rectangle of light, pulsing like a heartbeat. It rang again, and I could feel it searching for us, like something half-alive that had finally learned our names.

George answered after a little hesitation. At first, there was just silence. The empty, static-fuzz sound of someone sitting on the other end, not ready to speak. I could hear the hum of our minibar, and the low, static buzz from the streetlight outside; everything louder because of what wasn't being said.

"Hello?" George asked.

"George."

I heard Bobby's voice, and every cell in my

body wanted to lunge across, grab the phone, and tell the man to rot in the dark for the rest of his life—to never dare reach for ours again.

But George just lifted a hand, keeping me back. He stayed exactly where he was, sunk deep into his armchair, quietly unscrewing the cap from his whisky bottle. He took a slow pull straight from the neck, the glass catching the light from the lamp.

"Do you think," Bobby said after a long pause, "that Satan and his evil force look for men like you and I? Even after all these years?"

George swallowed his whisky, screwed the cap back on, and set the bottle aside like he had all the time in the world.

"If Satan punishes bad men," George said finally, "then doesn't that make him good?"

There was silence on the other end—an emptiness that seemed to stretch out forever, wide enough for all the world's sins to echo through.

"Satan punishes scum like you," George added. "That makes him the good guy."

Another long pause. I imagined Bobby on the other end, alone in a cold, windowless cell, trying to swallow his own reflection.

"I suppose," Bobby answered at last.

George left the silence untouched for a while,

letting the words find their own grave. Then, he picked up the thread of his thoughts.

"From all the people you could be calling right now, Bobby," George said. "You chose to ring me. Must be a sad life."

There was nothing but dead air for a beat—then the lone, final beeping sound of Bobby hanging up.

And that was it. The last word between them. No redemption, no forgiveness—just two men sitting on opposite ends of a line, both knowing that something had ended long before the call began.

George leans down once more and presses a kiss to the cool stone of Cornelia's grave. He rests his palm flat against her name and then uses that hand to push himself carefully back to standing.

He folds up his little stool and smiles at the sky. The wind is touching his hair as he begins to walk away. His heart looks so full that it might burst. I follow him.

Bobby is shot dead during the first week of November. The FBI detains Jacob Miller briefly, but he's released within 24 hours—insufficient evidence, they say. No charges filed.

And honestly? I still don't know how I feel

about Bobby's death. Did I hate him? I think so. But it wasn't just him. It was everything he stood for. Everything he twisted and broke and bent in people's lives. The damage wasn't his alone, but he was the root. Still, does his death truly undo any of it?

I wonder if Norina felt lighter when she heard. If Daniel did. If Jacob could finally breathe a little easier. If even a few of the hundred, thousands of people he hurt, manipulated, crushed… if any of them slept better that night. I hope so. I really do.

The arrests haven't stopped. One by one, the people who once called him a prophet are being picked off. This time, no one's rushing in to protect them. No more silence. No more cover-ups. No more saving.

But here's the thing: the world doesn't pause. It doesn't take a moment to think, "Let's not do this again." It moves forward, fast and messy. And if we're not careful, it finds another Bobby. Another tyrant in a suit with just the right words and the same old poison. The cycle doesn't break itself.

Did I think we could change the world? Maybe. Maybe I did. Maybe I needed to believe everything we went through—every lie torn open, every truth dragged into the light—might lead somewhere better. Not utopia. Just… better. Something quieter. Something kind.

Was I naive? Oh, definitely. Would I go back and do it all again if given the chance? Without blinking.

Because what I know now, what I feel in the soles of my feet, the root of my spine, in the deepest part of me, is that change doesn't show up with fireworks. It doesn't arrive clean or obvious. It's slow. So slow, you might not notice it at all unless you're paying attention. And sometimes, the real story isn't the one which gets told in courtrooms or headlines. It's the one playing out quietly, in the lives of people still stuck in the wreckage, still trying to crawl out.

Not everyone gets to walk away from something like this in one piece. Not everyone finds closure or courage or even words. There are families which will never heal the way they deserve to. There are people I'll never get to meet, whose stories I'll never get to tell, because the hurt went too deep, too long, too far.

And no version of this, no matter how I write it, could ever carry the full weight of that.

I wish I could rewrite this world like I could

rewrite a story—wrap it up with a clean ending, tie it all together in hope. But this is not how real life works, is it?

All I can do, all any of us can do, is tell the truth. Even if it's slow. Even if it's imperfect.

Because Bobby is gone. And now comes the hardest part. The part that always gets overlooked. The story of what happens after.

"My dad belongs next to my mum," Jesse says, his voice catching like he's bracing for me to argue, but I can only nod because I agree completely. "I know Cornelia will always be with him. And together, side by side, somehow, they've managed to leave their mark on this world. But my mother…" Jesse pauses, his jaw tightening just a little, "she spent her life cleaning up after a lot of messes. Quietly. Without applause. Without anyone noticing. She cleaned up what Cornelia started. To me, this makes her a hero as well. She did what she could with what she had. And for that, my dad—"

I notice it, how Jesse's eyes don't turn dark anymore when he calls George "Dad". It's a small detail. But it's everything.

"…he should be holding her hand too," Jesse finishes, a soft smile pulling at his mouth. "I hope you understand, Julia. My sister called, and she's worried too. We… we both need our dad."

"No, I was the one who was selfish when I tried to take him away from you."

"You didn't take him away. You gave him exactly what he needed, exactly when he needed it. You gave him a friend when I turned my back to him and for that, I thank you."

Jesse offers me a small, warm smile. People push in and out of the hotel.

"Dad," Alex calls, glancing down at his watch, "we should head out, boarding's in three hours."

Jesse gives him a look of understanding. I look over to George, standing there now beside me, his luggage at his feet, all packed up, all ready to go.

"I want you to have this," George says abruptly, almost shoving the *Meet The Beatles!* album into my hands.

I hesitate, trying to press it back towards him. "George, I can't. I can't possibly take this."

But he waves me off. "No, no—it's yours now. It's not like I'm getting buried with it or anything."

I laugh, soft, helpless. And I take it.

There's a pause. I'm unsure whether to step back, unsure what this situation calls for, but then George lifts his arms, reaching for me like a child blindly searching for their mother in the dark.

I step into his arms and hold him, knowing with every cell in my body that this is it—this is goodbye. Forever goodbye.

His arms are thin, his grip surprisingly strong. I feel his ribcage beneath my hands. This man who once danced in his living room, wildly alive, spinning to his records, now fragile in my arms, like he might dissolve into the air if I held him too tight. I feel his chest shudder, and I fear he might slip away like sand.

"This is goodbye," he says into my shoulder.

I shake my head. "It's not, George. I'll call you. I'll call you right after you land. And once Norina is settled and we know what's happening, we'll come visit. I swear. It won't be long."

Slowly, reluctantly, I pull away from him. My hair catches on his stubbled cheek and he lifts his hand to brush it away. Jeez, he looks older than ever. The last few weeks carved years into his face.

He looks up at me, his eyes clear.

"It is goodbye," he says, with absolute certainty. "We won't see each other again."

My eyes blur instantly. Because I know he's right.

"And you might think my words are ugly," he says. "But not everything has to be beautiful to bring you peace of mind. That what you've done is enough. And that everything you ever loved, everything that ever mattered to you, might mean absolutely nothing in the grander scheme of things. And yet, you deserve peace."

I look at him. My best friend. My brave, ridiculous, extraordinary friend, George.

"I'll leave it blank," George then says.

I stand there, waiting for him to go on.

"The blank space on my birthday letter," he says, smiling. "In the hopes we might all meet again someday—and fill it out together."

Alex waves down the Uber pulling up beside us. Jesse loads their luggage into the trunk. Alex gives me a final, silent wave before sliding into the backseat.

Jesse shuts the trunk and turns towards me.

"Thank you," he mouths, with a rare, genuine softness, then circles around the car to open the door for George.

George pauses at the open car door, glancing back at me one last time. His eyes, nearly translucent now, tired beyond words, are still the eyes of a man who, if he must, will walk straight into the storm.

"It's not that deep," he whispers.

I laugh through my tears. George smiles. And with one small, knowing nod, he gets into the car. Jesse closes the door behind him.

The car pulls away. Then, just before it's gone, the window rolls down. George leans out, half his small frame visible, and lifts his hand. Not a wave exactly. Something quieter. Something final.

I lift mine too, not just to wave, but to hold him there, for one second longer before the car disappears around the corner.

Chapter Twenty-One
"Now and Then"

I pull the handbrake, ease off the clutch, and turn the ignition off in the old rented VW Kombi. The engine shudders once, twice, then dies down with a sigh like it, too, has reached its final destination. Holding the keys between my hands, I glance down at them. My skin looks pale, wrinkled from dehydration. I squeeze the keys into my palms, and when I open them, deep red crescent marks from my nails stay imprinted on my skin.

"You sure you're allowed to drive this thing?" Norina looks at me from the passenger seat, one eyebrow raised like she always used to when we were kids.

"'Course not. But the law's got bigger fish to fry these days."

Every day, I learn more about my sister. Every day we catch up as we're racing against lost time, and somehow there's always still more to say. There are so many self-help books out there, all teaching you how to fix a broken relationship, how to win back a partner, how to heal. But nothing, nothing, really prepares you for rediscovering your sister after thinking you'd lost her forever.

We're sharing an apartment in Bushwick. Some friends of Norina's let her crash there, and for now, it means me too. I sleep on the living room floor, on an old mattress with a wonky spring, and I haven't felt this excited for my future in a long, long time. By the time my travel documents expire, Norina and I plan to move to London. Perhaps. She plans to rescue her adoptive brothers from their current families, and as long as my extended visa allows, I intend to be there to support her.

In the meantime, I'd also had some news from Auntie back in London. Turns out Fred's been arrested for sexual assault, and his old gym space has already been snapped up by a yoga and wellness studio; real aircon included. Auntie says they're opening next month, calling it something daft like *Breathe London*, and honestly, good for them. She also told me Fluf lives with her full-time now, and apparently, he couldn't be happier. She says she's slowly starting to come to terms with her husband's death, and that maybe, one day, she'll find it in herself to forgive herself for surviving him.

Norina squats down in front of Emma's grave. She leaves a small bouquet of forget-me-nots next to her name. Then she pulls out Emma's notebook, pages fraying at the edges, full of sketches and half-finished dreams. The wind flips through it, knowing exactly where to go, landing on the page with the Daruma Emma had started drawing.

Norina pulls the pen from behind her ear and leans in. Without rushing, she colours in the Daruma's right eye.

"I'm proud of you, Emma," she whispers. "It's not every day you help ruin a corrupt religious cult."

The truth is, Bobby didn't truly die this autumn. He still lingers in the quiet corners of people's memories; in the choices they made because of him, in the versions of themselves they never got to be. But maybe, maybe one day, all the holes he left in people's hearts will fade—to be filled not with silence or fear, but with love.

Cancer took George this same autumn. And if Bobby left holes, George left a canyon in mine.

But I don't want to fill it just yet. Not with love, not with anything at all. I want to sit in it. Feel it. Let it ache. And then, only when I'm ready, let it heal.

Cancer murdered George. But not his story.

I look up at the sky just as a single ray of sunlight cuts through the clouds, like it's reaching out for me. I feel it—the familiar, warm, unmistakable embrace.

"The things we can't explain with science, we explain with love," he once told me. The connection to this world is fragile, strange. Today we're here, cradling small wonders, eating salami bread. Tomorrow we're gone, scattered like dust, floating like lyrics of a forgotten melody.

Norina pulls the *Meet The Beatles!* album from my hands and uses it to shield my face from the sun.

"Don't stare at it. What are you, three?"

I glance over at her. She runs her palm over the worn album cover, still somehow bright despite the years. She flips it open and, tucked underneath the edge of the record sleeve, wedged right into the paper pocket like an afterthought only George would think of—a cheque flutters in the breeze. George wrote my name on it. Beside it, still folded the way he left it, lies Cornelia's letter from December 1964.

I grab the cheque before the wind can steal it from me.

"Silly old bastard," I mumble.

The maple trees along the edge of the cemetery sway gently, their leaves rustling like soft applause, like approval. Just as George found his way back, just as wild roses still bloom stubbornly over Cornelia's grave, I know things keep growing in their own time.

And I have my sister next to me again. For now. For always.

Now I understand. I finally get it. When life stalls, when you find yourself stuck, coasting without direction—all you have to do is shift gears at the right time. Ease off the clutch and give it just enough gas.

I clutch *Meet The Beatles!* tight to my chest and glance at Norina.

"Let's be happy before these pages we're writing turn yellow and smell like the past," I tell her. "Before we hold onto them like a sweet memory."

I stretch out my hand and she laces her fingers through mine. I look up at the maple trees swaying above us. And just like that, I can almost see *him*, dancing right there with the leaves.

"Let's go, George," I whisper, gathering my courage like a quiet storm.

All this time, we were the ones holding onto George. And now, forever, it's George holding us within his story.

So here it is. This is the whole story. The truth about my best friend, *George*.